P9-BZC-941

Helen
Elaine
Henderson

TAKEN FOR GRANTED

TAKEN FOR GRANTED

EARL SEWELL

sepia

BET BOOKS

BET Publications, LLC

SEPIA BOOKS are published by

BET Publications, LLC
c/o BET BOOKS
One BET Plaza
1900 W Place NE
Washington, DC 20018-1211

ISBN: 0-7394-3078-5

Printed in the United States of America

DEDICATION

In loving memory of my cousin, Anthony Studway

ACKNOWLEDGMENTS

Wow, where does one begin when a lifelong dream has become a reality? First of all, I must thank God for not putting more on me than I could possibly bear during the development of this project. If it were not for God's blessing, none of this would have been possible.

To my mother, Katie Sewell, who was right about everything all along. How I wish that I could turn back the hands of time just to see you once more. I miss you.

To my father, Earl Sewell, Sr., for all of the love he has given me and all of the wisdom he has taught me. My love for you is beyond words.

To Mary Griffin, for the time, support, dedication, and critiquing that you've given me. If not for you, I would surely have lost focus. Your tireless efforts to make this project a reality and see it through to the very end are truly appreciated.

To my wonderful editors, Gloria Grosvenor and Glenda Howard, for breathing life into my characters.

To Sandi Cook, Martina Royal, and Michelle Williams for going the extra mile to make *Taken For Granted* shine. To Barbara Collier, Lisa Davis, Sandi Denham, Denise Duncan, Yvonne German, Herlinda Monyak, Sarita Mulero, and Thelma Drawhorn for catching all of the little things that my eyes would have surely missed.

To the members of Escape Book Club, Mocha Moms Book Club, RPKA Book Club and Black Women with Books Book Club in Milwaukee. You guys are awesome.

To Ladoris Hope, Frances Utsey and Marie Walton for all of the hard work with helping me sell *Taken For Granted*. You ladies can sell bark to a tree, heat to sunshine, and wet to water. You're incredible.

To Daniel Burr for the generosity you've shown me. You came through with much needed necessities just in the nick of time. Thank you so much.

To Tyree Hayden for teaching me about the business of publishing. If not for you and your knowledge, I would never have found my way out of the forest. I cannot thank you enough for supplying me with all that you have.

To Linda Dominique Grosvenor, Renee Swindle, and Robyn Williams for taking the time out of your busy schedules to provide me with comments and support.

To Zane—girl, you're one bad sister. Thank you for taking the time to open a door and a whole new world for me.

To my agent Sara Camilli, you're an angel. Thank you so much for believing in me and my work.

To my family at Prolific Writers Group at (**www.prolific writers.org**). Thank you all for your support.

To my family at R.A.W. Sistaz Book Club (**www.rawsistaz. com**). Thank you all for your encouragement.

To everyone who supported me as a self-published author, thank you so much for helping me make a dream come true.

A special thank you to all of the following authors for your guidance and encouragement. You've all helped me in some way whether you were aware of it or not.

Tracy Price-Thompson
Timmothy B. McCann
Karen Quinnes Miller
Gwynne Forster
Kimberla Lawson Roby
Mary B. Morrison
Robert Fleming
Trevy McDonald
Victoria C. Murray
Nina Foxx

J.D. Mason
Vincent Tyler
Fredrick Cooper
J.D. Daniels
Cheryl Flood Miller
Shonell Bacon
Bernadene High Coleman
Denise Williams
Laurie Gilbert
Tanya Marie
Jamise L. Dames
Venise Berry

To Al Taylor, my friend for more than fifteen years, a big thanks to you for allowing me to sell copies of my book to clients at the hair salon.

To Riccaro Cunningham of the Cultural Bookstore in Chicago, a big thank you to you for giving me my very first book signing.

To the family at Books Inc. in Chicago for giving me my very first book signing at a major expo.

A special thank you to all of the commuters on the Metra Electric Train in Chicago who supported me by passing the word along about this book.

Please forgive me if I've missed anyone it was not intentional.

When you allow yourself to believe it, you can achieve it.

—Katie Sewell

1

Nina huffed as she plopped down on a booth seat next to the window at the Pancake House so she'd be able to observe pedestrians as they moved along Chicago's Rush Street. She was slightly irritated from the traffic jam she had encountered on Lake Shore Drive. Normally, the Sunday morning drive to her favorite breakfast spot was a pleasant experience, but today the police had blocked off the streets for a Walk-A-Thon. A handsome young waiter, dressed in a white uniform topped off with a flimsy white cap shaped like a submarine, set a glass of ice water in front of her.

"Hello, may I get you something to drink?"

"I'll have raspberry ice tea," she replied, gazing up from the menu as he scribbled down her request.

"May I have another moment to look over the menu?" she added, knowing the delay would allow her best friend, Rose, a little more time to get her perpetually late behind settled opposite her in the booth. Nina had no idea why she even bothered being on time when she knew damn well that Rose was the type of sister who would be late for her own funeral. For the twenty-plus years she had known her, Rose was always rushing to do some last-minute thing that she always claimed had to be taken care of.

The waiter returned with Nina's raspberry ice tea. "Would you like to order now? Or do you need a little more time?" he asked with one of the most pleasant voices Nina had ever heard. He had an announcer's voice, she thought. Not one of those voices that sound like a man has a needle stuck in his rear end, or a voice that makes a person sound as if everything he says is being forced up from his stomach and out through his teeth. Instead, his voice seemed to carry a hidden mystery.

"Give me a little more time. I'm waiting on my girlfriend, who is late as usual," she informed him.

He nodded his head, then moved along to greet the couple who had just sat down in front of her. She gazed out the window and observed Rush Street, which was quietly moving at a snail's pace. Nothing like it used to be, back in the 1980's. Rush Street at one point was a 24-hour, non-stop party boulevard, full of bars, dance clubs, and fast food spots like the Yellow Pork Chop Wagon. Nina had always refused to eat pork, but the way the owner grilled his food had made traffic on the strip come to a stop. The aroma from the restaurant enticed people to stop in for a sandwich and a flavored soda pop. She had been told on many occasions that after a night of stomping your feet and sweating to the beat of R&B funk music, the Chop Wagon's particular combination of barbeque pork with hot sauce was the best meal a person could eat. There was no doubt about it, on a Friday or Saturday night Rush Street used to be the most popular spot, jampacked with party maniacs on foot and in cars. Most people didn't mind the bumper-to-bumper traffic and the long delays; they loved being right in the middle of it all. Excited young people enjoying the festive night honked the horns of their convertible BMW's, Corvettes, and Mustangs to gain attention, and music seemed to be blaring from every direction. Women grooved to the rhythmic sounds heard along the strip, calling out from their cars to men whose physiques sang melodies to their womanhood.

Her friend Rose, clad in a Chicago Bulls T-shirt and blue

jeans, rushed up to the table, and Nina awoke from her day-dream.

"Happy birthday!" Rose called out as she tossed her purse on the seat, leaned forward toward Nina, gave her a hug, and then plopped down, releasing a huge sigh.

"Thank you," Nina responded dryly.

Rose interpreted Nina's tone as aggravation about her being late.

"Honest, honey, I left with plenty of time to get here but this damn freight train had Eighty-seventh Street all backed up. I had to sit there for twenty minutes while the damn thing crept along."

"Oh, it's not that, Rose. It's just—"

"Girl, I know, it's a bitch when you turn forty. But you just have to look at yourself as getting better. Besides, with the way you keep yourself together, you don't look a day over thirty. You look damn good for your age. Not that forty is old or any-thing. Hell, look at me. People think I'm around fifty. Can you believe that? Fifty! I'm only forty-three. Shit, I've got to do something about these damn dark circles and puff pockets under my eyes. And I don't even want to talk about my wide hips and huge behind. I've gained so much damn weight. I've got stretch marks everywhere, arms, legs, stomach, and all over my ass. If I keep this mess up I'll be bigger than Nell Carter."

Nina let out a holler of a laugh at Rose's comparison. "Let's hope that you don't let yourself get that far gone. I keep telling you to come on down and sign up for one of my classes. Between my aerobics and spin cycling classes, along with a bal-anced diet, I can take five years off of your look. You do realize that studies show that people who exercise on a regular basis have more energy and also look and feel younger, don't you?"

"Yeah, yeah, I know. But baby, it has been years since I've done any kind of exercise. I mean, look at me. Do I look like the kind of sister who's going to get up early in the morning for a quick jog? And I already know that smoking these damn cancer sticks is not helping my situation any. Heck, if the truth were to be told, the only times my heart rate goes up is during a sale or when Brian McKnight sings. That is one fine-ass brother, there."

Nina laughed so hard that the ice tea she was sipping almost ran out through her nose. "You are so silly," she coughed, while reaching across the table to pull a white napkin out of a metal container.

"Naw, not silly. I just like to keep it real, as the young people say nowadays. I've seen the way you work those people in your class. Remember that day I picked you up? I stood in the back of that dance room and watched you work people to within an inch of cardiac arrest. Step up, step down, kick your leg up, turn around, grapevine, run in place, toss your arms up, squat, one-two-three-four-shit! If I were in your class, I would just stand in the back of the room, look at everyone, and smoke me a cigarette. Everyone is going to die anyway; I don't see why everyone is fighting the inevitable so hard."

"Well, honey, that's where you and I see things differently. I'm going to fight this age thing for as long as possible. If I can prevent myself from having health problems in the long run, I'm going to do it."

"And that's cool," Rose said as the waiter placed a glass of water in front of her.

"Are you ladies ready to order?" asked the waiter in that soothing voice that Nina had taken a mild interest in.

"Yeah, sugar," Rose said. "I'll have scrambled eggs with cheese, hash browns, buttermilk pancakes, and beef sausage. And a cup of coffee with cream and sugar."

"I'll have the vegetarian omelet with wheat toast and orange juice," Nina requested, handing the menu back to the waiter.

"Okay, I'll put your orders in right away," he said as he headed off to the kitchen.

"Don't you think that he has the most soothing voice? It's deep, like James Earl Jones or Barry White."

Rose noticed a bit of gleam in Nina's eyes. "Who? that

young fella?" she said, "I wasn't studying him that hard. Now, getting back to what I was saying. It's cool that you workout and all—that's your thing, looking slender and slightly muscular looks good on you. I can respect all the hard work that you put into looking fit."

"I'll bet you as he matures, he is going to be a real ladykiller." Nina concentrated on the young waiter as he placed their order on the spin wheel next to the cook in the kitchen. Rose turned around in her seat to look back at the young teenager, then turned her attention back to Nina.

"What's wrong with you, Nina? That kid isn't a day over seventeen years old, not to mention that you have a daughter older than he is. Speaking of babies, how is Gracie? How is married life treating her?"

"Rose, I'm not interested in him like that. He's just handsome. Gracie is fine, I guess. Just turned twenty-two and believes that she knows the world. I wanted her to finish school—get a college degree and live a decent life. There was absolutely no need for her to settle down so soon. She shortchanged herself and doesn't even realize it."

"She sounds like somebody I once knew at her age. Are you two talking yet? Or are both of you still being stubborn with each other?"

"She has my number. I know how Gracie works, although she believes that I don't. When she needs me, she'll call."

"I don't mean to get in your business, Nina, but one of you needs to give in. How long has it been since you've spoken to each other? What, six months now? Gracie has been on her own for almost two years now, she's twenty-two, and a grown woman whether you want to admit it or not. You two have got to stop giving each other the silent treatment. You never know what the next day will hold. One of you may wake up and discover that death has come during the night. I just don't understand how you can't see that she's exactly like you were at her age."

"I was a mother at her age, Rose, she isn't." Nina's tone became sharp. "I had made a stupid mistake but accepted my responsibilities. Married with a baby by the time I was twenty, I thought I knew everything and didn't know jack! I had to learn everything as I went along. I didn't know a damn thing about caring for a baby, marriage, a husband, or a mortgage. Granted, Jay said that I didn't have to worry about anything, that he would take care of what needed to be done. He said it as if I were some type of burden to him. In my heart I knew that neither one of us was ready to settle down at the time. We were just doing the right thing." Nina let out a deep sigh. "Jay was nine years older than me, smart, handsome, and had a good job. I remember everyone telling me that I was so lucky to have a man like him. It was as if friends, family, and people in general thought that I was trying to trap him, or something, because he was fresh out of law school and working at a small law firm. But it was nothing like that, I was just incredibly naïve. As sad as it sounds, I didn't think that I could get pregnant my first time. In some respects I guess folks were right. Financially, I never worried about a thing. Whenever I needed anything, he just gave me the money for it. But Jay can be a very mean man when he wants to be. During the time I was pregnant, he would say crap like, I'd better have a boy because girls are nothing but trouble. Or even worse, he'd get me around his friends and insult me by saying that I was the most unattractive pregnant woman he'd ever seen. My skin broke out so badly during the time I was pregnant, and when Jay would embarrass me like that, it hurt my feelings. If the truth were told, that's one of the reasons why I made damn sure that I didn't become pregnant by him again." Nina stopped to think for a moment. " I don't know, Rose. I just see so much of myself in Gracie. I see her making the same wrong choices that I made. I just don't want her to go through the same difficulties that I did."

"I know that over the years you and Jay have had your share of ups and downs. We all have difficulties in our lives that change who we are. But you push through them; you grow and learn. However, I still say that you should be happy for Gracie.

She's young and in love with a man who loves her. He's made a good career in the military, and he is taking care of her."

"Yeah, that's what scares me. He's exactly nine years older than she is, and I don't believe that she fully understands all of the responsibilities of marriage. Sometimes a person can take advantage of you when they know they've got you just where they want you. She's just like I was. She isn't working because he doesn't want her to. He claims he wants to have a large family. I say, he's loading her up so that she can be barefoot, pregnant, and tied down with children while he has his woman on the side and his wife at home. After all of my hard work with Gracie, she's going to end up being a career housewife dependent upon some man for her livelihood."

"Maybe it will be different for her." Rose was being understanding of how Nina felt. "You can only teach your children so much. Then you have to let them walk and make their own path in life."

"I know that, Rose." Nina gazed out the window at the light foot traffic moving down Rush Street. She began to reminisce again.

"Girl, do you remember what Rush Street was like back in the early 1980's? All of the bars and clubs that used to be around here. How you could walk down the street and hear Kurtis Blow singing from every direction. You remember his big hit song, "These Are The Breaks"? There was so much life on this street. Remember how I would have to make up stories about you being sick, or about you having problems with your boyfriend, in order to get out of the house without Gracie?" Nina chuckled to herself, "Girl, you and I would sneak down here and have ourselves a good old time. We'd have to stand in a long line that looped around the corner in order to get into Gino's East Pizzeria, and when we went into the place, you'd see people sneaking to write and carve their names on the walls and the tables. There was a stupid myth that said your love would last if you did that."

Rose smiled, recalling the rare old times that Nina was

speaking of. "Now I understand what this is all about. You're going through one of those midlife things."

"Excuse me!" Nina was all set to get insulted.

"It's perfectly normal," Rose smiled. She folded her hands in front of her, and a moment later rested them on the table. Nina realized by Rose's body language that her friend wasn't trying to be insulting, just understanding.

"I don't know, girl, maybe I am. I don't feel forty. I feel like I'm completely free to do all of the things that I never had a chance to do. I never had the opportunity to party all night long or go club-hopping with friends. I used to love dancing but Jay had a fit every time I would bring it up, so I just let it go. I never had a chance to have my own apartment with a view of Lake Michigan. I moved out of my parents' house and directly into his. Nothing in his apartment at the time expressed who I was. He had album covers and Superfly posters all over the walls, beads hanging in the doorways, and bean bags for furniture. I never got a chance to date or meet different people. Jay and I came down here once and got into an argument because he felt that I should have been at home acting like a respectable mother instead of acting like some floozy in the streets. I got so pissed off with his ass! He could go out on Friday night with the boys but couldn't take me out dancing. Well, now things are different. For the first time in my life, I don't have any maternal responsibilities. I have my own money and my own car. Do you understand what I'm saying?"

Rose propped her elbows on the table and placed her hands in the praying position. "Of course I do. Look at me. I'm forty-three years old with no kids, never been married, and still club-hopping. Well, not like I used to, but I still get out there and do my stepping thing."

"I'm dying to learn how to step. When are you going to teach me?"

"Heifer, I keep telling you to come down on Thursday night when I have my steppers set. All you have to do is learn the basic six count, and you'll be dancing before you know it."

"Excuse me, ladies. The plates are very hot." The young waiter placed their orders in front of them and asked if he could get them anything else. Both of them brushed him off, not needing his services at that particular moment.

"I know, Rose, and believe me, one of these days I'm going to shock you and show up out of the blue." Nina paused for a moment in search of the right words. "Rose, it's difficult for me to express what I'm looking for. All I do know is I'm looking for something different, but I don't know what. I'm just tired of being bored all the time."

"Baby, I know exactly what you're looking for." Rose began pouring maple syrup onto her pancakes. "You want what our young waiter has."

"Rose, I'm not desperate!"

"I know that, but hear me out. From my point of view, the reason that you're looking at the waiter so hard is because of his youth and all of the possibilities that he has. Have you ever heard the saying, youth is wasted on the young and wisdom is wasted on the old?"

"Yeah, I recall something like that."

"What you want is the youth of that young man along with the wisdom that comes with turning forty."

Nina was all set to dispute Rose's claim, but suddenly she lost her words. Maybe she's right, Nina thought.

"Well, don't go get quiet on me now," Rose continued. "I'm not judging you. I have never done that, and I never will. And believe me, by no means are you the first person to feel like that."

"I know, Rose. It's just that the commonsense part of me says, leave the past alone. You've missed out, now move along—age, get old and die. Then there is another part of me screaming out with joy that I've reached the point of freedom again. It's like I have a second opportunity, and I don't want to let this one slip away."

"Well, excuse me for being so frank, honey, but you do realize that you're a married woman. You're speaking as if you're single, or about to be. Does Jay understand how you've been feeling?"

Nina had been holding back from Rose how her feelings toward Jay were changing. Their relationship had been reduced to routine and habit. Jay had become a couch potato, and let his once muscular body go flabby. He refused to control his eating habits and the gut he'd developed was too ridiculous for words. Nina felt like the odd couple whenever they were together. Odd, because he looked like he was nine months pregnant, and she looked like she was about to go run a marathon. Nina had spoken to Jay about his appearance and harmful eating habits. That had pissed him off; his sensitivity about the subject surprised her. "Everyone isn't like you," he growled. "When I was young there were twelve of us and there was never enough of anything, including food. Now I don't have that problem anymore, so I'm going to eat as much as I want! I enjoy eating, I love going to restaurants and trying different foods. And you should be happy that you have a man who likes to take you out and treats you as well as I do." Nina released a huge sigh as she thought about that conversation. It was one of those times in her marriage when she tried to express how she felt about something but by the time all was said and done, she was sorry she'd even brought the subject up. However, there was still that undeniable feeling somewhere deep inside that was screaming at her to break free and enjoy life to the fullest.

"It's difficult for Jay to understand how I feel about things. When I tell him that I'm bored, he really takes it personally. I want to do something other than go out to a movie and then to dinner to watch him stuff himself until he can't eat anymore, then head on home for him to climb his big ass up on me for a quick screw. And I do mean quick." Nina snapped her fingers to emphasize how quick Jay was. "We've had some good years and much better days, I can't deny that, but they seem so long ago. I mean honestly, Rose, how do I tell my husband of twenty years that suddenly he is a total bore? How do I tell him that he doesn't turn me on or satisfy me at all? How do I tell him that he's become self-centered and selfish without getting into a major dispute? The long hours he's working is something else that has been getting on my nerves. He is so absorbed in his job that he can't see, or refuses to see, that there is no time for us."

"Nina, this doesn't sound like something you've just discovered."

"No, Rose, it isn't. I guess over the years I had the job of taking care of Gracie to take my mind off of things. Then as she became a teenager and didn't want to be bothered with me, I occupied my time by going back to school to study accounting."

"Oh, yes," Rose said, "I remember how much he didn't like that idea."

"Could you believe that, girl? All of those years I was just a housewife. I would sit at home and cry my eyes out because I was so bored, scared, and lonely. I was an emotional wreck," Nina recalled, as she sipped her tea. "Then, the minute I wanted to expand my horizons, he tells me that I didn't need a college degree because he would always take care of me. And that there was no need for me to work because he made enough money. That crazy-ass man had me feeling like I still lived at home and that every time I wanted money for something I had to ask him for it just like I was a little girl asking my father for money. It's a damn good thing that I held my ground on that one."

Rose began laughing. "Remember how he called me and told me to stop putting ideas in your head? That he didn't need a college educated wife, and how you were happy with the way things were."

"How could I forget? He blamed you and Oprah for screwing up his entire life. Jay was raised on that old Southern way of thinking. A woman's place was in the house taking care of his kids and screwing him whenever he needed to be satisfied. I don't see how women back then did it. Heck, and believe me when I say that he was not happy about me going to night school. That man did not want me to finish. It took some doing but I finally got that degree, and when I did it was the wildest rush I'd ever experienced."

"You never told me—why didn't he want you to finish?"

"He was listening to his friends tell him how he shouldn't let his woman get more education than he had. With education I would get a better job, make more money, take business trips, and have affairs with men who were just as educated. Funny, it should not have surprised me, the way he felt. His father was the same way with his mother."

"Remember that time you wanted to learn how to drive, and he refused to teach you so you took his keys and taught yourself?" Rose was reviewing how much her friend had grown over the years.

"Oh, God, yes! He will never let me live that one down. He had come home late on a Friday night, drunk from a night out with the boys, and had fallen asleep on the sofa. I got up the following Saturday morning like I always did and fixed his breakfast. Gracie and I ate while he slept. I don't know what got into me. Something just told me to take his keys and go learn how to drive. I told myself that I'd seen him drive enough and it didn't look that hard."

"Girl, that man had a damn holy fit when he discovered that you not only took his car but that you left it in the middle of the street with the keys locked inside."

"I'd only made it about five blocks away from the house. Damn raggedy car. The fuel pump on it went out. After that, his evil ass blamed me for everything that went wrong with the car. But I discovered that driving wasn't as hard as he made it out to be," Rose smiled at Nina. "Jay kept telling me it was a man's job to drive a woman wherever she wanted to go. I realize now that that was his way of keeping up with me. He always knew exactly where I was. I think about how I accepted that mess back then, and I just shake my head. He had total control over me."

"Well, don't be so hard on yourself, Nina. Those were different times. Your thinking wasn't what it is today."

"I understand that, Rose, I really do. It's just that I feel like there are so many things I want to do and experience, but I don't know where to begin. I'm a forty-year-old accountant with no kids, a fat bank account, a sharp ride, and a whole load of free time. For the first time in my life I feel like I'm my own person. I can do whatever I want and not be afraid. When I look at that young waiter I see and understand what he may not yet—the possibilities that life has."

"Boy, life is so strange," Rose pondered. "Here I am, a forty-three-year-old nurse, with no kids, a house, and a nice car. And all I want is to find a decent man to share the rest of my days with. But the only type of men I keep running into are jerks, drug addicts, leeches, mommas' boys and ex-convicts. And here you are, my best friend. You have everything I could ever want, and you're telling me it's not all that it's cracked up to be. What's that phrase about how individuals think the grass is greener on the other side?"

"I'm not saying that Jay is a horrible man. I'm just starting to grow, and my fear is that I'm outgrowing him, and I don't know what to do about it. I'm no longer that frightened little girl that he has to take care of, but he can't see that."

"It sounds to me like you two need a vacation. Something to set off a new spark in your relationship."

"You could be right," Nina replied, thinking of places that she would like to go. "I would love to go to the Bahamas—Jay and I have never been there. You know his favorite vacation is going back to visit relatives in Arkansas. Girl, do you realize that in all these years, that is the only place we've gone for vacation?"

"See, now is the perfect time for you two to head for the Bahamas," Rose said, trying to carefully chew her food and talk at the same time.

"Girl, that is just a fantasy. You know just as well as I do that if Jay hasn't thought about taking me there in all these years, chances are he never wanted to go."

"Well, it's your call, Nina. But it could be just the thing."

"Yes, it could be, but I just don't see it happening. Once you've been with a person for as long as we have, you really know them, from balls to bone."

2

Richard stood in front of the Automated Teller Machine inside First National Bank. He glanced down at the receipt in his hand. Expressions of shock and disbelief were etched on his face. He read the receipt under his breath: "Insufficient funds . . . That's impossible, I just got paid." He reinserted his bank card, certain that this had to be a mechanical error. He heard an impatient sigh from a woman standing behind him in line. *She probably thinks that I don't have a damn dime,* he thought to himself. Once again, he attempted to withdraw fifty dollars from the machine and was immediately denied. He removed his wallet from the inside pocket of his suit jacket. He fumbled around searching for his Visa credit card, but quickly remembered that a few days earlier he had left his credit card at a department store. He'd called the credit card company and had the card cancelled and requested that a new card be issued, but it hadn't arrived yet. He took his bank card and marched over to the long line of patrons waiting to see a bank teller. While he waited he popped open his briefcase and pulled out his direct deposit payroll stub, which was confirmation that funds had been placed into his account.

"Next, please." He looked to his right and saw teller number two waving her hand for him to step down.

"Hello, I just tried to withdraw some money from the teller machine, and I got a message that said insufficient funds," Richard explained.

"Okay, sir," the teller answered with a pleasant tone. "Let me pull up your account." She began pressing the keyboard quick and hard. "Okay, here we go. A withdrawal for three thousand one hundred and twenty-eight dollars was made today by Estelle Vincent."

"What?" Richard couldn't believe what he was hearing.

"She took the money out," the teller continued, "at 12:01 P.M. today."

"So, what's available now?" Richard felt his eyebrows pinching together as his anger swelled. He couldn't believe that Estelle had done this without asking him if it was okay. He didn't have enough money to catch the Metra train home. He didn't even have his checkbook with him to write a check.

"Actually, sir, I'm showing a balance of negative three hundred and five dollars." She continued typing quickly, anticipating his next series of questions.

"Check number seven-eight-two-three posted late this afternoon. And it looks as if your savings account is showing a negative balance as well. Yes, it's showing a balance of negative one hundred and twenty-six dollars and four cents. The only transaction available to you is a deposit." Richard's mind began to race. He wouldn't even look the teller in the face, he was so embarrassed by his situation.

"Excuse me, I need to make a phone call," Richard replied, and marched as quickly as he could to a set of pay phones on the other side of the room. He made a collect call to Estelle at home but he only got the answering machine. "Goddamn it!" He slammed the receiver back down on its hook. His mind began racing—he didn't have a single dollar. He thought about rushing back to the office to catch his secretary and hit her up for a little cash. He'd make up some story about losing his wallet. But as he glanced at his watch, he noticed that it was now five-thirty P.M. and Sherri was definitely gone. *Wait a minute,* he said to himself. She'd mentioned she sometimes caught the five forty-five P.M. train. *Maybe if I rush over to the station I'll be able to catch her there.* He rushed out of the bank and headed south on Michigan Avenue. He kept flipping his wrist, glancing at his watch, keeping a close eye on the time. He had only eight minutes to make it to the train station, which was six blocks away. He started jogging through the thick crowd of window-shoppers, sightseers, and other professionals heading home. A slick sweat quickly formed on his brow as he picked up his pace, noticing that he had only three minutes left to get another two blocks. He reached Michigan and Wacker Drive, where the light was red. He didn't bother waiting for a green light to cross the street. Instead, he took his chances by darting out into traffic, narrowly escaping being hit by a taxi cab. By the time he reached the station it was just past five forty-five P.M. He'd missed her. Richard stood in front of a newspaper stand, staring reality right in the face. He dreaded the thought of listening to his back and feet scream at him all the way home. Walking ten miles in a pair of wing tip dress shoes would most certainly take its toll. However, the thoughts that were demanding most of his attention had to do with why Estelle would withdraw that type of money and not tell him. Why would she allow checks to bounce and be forced to pay overdraft fees? What had made her drain their account completely? Although his mind was asking a thousand questions, Richard knew the answer to them all. Rubylee! His overbearing and meddling mother-in-law was at the center of everything when it came to drama and Estelle. For years Richard had voluntarily placed blinders over his eyes, hoping that Rubylee would stop interfering with his marriage. Many a time, Estelle pulled outrageous stunts at the direction of her mother. On numerous occasions Estelle had gone against his wishes, all for the sake of pleasing Rubylee. He recalled a disagreement they once had, shortly after their marriage. Estelle had developed the habit of giving in to her mother's every demand. One particular day after running errands, Estelle was exhausted and needed to rest. No sooner had Estelle gotten undressed and into bed than Rubylee phoned and commanded her to get up and take her someplace she needed to go.

"Momma I'm tired." Richard listened to Estelle as she spoke on the phone. "Why not? Because I don't feel like it. It's not my job to drive you everywhere you need to go." There was a long pause and Richard could hear Rubylee shouting at Estelle through the telephone. "Fine Momma! Just come over and pick up the keys to the car."

Estelle was forced to loan her mother her car so she could handle her affairs. Rubylee's influence surfaced again when Justine, her irresponsible, criminally inclined, and emotionally unstable younger daughter, got hold of Estelle's car keys and disappeared with the car. Justine was on probation; Estelle refused to report the car stolen as Richard suggested because she didn't want to be the cause of her sister returning to jail. Three weeks later, the police department sent Estelle a certified letter informing her that her car had been stripped, abandoned, impounded, and was slated for the wrecking block. Estelle still had two years left to pay on the car, and Richard was furious about it and wanted her to press charges.

"Let it go Estelle, you know your sister isn't quite right in the head," is what Richard recalled hearing Rubylee say when he and Estelle went over to Rubylee's dingy, cluttered apartment to talk about what had happened. "Besides, you know that she's on probation for check fraud, burglary, and theft. The judge said that if she saw her again she'd see to it that Justine did hard time. And if they locked your sister up, I'd never forgive you for turning her in."

"What do you mean you'd never forgive her? It's not Estelle's fault!" Richard got loud. "Justine should have thought about that before she stole the car!" Richard shouted.

"Who are you raising your voice at, Richard?" Rubylee asked, daring him to step out of line again. "I hope you don't think that you can walk into my house and snap off like you've lost your damn mind." Rubylee's words and nerves were as sharp as a razor's edge. Richard was about to completely unload but Estelle stopped him from doing something that Rubylee would make him regret later. Estelle had learned long ago to always stay on Rubylee's better side. Even if it meant going against her husband's wishes.

Estelle never pressed charges, and continued to pay for a car she no longer owned so that she wouldn't default on her loan. Eventually, when some of the tension in the air cleared, Justine returned, wearing raunchy clothes and extremely tasteless jewelry and acting as if she'd been away traveling and had nothing to do with the missing car. It was then that it dawned on Richard that Justine more than likely took the car to some alley chop shop, got whatever money she could get for it, then left it up to the chop shop thugs to dispose of the remains. Shortly after the incident, Estelle began using Richard's car to handle her mother's affairs. It wasn't long before scheduling conflicts arose. When Richard needed his car, Estelle had already scheduled to use it. However, Estelle knew exactly how to handle Richard. Sex! Every time he got mad, all she had to do was arch her back, press her behind across his manhood, tell him that she was all his, wait for it to rise, squeeze it with her hand, and take him to bed for a night of passionate lovemaking. It was so easy. After it was all over, Richard would be angry with himself for allowing Estelle to control him. Allowing himself to be manipulated by Estelle with sex was Richard's weakness and his biggest flaw.

Richard's feet were starting to throb, and his lower back and knees ached from walking on the hard concrete. He had taken off his suit jacket, undone his tie and unbuttoned a few buttons on his shirt. The hot June sun was taking its toll on him. He could see a temperature reader on the side of a building in front of him that read ninety-one degrees. Sweat was dripping off of him from everywhere. This stretch of Michigan Avenue was a depressed commercial area. There were no homes, no business offices that he could duck into to cool off, and no fast food restaurants that he could walk into for a cup of water. There were only a few scattered dilapidated buildings and a couple of parking lots. He silently wished for a gas station with a small bathroom where he could wet a paper towel and wipe his face. Once Richard reached Eighteenth Street and Michigan Avenue, he decided to head over to the lakefront and take the bicycle path the rest of the way. At least there were drinking fountains along the path.

Richard began to think more about the relationship that he and Estelle had. It was difficult for him to swallow the fact that they had been married for eight years now. At times like this he couldn't help but wonder if the person that he'd chosen to be his wife was indeed the right person. Did she love him? Or did she take his kind, quiet, and simple ways as a weakness? It was the question of respect that kept his wound of anger open. What had happened to the way he used to feel about her, he asked himself. Why was it that he didn't like coming home the way he used to? What had happened to those feelings of just wanting to hear her voice or see her smile? Absent were the feelings of just wanting to do something special for her, like buying flowers or taking her out to dinner and a play.

There had been days when Estelle would come home feeling awful due to a chaotic day. Richard didn't mind turning off the Bulls game to rub her shoulders and listen attentively to the events of her day. He used to adore the way she expressed herself. But his feelings toward Estelle had changed somewhere along the line, and he wasn't quite sure when or how. It just seemed as if all of a sudden he couldn't stand the sound of her voice any longer. Whenever she spoke to him she reminded him of a street hustler pushing her opinion on him, trying to gain a larger degree of control over him. It was as if she wanted to be the sole decision-maker. She wanted him to think exactly like her and not for himself. He began questioning her reasoning and she took it personally. Estelle didn't like having her views challenged by him. It wasn't until recently that he'd fully understood that it was her way of saying "how dare you question my domination over you." Whenever there was a disagreement between them, he always ended up on the defensive, explaining himself to her and waiting for her approval. It bewildered him that she was able to do that. However, the greater reality was that he had grown tired of Estelle and her ways.

At the start of their relationship he had wanted to be her Prince Charming and take her away from inner-city life and move her into a nice house in Barrington, which was a beautifully landscaped suburb outside the city. "Just wait until I finish dental school," he kept telling her, "I'm going to build a beautiful castle for us to live in and raise a family." Family arrived a bit earlier than anticipated when Estelle became pregnant with their son, Nathan, during Richard's last year of dental school. Richard married Estelle because he felt that it was the proper thing to do. It was difficult during that last year, but through sacrifice, struggle, and determination, Richard completed the training necessary to start his career. After he completed his residency, he took a job as an associate in a local practice. Then, with both barrels loaded, he set out to fulfill his dream of owning a home with a front and back yard, a garden, a fireplace, vaulted ceilings with skylights, and a spiral staircase. He wanted Nathan to grow up in a safe neighborhood and attend the best schools.

Richard's dream was not what Estelle and Rubylee had in mind. "Why do you want to go way out there in the middle of nowhere with a bunch of white folks and be the only darkies in the neighborhood?" Rubylee objected to his plans for the future. According to her, the problem with black people was that "when they get a little money in their pocket they rush off to be next to the white man." Richard became annoyed with Rubylee and her intrusiveness. He ached for the opportunity to criticize her round-as-a-barrel figure and the raspy breathing that made her sound like Darth Vader. He longed to argue with her over her non-existent credentials and education that she believed gave her the right to interfere with the plans he had for his family.

Richard felt that his education gave him a certain amount of superiority over Rubylee but what he didn't realize was that

Rubylee had a different type of education, a shrewdness learned from the streets that gave her an equal amount of superiority over him. "What you need to do is get yourself one of those old buildings with six flats over in Englewood." Rubylee advised with labored breathing. Richard almost had a heart attack— Englewood had burned to the ground in 1968 after the Martin Luther King assassination and had never been rebuilt to its full potential.

"I could take the apartment on the first floor on one side and you, Estelle, and Nathan could live right across the hall from me. You could rent the rest of the units out to Section-8 tenants. Make yourself a little extra money that way and the government will help pay for it." Richard's neck and shoulders grew extremely tense as he prepared for a fight. There was no way he was going to let Rubylee, of all people, alter the plans he'd made. He sensed a storm coming, he just didn't realize how big a storm it would be.

Richard directed Rubylee's attention to his newly acquired diploma on the wall and put his words in plain English. "That piece of paper means that I don't have to deal with the unpredictable profession of hustling the government!" He barked at her in a tone that was filled with anger and confrontation. Then, like a true fighter, Rubylee came out swinging and counterattacked, informing him that she and Estelle had already discussed her plan and decided it was the best course of action.

It was at a time like this that a man expects to receive the full support of his wife, and Richard refused to believe that Estelle would make alternate plans after the many nights they had sat in bed planning out their future. There was no way she would do such a thing to him. However, the guilty look on Estelle's face confirmed that she had made different plans without consulting him. The feeling of betrayal hit Richard like a huge blow and he was momentarily paralyzed by the mental anguish. Estelle argued her case, asserting that they needed a babysitter, pointing out that Rubylee didn't own a car to make it out to the suburbs, and saying how she didn't want a strange person looking after Nathan while the two of them worked. Soon he could no longer distingiush her words, and felt his shoulders slump forward in defeat. Richard never recovered from that act of disloyalty.

That was four years ago. Richard had never purchased his home or Rubylee's building. He'd hoped that Estelle would come to her senses, but that didn't look likely anytime soon. And now this. Richard tried to rationalize things. He tried to tell himself that there had to be a perfect explanation for this type of deceit. "What the hell is going on?" he shouted out as he walked down the path. *No*, he thought, attempting to calm himself, there was no rational explanation for this. This was clearcut deception, no doubt about it. Estelle was not going to worm her way out of this one. It was time to start getting even. Now things were starting to come to light in his mind. It was the mistrust that Estelle had aroused that made him not want to discuss his day with her. It was her lack of respect that made him not give a damn about her day. It was the very sight of Rubylee and Justine's young daughter, Keysha, that made the hair at the nape of his neck rise.

"Richard, is that you?" A female runner heading in the opposite direction started to slow down her pace. Richard looked in the runner's direction as she slowly approached him. It was Nina. Richard recognized her walk and her beautiful sweat-covered, honey-shaded skin immediately. His eyes traveled slowly over her, stopping at her muscled abdomen, which was left exposed by the sports top she was wearing. His eyes made a quick series of stops at her belly button, wonderful hips, strong thighs, and defined calves.

"Hey, Nina." Richard forced a smile. Nina stopped and began jogging in place.

"Why haven't I seen you in my aerobics class?" She spoke slowly, regulating her breathing, and then made a playful motion as if she were about to hit him in the stomach.

"Looks like you've been letting yourself slip a little. I hope you can keep up with me when you do decide to return."

Suddenly, all of the issues that were plaguing Richard took a quick back seat. Running into Nina was a much needed diversion from all the turmoil that was going on in his mind.

"Nina, where do you get all of your energy?"

"A little pink bunny rabbit," she said, watching as Richard's naturally beautiful smile gave way to a wonderful laugh that was like music to her ears. Nina was feeling flirtatious, not that she intended to flirt with Richard. She knew he was married. It was the way she'd caught his eyes scanning her that rushed a small wave of excitement through her. Besides, she didn't see any harm in flirting with this tall glass of water.

"Turn around; where are the batteries you took from the poor thing?" Richard said, completely embracing the moment.

"What are you doing out here in this hot sun walking in a suit?" Nina inquired. At that instant Richard's thoughts traveled back to Estelle and his rage. Nina noticed his sudden change of expression.

"Are you okay Rich?"

"Yeah, it's just that . . . Well, you know how it is when you leave your wallet at home and don't discover it until you go looking for money?"

"Oh, yes, been there and done that."

"Well, anyway, that's why I'm out here. I'm walking home."

"Man! How far do you have to go, sugar?"

"Oh, I'd say another four miles."

"Richard, that's too far to walk in all of this heat. Look, my car is right up here at the exit you just passed about a quarter mile back. It's a short walk, and it's air-conditioned. I'll give you a ride home." For a moment Richard wanted to do the courteous thing and say, "oh no, I couldn't inconvenience you that way," but he didn't, he wanted that ride more than a kid wants a toy for Christmas.

"You're an angel, Nina. I owe you big time. You just don't know how badly my feet are killing me."

"Richard, please! You don't owe me anything. I'm just glad I'm able to help you out. Come on, I'll give you a piggyback ride—oops, just kidding." Nina had always been able to read body language well. And she knew that Richard had an extraordinary amount of concern running through his head. That expression on his face was familiar—she'd seen it plastered on her own. Although she didn't mention it, she truly hoped that he'd be able to work it out.

3

Nina stood in front of her dresser mirror putting the finishing touches on her makeup. She opened a tube of honey-colored lipstick and applied it to her bottom lip. She puckered her lips inward, then made a small smacking sound as if she were kissing someone. She studied the color against her skin and agreed with the saleslady at Marshall Field's. The color did complement her coloring; it had just the right amount of contrast. She stood proudly in front of the mirror because although she'd been out running earlier, she'd spent a considerable amount of time fixing the tight curls on her short hair. She'd gotten the top to curl just so and her bangs to come down over her forehead just right.

A steady flow of water was coming out of the shower. She listened as it stopped, and heard the shower curtain rings slide against the curtain rod. She stepped away from the mirror and began putting on her heels. Jay despised having to wait for her to get dressed, so in order to avoid listening to his ranting she made sure she was fully dressed by the time he was out of the shower.

"What time is it, Nina?" Jay bellowed from the bathroom. She glanced at the clock.

"Quarter to eight."

"Why didn't you say something? We're going to be late for our eight o'clock dinner reservation." It was Friday night and Jay was determined to take her out for her birthday ahead of time since he was going to be out of town on the actual day. Nina assured him that there was no need, she did not want to make a production out of turning forty. Besides, she wasn't even all that hungry. But Jay insisted on having his way, saying he had something special to tell her.

"I didn't know that you had reservations for eight P.M.," Nina replied, as she watched Jay walk out of the bathroom naked and wet to pick up the phone and call the restaurant. Oftentimes she would inspect Jay and wonder what had happened to the man she once knew. He'd been such a tall, slender man, with broad shoulders, a wide chest, and strong arms that she loved being held by. Now his long legs were just that, long legs, like branches on a tree. The almond beach-ball belly, riddled with stretch marks, was a complete turnoff to her. As she thought about it, a sense of guilt slowly started taking hold of her. Was she wrong for feeling completely unattached to him? She didn't mind the aging process, and knew that no one could stop Father Time. But in her mind, you could damn sure slow him down.

They arrived at Nick's Fish Market, which was an expensive seafood restaurant downtown. As Nina searched the menu she could feel Jay's eyes on her. For a moment she felt a twinge of excitement. Maybe he was going to be more attentive to her, like they'd discussed a thousand times before. Maybe he was noticing how nice her hair looked or the new lipstick she'd purchased. Maybe he'd notice that although she was forty she didn't look a day over thirty, just like Rose had said. Nina folded the menu so she could focus her attention on him. She studied his smooth maple brown skin and teddy-bear eyes. She anticipated him saying something wonderful, somehow finding the right words to express his feelings for her. Perhaps he'd tell her that he didn't have to work so many hours or travel so much. Or even better, maybe he'd put some thought into getting a present instead of just giving her money and telling her to go buy herself something.

"I talked to Gracie yesterday," he said, smiling like the cat that ate the canary.

"Oh, how is she?" Nina felt her heart sink. "Is everything okay?"

"Oh, yes, just fine. The surprise is, she's pregnant! You're going to be a grandmother!" Jay boasted proudly. Nina felt her face fall to the floor. That's what his surprise was?

"Well? Aren't you excited? We're going to be grandparents. We get to spoil the child rotten and then send it home." Jay had an enormous smile on his face. Before Nina thought about what she was saying, she blurted out, "I'm not taking care of her kid!"

"What's the matter with you? And why do you have an ugly attitude all of a sudden? I thought for sure you'd be happy." That just went to show how much attention he paid her. The last word Nina wanted to hear was grandmother.

"If that's what Gracie wants, then I'm happy for her. However, I'm not ready to be anyone's grandmother," Nina snapped. She picked up the menu and focused on what she wanted to eat so that they could get out of there and go home. She was angry at herself for even thinking that Jay would notice all of the effort she put into making herself look good for him.

"Nina, it's not your choice. This is Gracie and Mark's child. She's starting a family and that's a wonderful thing. What is it with you and Gracie?"

"Nothing, Jay," Nina answered with a sharp edge in her voice.

"Humph," Jay replied suspiciously. He knew something was going on but didn't want to attempt to figure out the details. He chalked it up to one of those mother-daughter things that he couldn't possibly understand. One thing was undeniable, though: Nina had changed so much over the years that at times he didn't know who she was.

"Whatever it is between you two, you need to fix it. I know

that you're upset about her not finishing school. Hell, I am too, but I don't dwell on it. I let it go and you need to do the same."

The waiter came, and she ordered a chicken Caesar salad. Jay ordered the catfish dinner, which included greens, macaroni and cheese, and cornbread. He ordered a beer to wash it all down. Before long, the waiter placed their orders in front of them. Nina sat silently. Every now and then she glanced up and watched Jay sweat as he stuffed himself, perfectly content, not noticing her or speaking to her. Nina's thoughts then switched over to Gracie and how the relationship between the two of them had gone sour. She had become disappointed, then heart-broken, and finally angry with Gracie for not holding up her end of the agreement they'd hammered out for her future. The letdown had cut Nina deep in her heart, and although Gracie didn't live in the house anymore, the wound was still very fresh.

Nina began to think about the many nights, when Gracie was still a teenager, when she would come into her room, sit on the bed, and talk with her about whatever. Gracie wanted to go to law school like Jay and eventually become a judge. Nina's heart swelled with such pride; she was so proud of her little girl for making such grand plans for her future. Her little princess, whose hair she'd washed in the kitchen sink, would sit between her legs every other school night while she combed her hair and oiled her scalp with Royal Crown hair grease. During Gracie's childhood, Nina loved holding her small hand as she walked her to school in the early days of her primary education. She'd felt such joy watching Gracie run up the school steps with her Wonder Woman backpack on. Gracie had such wild excitement about learning new things. Nina could still hear herself calling out to Gracie "Have a good day; learn something new so you can tell me all about it."

By the time Gracie reached the seventh grade she'd become an honor student. She'd won the local school district spelling bee, and after that, an essay contest. Gracie became president of her student council and editor of her school newspaper. Nina was there every step of the way, guiding, giving encouragement, and reinforcing the power of a positive attitude. "You have a beautiful mind, Gracie; it would be a terrible thing to waste it," she would always tell her. Nina had borrowed the phrase from the Lou Rawls' Parade of Stars, which was a telethon to raise money for historically black universities.

By the time Gracie reached the eighth grade, Nina had discussed with Jay that she herself needed to go back to school. How could she tell Gracie not to waste her beautiful mind when all she had accomplished at the time was making a baby and becoming a housewife. Jay fought the whole idea, but Nina held her ground and enrolled in Roosevelt University downtown. It was tough being a full-time mom and student. Nina took classes during the day while Jay was at work and Gracie was in school. Some semesters, Nina took night classes and took Gracie along with her. Gracie enjoyed going to college with her and sitting in the classes listening to the professors speak. The two of them would spend their entire Sunday at the library working on projects and term papers, strengthening their bond. Nina was feeling such a sense of accomplishment during those four years that she remained a full time student even during the summers. By the time Gracie was graduating from high school, Nina was graduating from college. Ironically, both graduations were on the same day. Nina did not attend hers, however. In her mind, what Gracie had accomplished was far more important. Gracie graduated as president of her class with a 4.0 grade point average, was voted most likely to succeed, and received the school's first award granted to a student for perfect attendance.

The two of them made plans for Gracie's college career. Although Jay was proud of his little girl, he feared the soaring costs of a college education and wanted her to attend a community college and take a part-time job. After all, he'd just helped Nina get her degree. But Nina would not have it. She explained to Jay that there was no way Gracie would be going to go to a community college when some pretty impressive universities had already accepted her. By arguing that they could find educational scholarships and reminding him of her eventual employment, Nina won Jay over to the idea that it was possible for Gracie to attend the black university of her choice, which was Howard University. Nina was proud that through sacrifice and commitment, Gracie was going to go to a university and live the dorm room life. It wouldn't be exactly living on her own, but it would give her a taste of what independence felt like. She didn't want her to attend night school like she had. Once Gracie's undergraduate studies where finished, Nina would find a way to get her a part-time job in an office to help with the cost of law school tuition. A week before Gracie went away to school Nina landed herself a job at a well-known accounting firm. She'd held up her end of the bargain. Her little girl was on her way to becoming Judge Gracie Epps and Nina's pride was running high. She'd gotten Gracie through high school without her becoming pregnant. She'd kept Gracie focused and on the right track. She wanted Gracie to go out into the world and cut a path for herself, not depend upon a man for her livelihood like she herself had. She wanted Gracie to make her own money, travel the world and see new and exciting things. Take exotic vacations instead of the ones like she'd taken to Arkansas all of her life. Nina wanted Gracie to have the chance to experience the life that she had always wanted. She imagined Gracie becoming valedictorian and graduating at the top of her class.

Gracie's first two years of college went well. However, something went terribly wrong in the third year. Suddenly Gracie didn't call home as much, which was totally unlike her. Whenever Nina did reach her, Gracie was curt with her, and Nina didn't understand why. Whenever she tried to communicate with Gracie about the future, she didn't want to discuss it. Finally, after not hearing from Gracie for a month, Nina flew out to see her. Something was going on, and she aimed to find out what it was. She discovered that Gracie no longer lived on campus. She'd moved into an apartment with a boyfriend and was currently on academic probation. Nina knew right then what the problem was. Plain old sex! Intercourse had been responsible for Gracie losing her damn mind. The thought of Gracie not succeeding was too much for her to bear. She did all that she could to convince Gracie that she was destroying the plans they'd made. She told her that she'd go talk to the dean of students about her probation; after all, she'd dumped twenty-four thousand dollars into the institution over the past two years, and someone was going to listen to her. She pleaded with Gracie to pack her things and come with her, but Gracie stood up against Nina in pure defiance. Gracie insisted that she was a grown woman and that she wouldn't allow Nina to control her anymore. She told her mother that she had a man who loved her and that's all she needed.

Nina felt a strong urge to snatch the naps out of Gracie's head but she didn't. She attempted to reason with Gracie woman-to-woman. It was okay that Gracie had discovered passion and lust and all that went along with it as long as she remained responsible. She reminded Gracie to keep her eyes on the prize. To get focused again like she knew she could, finish school and continue on to law school. If the man she was sleeping with truly loved her, he would let her complete her education. None of what Nina attempted worked, and it was only a matter of time. Gracie eventually flunked out in her third year. That's when she decided to come home and introduce Mark and announce that she had married him. From the moment Nina set eyes on him she knew that he was a slick, fast-talking, pimp-daddy type of man that she didn't care for.

"So what was Rose talking about when you two went out Sunday?" Jay broke Nina's train of thought, tossing out a question in hope of starting a conversation.

"Huh? Oh, nothing really—she took me to breakfast and afterwards she took me to the spa; I got a massage and facial, then we did some shopping, ate dinner, and I came home." Nina didn't feel like talking. Thinking about Gracie was giving her a migraine. She welcomed the sight of the waiter bringing the check.

As the two of them drove back home Jay placed his hand on Nina's thigh and began to slowly rub it.

"You look nice tonight," he complimented her. "Did you like the food?"

"It was okay," Nina answered, knowing Jay's intentions all too well. His passions were stirring; she could hear it in his voice. The only time he complimented her was when he wanted to get a little action. In Nina's mind their love life had deteriorated to a low that she never knew existed. She wanted to snatch his hand off of her thigh, but instead her thoughts took her to what was going to happen later that evening. He would come to her wanting to satisfy himself and afterwards he'd quickly drop off into a deep sleep. Jay only cared about himself and his needs. He didn't like to put out the effort to turn her on. He would crawl on top of her and pry her legs apart with his own. Then he'd thrust himself into her while she was still dry and proceed to have some of the most uncomfortable sex known to woman. He'd rest all of his body weight on her, which would make her feel as if he were crushing her. She'd have to push up on his chest so that she could breath. It's at that point that she'd pray for him to hurry up because the pain of dry penetration was unbearable. Whenever she mentioned the fact that he wasn't pleasing her, he took great offense, and told her that it wasn't him, something must be wrong with her. This hurt Nina in a way she'd never imagined. Attacking his manhood is what he accused her of, and to him that was a federal offense. The thought of him maneuvering his body on top of her made her stomach go sour. She would have to endure the smell of beer on his breath. Nina didn't want to think about Jay anymore, so she allowed her thoughts to drift and focus on more pleasant things, like Richard and his wonderful smile.

4

It was eleven P.M. when Richard finally heard Estelle's key in the lock. She walked through the door with Nathan, who was beaming with energy and excitement. Richard sat on the sofa with his eyes fixed on her like an animal ready to attack its prey. He didn't want to ask questions right then; all he wanted to do was go with his anger and knock the hell out of her. The idea was so inviting that he clenched his fists as hard as he could.

"Daddy!" Nathan, his four-year-old son, rushed over to Richard and jumped up on his lap, then locked his arms around Richard's neck for a tight hug. "Guess what?" Before Richard could answer, Nathan blurted out. "We got Grandma a new car today. It's brown, and has a radio and—"

"Nathan, why don't you go to your room and get ready for bed," Richard said through clenched teeth. "Your mother and I need to talk."

"Okay, but will you come in and read me a story before I go to sleep?"

"Yes, I'll be there in a second or two." Nathan hopped down and rushed past Estelle, who told him to run himself some bath water.

"What the fuck happened to all of the goddamn money?" Richard stood up and approached Estelle.

"Why are you looking at me like you're crazy and want to hit me? You'd better think about that before you do it. And don't you curse at me!" Estelle stood up to him boldly, attempting to gain control of the situation. The last thing she needed to deal with was abuse. She placed the palm of her hand on his chest and slowly pushed him back far enough so she could move around him and head for the kitchen. She was nervous as hell because she'd never seen that look in Richard's eyes before. *This may be the straw that breaks the camel's back,* she thought.

Richard followed close behind her. She went through the cabinets in search of a pot to boil water for tea, then grabbed an apple from the basket on the table. Estelle opened the knife drawer and pulled out the biggest one inside to peel the skin off of the apple. She was no fool, and under no circumstances was she going to start letting Richard beat up on her. No, if he wanted to get physical about this, she would burn him with the hot water or stab him, if it came to that. Richard hadn't even noticed Estelle peeling the apple with the large knife. He pinned her against the sink counter and placed one hand at each side of her hips so that she was unable to move. Estelle lowered her arms to her sides, gripping the knife tightly in one hand and allowing the apple to fall to the floor. Richard got in her face.

"I said, what the fuck happened to all of the money?" Richard roared. "I'm not playing with you Estelle!"

"I was out at a car dealership today with my mother and Justine. Mom has saved herself up a little money to buy a car so that she won't have to depend on me driving her everywhere. The first car that we looked at in her price range seemed to have a lot of mechanical problems so the salesman showed us a better car that cost a little more. Mom test-drove it, and she really liked it. So she asked me if I would give her the money to get the car. I told her that I didn't have it right then, but my sister

Justine said that tomorrow she would give me back the money I loaned Mom for the car. Justine has her little street hustle on the side and said that she could have the money back to me in the morning. So I went down to the bank, and got the money so that she could get the car."

"That is the dumbest shit I've ever heard!" Richard began barking at Estelle like a dog gone mad. "You could have waited until tomorrow to get the car if that was the case. Do you know how many goddamn checks bounced today? Do you have any idea of what we are going to owe in overdraft and bounced check fees? Do you realize that I had to walk home today because I couldn't get any money for the train? And what in hell makes you think that your sister is going to give you four thousand dollars? Come on, Estelle, I'd love to hear this one!" Richard felt himself losing the small amount of control that he had left. He was angry like he'd never been before, and he wanted to fight, he wanted to swing and hit. Estelle could see it in his eyes, his posture and tone of voice. She attempted to push him away from her again with her free hand but he wouldn't move.

"Get your goddamn hand off of me!" he snarled at her with a razor-sharp tone. Estelle tightened her grip on the knife, fearing that she would be forced to protect herself. "Tell me, Estelle, because I'm just dying to know. What was it that Rubylee and Justine said to you that made you drain out the account, bounce checks, and leave your husband without a dime? I want to know, because the two of them need to go into fucking business. Tell me, please! I want to use the same pitch on some people I know! And why didn't you call me before you did that?"

"Because I knew that you would say no! Besides, part of the money was my own, you know." Estelle was barking back at him now.

"No, seven hundred and sixty-four dollars of it was yours. The other thirty two hundred dollars belongs to me!"

"I've always helped my mother and whatever I can do for

her I'm going to do, regardless. I don't want her to have to catch the bus or pay those high-priced cab drivers. But you wouldn't understand that because you are so damn selfish and self-centered! I knew that we had the money in the bank so I gave it to her. I'm tired of driving her every place she needs to go. Don't you see how this is going to help us?"

"How in the hell is this helping us? You've put us in a fucking hole!"

"I've already asked you once to stop cursing at me, I'm not going to ask again. Like I told you, Justine said that she would have the money back to me in the morning. I will take care of the overdraft fees, end of conversation."

"Oh, by no means is this the end, Estelle. No! You've gone too far this time. What you've done was completely disrespectful to me. There is no way in hell I would have done something like that to you. When I married you, I didn't know I was getting a package deal, but I see now. You will put your mother before our marriage."

Now Estelle roared back. "Richard, grow up and get over it! It's not the end of the world. My mother and I are very close and you seem to have a problem with that. Don't make me choose between you and her. Now, you need to back up away from me." Estelle angled the knife toward his thigh.

There was a voice in the back of Richard's mind telling him that she needed to be put in her place. She had gotten too bold. She didn't know how to back up and bow down when a man was about to lose complete control. A voice in his mind kept encouraging him to hit her one good time right in the mouth. It told him he would feel better if he did. It would teach her the lesson she needed to learn. Hitting her would let her know who was in charge here. Richard clenched his fist into a tight ball and narrowed his eyes. He could feel the adrenaline rushing through his chest, arms, and fists. He gritted his teeth and locked his jaws as the rage took him over. Estelle could feel the air around her turning thick with danger. Something horrible was about to happen, something she hadn't planned on dealing with. She was set to thrust the knife into his flesh if he hit her. Richard raised his arm and cocked it back. Estelle braced herself for the impact but just then Nathan entered the kitchen crying.

"Please, stop yelling," he pleaded with both of them. Hearing Nathan's tiny squeaky voice and seeing the tears running down his face, Richard realized he needed to back off. One thing he didn't want was to emotionally upset Nathan by beating on Estelle.

"Now look at what you've done, Richard. You've gotten him all upset with your shouting. Move!" Estelle dropped the knife on the floor and pushed Richard away. It was the first time he'd noticed the knife and how critical the situation could have become. He collected himself, walked out of the kitchen and out the door. He needed some fresh air and space to calm himself down.

Estelle grabbed a paper towel and dried Nathan's tears. Things hadn't gone as she had planned. She wanted Richard to accept what she had done and forget about it like he'd done so many times before. She had never seen that type of fire in Richard's eyes. But she knew him, and knew that he would get over it. Like he has always gotten over things like this. That was her security blanket. The fact that Richard could be pushed beyond the line drawn in the sand. She liked that weakness in him. It gave her the chance to take liberties that she knew no other man would stand for. A bath would make Nathan fall asleep quickly, which would be good, and it would give her time to prepare for Richard's return. She would apologize to him in her special way. She knew that he would want a good release when he returned, so she would prepare herself to be all over him when he got back. She would fix up a quick meal, something heavy that wouldn't take long to cook. Two cheeseburgers with grilled onions and mushrooms should do the trick. She would have a nice hot bath waiting for him so he'd be able to soak. *Yes,* she told herself. She would get Richard to go along with her like he always had. When he walked through the door, she'd throw her arms around his neck and whisper in his ear that she didn't want to fight anymore. She'd move her hand down over his manhood, squeeze it a few times and as usual his body would betray his current mood and she'd have him where she needed him to be, relaxed and agreeable. She couldn't believe that Justine tricked her like she had. Justine never had that type of money to give back to Estelle and told her so after she'd gotten in the driver's seat of Rubylee's new car and was about to pull off. Now, in typical Justine fashion, she'd disappeared. Rubylee offered to try and help Estelle put the money back but Estelle knew that her mother would be unable to do that. Estelle had no idea how she was going to take care of all the bounced checks and overdraft fees.

5
_____

Rubylee lay flat on her back in bed, gazing up at the ceiling and listening to Keysha, her granddaughter, making a raucous noise with her snoring. Keysha was now fifteen years old but still slept in the fetal position like a needy infant. Rubylee tossed the covers back and swung her feet over the side of the bed and onto the floor. She rocked a few times, then heaved herself to her feet, for she was no longer a tall slender woman like she once was. She stretched and yawned, then slipped her swollen feet into her slightly torn pair of house shoes and shuffled out of the room toward the kitchen.

Scratching her drooping breasts, she filled a kettle with water and placed it over the burner on the stove. She turned the flame up and opened the cabinet to pull out the coffee can. She made her way over to the back door, unlocked several locks, swung the door open, and greeted the yellow Sunday morning sun. Scooting a chair away from her wooden kitchen table, she placed it on the back porch next to the banister. She moved a curtain aside and took her radio off the windowsill—it had a coat hanger for an antenna. She sat in the chair with the radio in her lap and began adjusting the knob. She noticed on the frequency dial that a cockroach had crawled inside and died. So she slapped the side of the radio a few times, hoping to knock it out, but it was no use, the bug was stuck inside. She found the AM radio station she had been searching for and listened as Billy Holiday sang "Good Morning Heart Ache," propping her arm up on the banister of the porch and looking out over the vacant lot below her, which was full of broken glass, hard dirt, and broken chunks of concrete.

Reaching inside the pocket of her robe, she pulled out her cigarettes and lighter. She spun the wheel on the lighter, watched the flame shoot up, and ignited her smoke. As she exhaled, she felt the nicotine relax her. Justine had wronged her grandbaby by abandoning her the way she had. Justine had mistreated Keysha from the day Keysha could kick inside of her belly. Justine fed baby Keysha sour milk, screamed at her to be quiet when her little squeals got on her nerves, and refused to change her diaper on a regular basis. Rubylee had never seen such a horrible example of diaper rash as she had seen on baby Keysha.

Rubylee did not bite her tongue about how Justine was treating her grandchild. She got on her ass every time she saw Justine. However, Justine was just like her father, Stanback. Just like him, she carried anger around like a purse on her shoulder. She had a short fuse, a hot temper, was prone to violence, loved to hustle, hated authority, didn't like to be told she was wrong, and accepted no responsibility for her actions. Rubylee had raised Justine the best way she knew how, but she was completely unequipped to supply Justine with the nurturing she needed. So she did the next best thing. She made excuses for her and carried the responsibility for Justine's malicious acts and ugly ways. Rubylee was convinced that Justine was unable to help herself because she had inherited so many ugly traits from her father, Stanback, who was nothing like Estelle's father, Albert.

Albert was the only man that Rubylee would admit she truly loved. In her mind, a woman could only fall in true love with a man once. If he broke her heart, she would never be able to fully trust any other man ever again. She and Albert had known

H. H.

each other since they were children. They lived next door to each other in a slumlord building on the corner of Jackson and Pulaski Streets in the westside neighborhood of Chicago. Rubylee's mother and Albert's mother both came to Chicago together in 1944 during the great migration of blacks from Mississippi during World War II. After arriving at Central Station on Roosevelt Road, they settled into the poverty-stricken section of Chicago known to black natives of Chicago as Jew Town. Before blacks began inhabiting the area, it was where Jewish immigrants settled when they arrived from the old country. The two mothers found work as maids in the nearby community of Hyde Park, known for its million-dollar mansions. Rubylee surrendered herself for the very first time to Albert on the night of his senior prom. He was a year older than she was, and made her feel so special that night. When she later discovered she had become pregnant with Estelle, she was happy because she knew that Albert was the type of man who took care of his responsibilities.

Upon graduating from high school, Albert received orders that he was going to Vietnam. His best friend Henry volunteered to go and before long, they were shipped directly into the service and rushed off to the war. Albert promised her that he would take care of everything as soon as he returned. They'd get married, he'd apply for the GI bill, buy the three of them a house so they could live a decent life. Rubylee promised to wait for him, and pledged to always be true to him. Albert was her first love, the first man that had made love to her and told her that he loved her. Rubylee knew that he was a man of his word. During the summer of 1966, Rubylee gave birth to Estelle. She never finished her senior year because she had to take care of Estelle. Albert wasn't there for the birth, but Rubylee mailed him several pictures of baby Estelle. He regretted that he wasn't there helping out like a man should. By that point, Albert had volunteered to stay overseas longer in order to make more money. He promised that he would be extra careful to stay alive because he loved her so much. Rubylee loved reading his words and it filled her up with such pride. She prided herself on having a man in the military who could take care of a woman. She was so proud to have a man who had finished high school. There were so many men around the neighborhood who hadn't graduated and fell into the only things available to uneducated black men—hustling, gambling, drug dealing, and robbery.

Both Albert and Henry were due home in the fall of 1969. Albert had been gone three long years by that point and Rubylee couldn't wait to toss her arms around him. But only Henry came back, missing both of his legs. He told the horrific tale of how Albert had been gunned down by the enemy while attempting to lift what was left of Henry onto a helicopter. Listening to Henry that day, Rubylee suddenly felt light-headed, as if her brain itself had somehow fallen out of her body and left it alone and bewildered. How would she survive? Then in an unexpected turn of events, Rubylee's mother had a heart attack in her sleep and died the very same night she heard the news about Albert. The only thread that could have held Rubylee together was now gone. At the age of eighteen she was tossed into the world—with minimal education, a baby, and a poorly paying part-time job that didn't even cover the rent.

Stanback was a large brown man with a prominent nose, large eyes, and a bad scar on his left cheek. Rumor had it that his old lady had cut him with a straight razor while he slept for beating her in one of his drunken rages. He was the type of man who loved to boast about all the grand plans he was making. He loved to talk about the day that his ship would come in and how he would have tons of money, a big car, and a large home. Stanback's only problem was that his drinking came before everything. Stanback never was very appealing to Rubylee, but over time, her lack of money and desperate situation caused her to give in to Stanback and accept the unacceptable. Rubylee would step out of her doorway and make her way past him on her way to work every morning. Stanback would wait for her to come past him and his street corner, wine-head singing group who had grand dreams of being discovered by Motown. As soon as he saw Rubylee step out of the building doorway in her white uniform with baby Estelle riding her hip, he'd screw the cap on his liquor bottle, being extra careful not to spill a single drop of his precious drink. One day, he stuck it in his back pocket and walked alongside of her. Any other time she would have ignored him, but on this particular day she was at the end of her rope.

"Miss Lady," he said, slurring his words as he tried to explain to her the best way he knew how that she was pretty. The strong aroma of alcohol so early in the morning made Rubylee's stomach turn.

"Miss Lady, I heard about your mom. You got my sympathy." Then, in a completely unexpected move, he handed Rubylee three hundred dollars from his pocket. In her heart, she didn't want to take his money, but the reality of her situation left her no other choice. The only thing her mother left her was alone. She was four months behind on rent and was due to be set out on the street. The lights were off, the phone was off, and baby Estelle needed new clothes and shoes. Estelle's feet grew so quickly that Rubylee used socks for Estelle's shoes. The soles of Rubylee's own shoes had holes in them from walking to work everyday. She'd taken to putting newspaper in the bottom of her shoes to keep her toes from scraping the ground.

"Here, take it, Miss Lady," Stanback offered again. "I haven't met a woman yet who couldn't use a little extra money."

Rubylee took Stanback's money against her better judgment. Later that night there was a knock at her door. Rubylee answered, and found Stanback leaning in her doorway smelling of fresh whiskey and old cigarette smoke. He plopped his large rough hands down on her shoulders and began squeezing. Fear instantly consumed her.

"Did my money help you out?" he asked with an aggressive tone in his voice. He could see the fear in Rubylee's eyes, and he liked that. It would give him the amount of control over her that he needed.

"I'm not able to pay you back," she squeaked, looking into

his red eyes. Rubylee shook as a sinister-looking grin plastered itself on his face. He let himself in.

"I'm sure that we can find a way to work something out." Rubylee gently shut the door behind him. She was afraid, alone, vulnerable, and very confused. She understood that Stanback's purpose for being there was to have his way with her. Her innocence and inexperience told her that it would only be this one time that she would have to give herself to him and then send him home to his wife. However, Stanback had other plans. Not only was Rubylee going to be his woman on the side, she was going to help him with his hustles, which included gambling, drug dealing, prostitution, and robbery. After her first month with Stanback, Rubylee became pregnant with Justine.

Over the years of their turbulent relationship, Stanback taught her how to shoot a pistol and how to swindle and bamboozle people out of their money through get-rich schemes. They hosted extravagant house parties that involved gambling and prostitution as well as drug use and dealing. He taught her how to hold her liquor like a man, fuck like a man, and smoke cigarettes like a man. He schooled Rubylee on how to spread her legs open to turn a trick and rob a man while he lay on his back. He taught her how to cut a person up with a knife, how to torture and collect from a person who owed her money. Over those years, Rubylee saw, did, and experienced just about everything. She went to jail five times over their years together—once for prostitution, once for shoplifting, once for carrying a controlled substance, once for assault on Stanback's wife with the intent to kill, and once for shooting Stanback in the leg for beating her in one of his drunken rages. Then, in the early eighties, Stanback was shot and killed during a drug exchange that had gone sour. The rumor on the street was that Rubylee had set Stanback up. Once again Rubylee was thrust out into the world with no job, no education, two children, and no money. On top of that, Justine who was just about to turn thirteen, had gotten pregnant. The only things that Stanback had left Rubylee were the tools for survival in the ghetto.

She took over Stanback's operation for a while and earned herself a dangerous reputation. However, the lifestyle that she was leading backlashed on her when she blackmailed a crooked married lawyer into committing insurance fraud by setting fire to property he owned in exchange for her not sending his wife photographs of them together at one of her and Stanback's house parties. With the money, she purchased a two-flat rental building to raise Estelle and Justine in. To make ends meet, she continued to hustle any way she could. Then, in the winter of 1987, an arsonist used lighter fluid to set fire to her building, burning her out. It was payback for swindling the wrong somebody out of their money. That was a major turning point for Rubylee, and the start of her complete dependency upon Estelle, who at that time was twenty-one and about to graduate from community college. She forced Estelle into taking care of her because she was tired of running con games. Without thinking twice about it, Estelle took a full-time job and found a place where she and Rubylee, along with Justine and her five-year-old daughter, Keysha, could live.

A short time later, Justine, who was twenty, took Keysha and moved in with her boyfriend, and life was really grand to Rubylee. She didn't have to work, didn't have to scheme, and didn't owe anyone a damn dime. She'd become content with living in a little room off of the kitchen. She had a bed, a dresser, a small color TV, and the privacy to smoke a reefer whenever the mood hit her. She didn't bother with cleaning up her personal space. Bending over to pick up her clothes and hang them up hurt her knees and back too badly. It was much easier to leave them in a pile at the foot of the bed. That way, when Estelle did her washing everything would be in one place. She left dirty dishes on her dresser for days at a time, waiting for Estelle to pick them up and wash them.

Then Justine and Keysha had to move back in with them. Her boyfriend had put them out on the streets when he discovered that Justine was a compulsive thief, swindler, and liar. Just like her father. The final straw came when he went to cash his check, brought the money home, and placed it in his drawer. He ran out of the house for a moment, and when he returned he discovered that Justine and all of his money were gone. He packed their things and told them never to return. Rubylee had the power to persuade Estelle to do pretty much anything she wanted her to do. It wasn't difficult for her to convince Estelle to let them move back in.

It wasn't long before Justine and Estelle started bumping heads the same way they had as children. Justine started out by wearing Estelle's clothes, so Estelle put a lock on her bedroom door. Justine kicked the door open one day while Estelle was at work and started selling her clothes in order to have some cash in her pocket. Then Estelle fixed the door and placed an iron security gate up in front of it to keep Justine out. It was clear from the beginning that Justine didn't want to take care of her daughter the way a mother should. Justine wanted to party and run in the streets just as she'd seen Rubylee do. It started with Justine going out for an evening and leaving Rubylee with the baby. One evening became a full day, a day grew into several days and eventually into weeks at a time. It was this kind of madness that wrecked Rubylee's sanctuary. A year later Estelle had had enough and moved in with her boyfriend, who had come from money and was in dental school. Eventually, she married him. Rubylee didn't let her gravy train pull off without getting her survival needs met, however. She convinced Estelle to sign a new lease and pay the rent since her new man would be taking care of her.

After Richard finished dental school, it was Rubylee who spoke with Estelle and gave her instructions on how to get Richard to open a joint checking account so that she could have access to his finances through Estelle. It was Rubylee who told her not to tell him or his family about the things she had done when she was with Stanback. "That information is for us to know only. There is no need to talk about the past at all." It was Rubylee who showed Estelle how to gain control over Richard by using what she had between her legs.

"Circle your ass in a figure eight pattern until his toes curl and his mind blows," Rubylee told her. When it came to something Rubylee wanted, her true colors showed. She was a user, con artist, and a schemer with a by-any-means-necessary attitude.

Now Rubylee was thinking about the future. She started visualizing plans that included a six-flat apartment building where everyone could live. She was going to use Estelle and Richard to get what she wanted. She'd already completed the first phase of her cunning scheme, and she smiled—like the Grinch who stole Christmas—at the thought of how clever she was.

6

Nina looked around the dance studio at the students in her aerobics class as they waited for her to start the music. She'd noticed Richard's presence immediately and acknowledged him by winking her eye at him. She started the tape and put on her microphone headset.

"Okay, you guys, we are really going to work tonight. I have a ton of stress that I need to work off," Nina said as she began giving instructions. Richard was happy to hear that, because he had a ton of stress that he needed to work off as well. After class Richard hung around to speak with Nina privately, and to thank her once again for the ride home the other day.

"No problem, Richard," she replied, "I was more than happy to help. Besides, you looked as if you were melting out there in that suit."

"Boiling is more like it," Richard responded with a grin.

"Listen," Nina said, standing in front of him and placing her hand on his shoulder as she looked directly into his eyes. "I hope that you don't think I'm trying to get in your business, but you looked like you really had a lot on your mind the other day. Is everything okay?"

Richard let out a deep sigh. "It was just one of those days, you know. Things just weren't going my way."

"Well, from the way you kept up with me in class tonight, I gather that whatever it is, it's still got a hold on you. I say this to you as a friend; if you need someone to talk to, I know of a great cafe we could go to. I'm a great listener."

"You know, Nina, considering all that's on my mind. I would love to take you up on that offer."

"Great. Let me run to the locker room, take a quick shower and change back into my street clothes. I could meet you at the front desk in about twenty minutes. How is that?"

"It's a deal, Nina," said Richard, smiling at her.

Nina felt a twinge of nervous energy rush through her as she ran back to the locker room. Suddenly she felt like a teenager and didn't know why. She wasn't sure why she had offered to go out with Richard, except that there was something about him that was compelling to her. Maybe it's that sexy-ass walk of his that reminded her of the way Lawrence Fishburne walked. Those long, smooth, confident steps were a huge turn on to her. Deep in her heart she wanted to know Richard better than she did. After she'd given in to Jay's pleading to make love to him the other night, she did what she had to do in order to get him off. Then she got up and ran herself a bath as he lay on his back snoring. She slipped into the warm tub and let her fingers work their magic on her center. It was then that she longed for her hand to turn into Richard's. She realized that she shouldn't feel that way, but she couldn't help it. And she did realize that by going out with him she was acting on some deep hidden attraction to him. What the hell, you only live once. Besides, a drink with him wasn't against the law. Nina decided to take him to After Thoughts, which was a small club on the other side of town where Rose would be hanging out. Wouldn't she be surprised when Nina strutted in there with Richard. Nina knew that kind of bold move would send all kinds of questions through Rose's mind. But she knew how to handle Rose and keep her at bay while she got to know Richard. *Hopefully, Richard knows how to dance,* she giggled to herself. If she was lucky, she would be able to dance with him. The thought of the two of them dancing was enough to make her speed up her shower and not keep the man waiting.

Richard was by no means in a rush to get home. Especially since he and Estelle had had that horrible fight the other night. He'd dropped by the house for a hot minute on his way to the health club to check the mailbox for his replacement credit card. He was happy when he found it had finally arrived. Home hadn't been the same for some time. He and Estelle had a major communication problem, and he had no idea how to fix it. He'd been thinking of going to a therapist but after his recent strong, undeniable urge to do her bodily harm, he wasn't sure if that would help. And the memory of that butcher knife she had held in her hand didn't make him rest easy at night. In his mind, a date with Nina should at least allow enough time to pass for everyone in his house to be asleep when he returned. He would come in the door and go to sleep on the sofa.

After Thoughts was a cozy black-owned place that served traditional American soul food. At the rear there was another room that offered good stepping music, a cozy dance floor, and any kind of liquor you needed to put you in a dancing mood. Since neither of them was particularly hungry, even after Nina's killer workout, they decided to sit down at a booth next to the dance floor. As Richard led the way to an empty booth, Nina spotted Rose, who had a pleasant look of surprise on her face. Nina winked at Rose, then focused her attention on following Richard. The wink was to let Rose know she would talk to her a bit later. Rose let her eyes follow Nina to the booth where Richard was. As Nina sat she looked back at Rose, whose facial expression was asking a million questions, just as she had known it would. Nina smiled at her, then scooted over in order to sit at the table's center.

"Would you like anything to drink?" Richard inquired.

"Uhm, I'll just have a Coca Cola," Nina replied.

"Are you sure? I promise not to take advantage of you if you have something a little stronger," Richard said playfully.

"I'm sure." Nina said, and watched him head toward the

bar, paying particular attention to his slow sexy walk and tight behind. The DJ was playing a slow jam by James Ingram, "One Hundred Ways." James Ingram had a strong soothing voice that had a way of putting Nina in a mellow mood. *Love her today—find one hundred ways,* James Ingram crooned. Nina adored the fact that Richard was starting to loosen up. She'd known Richard a little over a year, and had watched him transform from a pudgy couch potato to a nicely defined, incredibly handsome, almond brown sweet-thing that she had an undeniable crush on. Her private moment in the bathtub the other night had raised her curiosity about him to an alarming level. Richard returned with two Cokes and sat down across from her.

"So, King Richard," Nina spoke as she stirred the straw in her glass. "I'm all ears." Richard smiled, enjoying Nina's reference to European history with respect to his name. Nina smiled back at him showing all thirty-twos. "It's okay, you can talk to me." Richard loved how beautifully her smile lit up the space around them and how one look at her face would make any supermodel rush to a plastic surgeon in order to obtain her striking features.

"No, Queen Nina. I want to know about you. What made you become an instructor?"

"I wanted to do something different, something that I liked. Something that made me feel alive. What about you? What was the deciding factor that made you get serious about losing weight?"

"I got tired of my wife lying to me. Telling me how good I looked to her with a size forty waistline. When I met her, I was a slim and toned 195 pounds. The next thing I knew I was 240 pounds and could barely walk up a flight of stairs. So I decided to do something about it. Would you believe that she tells me I need to put the weight back on? She says that she likes a man with plenty of meat, and that a dog doesn't like a bone because he buries it."

"Well, I can tell you why she wants you to pick up weight."

"Enlighten me, please." Richard placed his elbows on the table and leaned in toward her, curious as to what Nina was about to say.

"You men," she teased. "It takes you guys forever to figure out the simplest thing. If you're fat and dumpy, sugar, other women will not pay attention to you. Do you know what I mean? Yes, it's true, a dog will bury a bone, but a dog also doesn't like fat. He'll spit it out."

Richard laughed, "I know what you mean. Although I must admit I didn't realize that was her motive for wanting me to pick up weight."

"Honey, that's a trick many women use to keep their man in line," Nina responded with a matter of fact tone.

"So, may I ask how you keep *your* husband in line?"

"Oh, I don't have to work hard in that department. Jay loves to eat and hates to workout. You thought *you* were a big man— he's about ten pounds heavier than what you were."

"No shit?" Richard tried to get an image of Nina with a man that large. The only image he came up with was of Ralph and Alice Kramden of the once popular TV show *The Honeymooners*.

"He doesn't need me to tell him to eat. He does that all by himself. I've been encouraging him to lose weight for some time now, but I haven't had any luck. But enough about me, my friend, we came here for your peace of mind. I'm all ears if you need someone to listen to you or just get things off your chest. Carrying around anger is not good."

Richard was silent for a moment, putting his thoughts in order and searching for the right words to begin with. Then he explained the week's events to Nina. She paid close attention to him as he spoke of his frustrations. Nina sympathized with Richard, wanting to help him any way that she could. The kind of madness Estelle was locked into would have driven her crazy. She studied the pain in Richard's eyes as he spoke of Rubylee, who he said had to be the most bossy, two-faced, nosy, controlling, conniving, and sneakiest woman he'd ever known. Rubylee's personality struck a nerve with Nina. Rubylee had the type of personality that power-hungry or otherwise controlling men had. She should know, Jay was one of them. Nina couldn't stand for one person to take advantage of another. After hearing about the disrespectful act that Estelle and Rubylee had commited, she understood why Richard had been so angry when she ran into him on the jogging path.

"Have you thought about what you're going to do about this? I mean, if it were me, I would not take this lightly." Nina wanted to fight even though it wasn't her problem. She wanted to put on her gloves and jump right in the middle of it.

"I don't know what I'm going to do, to be honest. I've never had to deal with a situation like this before in my life. Instinct begged me to beat the crap out of her, but I'm not that type of man. That would not have solved my problem, and I guess I'm still in shock about the situation. I trusted this person and now I don't. I mean honestly, how does a person deal with something like this?"

"Well, I'm speaking to you now as an accountant. The first thing I'd do is close out that joint checking account before she puts both of you in the poorhouse. Then I'd call the credit card company, remove her name from the account, and have them issue new plates. Then I'd . . . You know what, why don't you come down to my office—bring all of your joint financial information, and we'll see what we can do. Because honestly, you can do bad by your damn self. How long have you been married Richard?" Nina asked.

"I've known her for nine years, I've been married eight. But it feels as if I've been married to her forever." Richard picked up his drink and took a large gulp, wondering if he should explain that Estelle kept all of their financial information. She'd convinced him long ago that she could manage money better than he could. Richard knew at the time that it wasn't something he felt comfortable with, but he allowed Estelle to have her way. He just closed his eyes and told her he trusted her.

"How did you meet her?"

"I met her during my first year of dental school. I was sitting on the lawn outside the dental school building, studying, when her clunker of a car broke down with a flat in the middle of the street. She didn't know how to change it, so I offered to help. Next thing I knew we were dating, and the rest is history. Although now I realize that what my mother said when she first met her was absolutely true. She explained that Estelle was not the woman for me. "Take her back to wherever you found her," she told me. "She is not of your caliber." At the time, I chalked up my mother's view to her being uppity. You see, both of my parents could be so arrogant at times. My mother was a surgeon and my father a pediatrician. God bless their souls, because over the years with Estelle, I have come to understand what my mother was trying to tell me."

"Are your parents still alive?"

"No, they died a few years ago—back in 1989 during the San Francisco earthquake."

"I'm sorry to hear that, Richard."

"Well, there was nothing anyone could do about that. I was a second year dental student at the time. I inherited a nice amount of money that I used to finance the rest of my education. The remaining amount I set aside for a rainy day."

"Does Estelle know about that money?"

"No, she doesn't. That's tucked safely away at another financial institution." *Thank God,* Nina thought, relieved to see that he wasn't a total fool.

"If I'd only known then what I know now." Nina's heart sank a bit when he said that because she'd felt the very same way so many times over her twenty years of marriage to Jay. Richard saw Nina's smile fall from her face, and he desperately wanted to pick it up and put it back on but he had no idea how to do so.

"So, will you come down to my office? If nothing else, I'll find a way to get you out of debt." Richard knew that Nina was sincere about offering her help. She really wanted him to get through this and prevent it from happening again. After a short pause, he agreed. In light of recent events it would be best if he took over all of the financial matters. Estelle was going to have a fit, but he was no longer going to put up with this type of deceit.

"Good. I promise, you will not be sorry. You can trust me, I will not steer you wrong."

"I hope so. I'm going to follow my instinct and see what you can do for me. Well, now that I've spilled my guts out to you—which is very unusual for me mind you—tell me more about yourself."

"Let's see, I've been married a little longer than you have." Nina replied. "After twenty years, my husband still thinks I'm that eighteen-year-old girl that he got pregnant and needs to take care of. He still treats me like a kid sometimes. It doesn't matter that I've gone back to school, obtained a college degree, have my own job, and make my own money. Jay is the type of husband who likes to be the sole breadwinner. He loves power, authority, and control more than he loves tenderness and affection, if that makes any sense. What I mean is, if a woman has more credentials than he does or makes more money than he does or has a strong sense of independence, his manhood is threatened. For years he had me just where he wanted me. I was young and didn't know much about anything. About the only thing I knew for sure was that I was pregnant and being pressured to get married and settle into family life. He's nine years older than I am and I thought he knew so much more than I did. So everything he told me I took as the gospel truth. At the time we married, he wasn't exactly ready to settle down. He had his young thing at home taking care of his baby, and his other life, whatever it was, out in the street. Or at least I had my suspicions about another life out in the street. I didn't know how to handle that sort of thing so I just sat at home with my baby and cried more times than I care to think about. I was so dim-witted back then. He would come home and I'd ask where he'd been and he'd just say "Out." But whenever *I* went anywhere I had to take my daughter and be accused of seeing another man if I came home one minute late."

"Well, are you happy in your marriage now?" Richard asked, completely amazed that Jay had a woman as beautiful as Nina and mistreated her.

"I wouldn't say happy. I'd say my marriage is just comfortable because of habit and familiarity. What about you? Are you happy?"

"I feel that I love my wife, but I'm no longer in love with her. If that makes any sense. We have such horrible communication and I'm not sure how to fix it or even if I want to fix it."

"Oh, no, it makes plenty of sense. I feel sort of the same way about my husband. It's not one particular thing that I can just point to and say here is the problem, let's fix it. It's a combination of unresolved issues that have been going on for some time." Richard studied Nina the entire time she talked. He let his mind drift a bit toward thoughts of how his mother would have viewed Nina. She was so pretty, intelligent, and confident. The fact that her experiences had made her who she was today intrigued him because he himself was being changed by experiences.

"Your voice has a wonderfully sweet sound, has anyone ever told you that?" One of Richard's private thoughts somehow got past his wall of reserve.

"No, but what a sweet thing to say." Nina felt that the mood and the subject at hand were about to change. She paused for a moment, searching for the right way to find out more personal information about him without seeming too intrusive.

"So, how is Estelle keeping up with the new and improved Richard? Can she handle all of the energy you have?"

Nina couldn't believe that question had actually come out of her mouth. She prayed that she wouldn't regret asking it. But Richard didn't make her feel foolish at all, he answered the question without even thinking about it. He'd already reached a certain level of ease and comfort with Nina that made him feel good.

"There is much room for improvement on her part, that's for sure. It seems as if I've matured more than she has over the years. Things that I accepted as a young man, I can no longer accept as a mature man."

"Explain, please."

Richard instantly picked up on Nina's enthusiasm about this subject. He let down all of his defenses and spoke freely. "My sweet, dear Estelle likes to use sex as a method of manipulation and control. She's one of those people who likes to fight and fuck, to put it bluntly. If we have a disagreement and then have sex, during the middle of it she'll bring up the subject of the argument again. It is the most annoying thing I've ever experienced. I'll be the first to admit, that in the beginning of our relationship I let her have her way every time. But now, I've grown tired of her tricks and tactics, and I refuse to be manipulated anymore. So as far as life in the sack goes, it may have been laced with a bit of passion at the start of our relationship, but now it's used as a weapon of choice. Am I making any sense?"

Nina was totally amazed at what he was telling her. A man as fine, handsome, and educated as Richard could have his choice of women. She was dying to ask why he was still with Estelle, but thought better of asking such a question. "I understand you," she replied.

"Just like now, we are having major problems in our marriage, and I know that she's going to try and sway me to her style of thinking through sexual manipulation, but I'm not that pussy-whipped man anymore. I've changed and matured so much, but she doesn't even realize it. I feel that the only thing she truly wants is to have me return to the overweight, docile man I once was."

"I understand," Nina sat straight up in her seat. "Do you have any children?"

"Yes, a little boy, Nathan, who is four. What about you?"

"I have a twenty-two-year-old daughter named Gracie who is married and lives in another state."

"I bet if the two of you were in a room I'd mistake you for her younger sister. My goodness, Nina, you look absolutely wonderful. What issue of *Jet* magazine will I be able to find your centerfold in?"

"Stop that! You're making me blush. Thank you for the compliment, though, that's such a nice thing to say. I'm glad that you appreciate how hard I work to keep myself together."

"Oh, believe me, I appreciate it. I've noticed for some time now, I've just never mentioned it."

"Oh, really?" Nina detected Richard's flirtatious tone. "What have you noticed?"

"Well, for one thing, you have the most beautiful skin I've ever seen. I notice how you get your hair done every week, how you dress, how you walk, and how the men at the health club are always asking if you're single."

"So, have *you* ever wondered if I was single and available?"

"You know, Nina," Richard lowered his voice and added a bit of bass to it. "If I didn't know any better, I'd say that you were flirting with me."

Nina propped her elbows on the table and leaned in closer to Richard and gazed directly into his almond eyes. He had the most beautiful eyes. "What if I am?" At that moment, as if he were waiting for his cue, the DJ put on "Just my Imagination (Running away with Me," by the Temptations. *Wooooo, whooooooo, each day through my window I watch her as she passes by,* the Temptations crooned. Both Nina and Richard lost their train of thought as the sweet mellow sounds grabbed their attention. Nina bowed her head and instantly began rocking to the groove. Richard was apprehensive about asking her to dance to such a romantic song, but Nina's sensual movements to the music and the stirring of his passions forced him to cross the line and ask for a moment of intimacy. Without even thinking, Nina gave him her hand and they moved to the center of the dance floor where it was just the two of them.

Rose, who was seated at another booth across the dance floor with other friends, directed her attention to her best friend Nina, who had wrapped her arms around this strange, but fine-as-hell man's neck like he was a lover she hadn't seen in a long time. Rose watched as his brown hands slid around Nina's waist, pulling her closer and locking her in. "Look at this shit," Rose quietly mouthed to herself. Nina looked up into Richard's eyes, smelling the luscious scent of his cologne for the first time. *What a beautiful smell,* she thought. *It works so well with his body chemistry.* Goodness, here she was talking about chemistry already, but that's what it felt like. They'd slipped into each other's arms like missing pieces of a jigsaw puzzle. It had been so long since either of them had enjoyed a slow dance. Richard felt Nina's fingertips lightly stroking the nape of his neck. Her touch was so dear to him, she was rubbing away all of his stress. Richard exhaled and drew her even closer to him, holding her tighter.

"What's that you're wearing Richard?"

"It's called Joop, do you like it?" Nina was turned on by the scent of it. "Yes, I really like it." The two of them rocked slowly back and forth while the Temptations lulled them into a blissful state of euphoria. The song ended and it was apparent that neither one of them wanted to let go. But Nina placed her left hand lightly on his chest and slowly pushed herself back. Being inside of his arms felt more comfortable than she'd anticipated, and it would be all too easy to get caught up in the moment.

"I'm going to go freshen up," she said, heading toward the table to get her purse.

Richard followed. "Would you like another drink?"

"Yes, that would be nice."

Rose watched Nina as she headed for the ladies' room. She quickly excused herself, jumped up from her seat and hustled toward the bathroom. Nina pulled her makeup pouch from her purse and set it on the counter.

"Baby girl, now you *know* that you have to talk to me," Rose said after she rushed in and stood behind Nina. She placed one hand on her hip and began working her neck the way that a sister can do when she's trying to get her point across. "I want details. Who is he? How long have you known him? Why haven't you told me about him, and how good is he in the sack?"

"Rose, he's just a friend and a potential client," Nina coolly replied while applying more lipstick.

"Uhm, excuse me! But do I look like Booboo the Fool? There has got to be something going on, the way the two of you were just out there all hugged up. Naw, I'm not buying that one. What's his name, Nina?"

"Dr. Richard Vincent. He is one of my students. After class tonight I asked him if he wanted to hang out, and he said sure. We sat, talked, discovered that we have many things in common, and shared a slow dance. Is there any law against that?"

"No, not yet." Rose paused, noticing how Nina was really taking her time with that lipstick. She put on a little more cologne, played with her hair a bit, and then adjusted her clothes.

"Nina!"

"Yes."

"You've got the hots for him, don't you?"

"Rose, what are you talking about? We're both married people."

"Hey, that doesn't stop a sister from getting the hots. And just because a man is married doesn't stop his you-know-what from getting hard. Now, you know me, I'm going to call it like I see it whether you like it or not. So be honest with me, you've got the hots for him, don't you?" Nina could have just choked Rose for making her supply more information than she wanted to give or admit. But Rose had been her best friend for as long as she could remember and if anyone knew her, she did.

"Yes, I've got the hots for him, are you happy now?"

"I knew it! I could see it all in your eyes. That man has got your ass hooked! I'm not mad at you though, because that brother is fine!" Both Nina and Rose giggled and then laughed like two schoolgirls chuckling at a dirty word.

"You are so damn silly," Nina responded.

"All I want to know is, what are you going to do about it?"

"Do about what?" Nina asked.

Rose shifted her weight from one foot to the other and put an expression on her face that said "you know damn well what I'm talking about."

"I'm just going to be his friend, and that's all."

"All right, if you say so, but I know better."

Nina zipped up her pouch and placed it back inside her purse. "So, would you like to meet him? Maybe I can convince him to stay long enough to take your steppers class."

"Now you know I've got to meet him. For all you know he could be Dr. Jekyll. I'll check him out for you and make sure he's okay."

"Rose, it's not like that."

"Well, not yet, anyway."

"Girl, please! I'm not crossing any lines like that," Nina said with a mischievous smile on her face. "But let me get back out there before some hoochie momma tries to take him." Nina giggled, then pulled Rose by the wrist and out the door.

7

Estelle had just opened the safe and had begun counting the money before she opened the store. When the phone rang, she had half a mind not to answer it—she hated being interrupted when she was counting money. But it could have been William Holiday, her district manager, so she picked it up. "Good morning, Dollar for Dollar—how can I assist you?"

"Estelle!" The voice on the other end hollered at her through the receiver.

"Hello, I think we have a bad connection. Who is this?"

"Can you hear me now?"

Estelle recognized the desperate sounding voice. It was her sister, Justine. "Justine? Where are you? And what's all of that noise in the background?"

"It's a passing fire truck. I'm at the pay phone around the corner from Mom's house."

"What do you want, Justine?" Estelle didn't have time for Justine's bullshit today. She was short staffed and was expecting a store visit today by her district manager and the regional manager. Besides, she was still pissed with Justine for not giving her back the money that she'd taken from the account. Thinking about the entire thing gave her an awful migraine.

She was still trying to patch things up with Richard, but he'd been acting so distant with her lately. It was like her very presence in the same room disgusted him. By now she was supposed to have Richard eating out of her hand like she'd always been able to do.

"The Cook County Sheriff's Department and the landlord are over here setting all of Mom's shit on the street," Justine responded with aggravation in her voice.

"Wait a minute. What do you mean, they're setting her stuff outside?" Estelle set the money from the safe down in front of her.

"They came by early this morning with eviction papers, talking about how she hasn't paid her rent. Momma got to fighting with the police, and they wrestled her down to the ground and handcuffed her. She tried to get up, but one of the police officers held her down on her stomach by putting his knee on the side of her neck. You've got to get down here and do something! Some dudes have already come by and snatched the VCR. This shit is fucked up, Estelle! Why didn't you help Momma pay the rent like you were supposed to?"

"Pay her rent!" Estelle was confused.

"Please deposit twenty-five cents for the next minute." A recorded message from the operator interrupted them. The message repeated, and then, before Estelle could answer or ask more questions, the connection was severed. "Shit!" Estelle rubbed her temples trying to ward off an ensuing migraine. None of the hourly workers were due in the store for at least another two hours. The only person that would come in on short notice was her assistant manager, who didn't have a car. Estelle didn't feel like waiting for her to catch a bus to work, it would take too long.

"Shit! Shit! Shit!" she hissed again and again, then grabbed some of the money from the safe. She left the rest sitting out in the open. She picked up her purse and rushed out the door, wondering how much it would cost her to fix this latest crisis.

* * *

Estelle pulled up in front of her mother's house on Parnell Street an hour and a half later with a rented U-Haul truck. She saw her mother sitting on her worn-out sofa, which had been placed under a tree. Rubylee was smoking reefer and staring blankly at the ground in front of her. Keysha, Estelle's niece, was sitting on the steps of the building while her sister Justine stood in the center of the street shouting obscenities at the heckling neighbors. Her hair was all branched off, in desperate need of a perm. The gold spandex biking shorts she had on were way too tight and wedged in the crack of her behind, accentuating her ass and making it appear larger than it actually was. Estelle got instantly angry with Justine. The least she could have done was walk around the corner to the grocery store and get some empty boxes to put their clothes in.

"Justine!" she yelled out of the window of the truck. "Get out of the goddamn street and start loading this stuff up." Justine walked around to the rear of the truck and opened the door. Rubylee looked absolutely pathetic, she just sat there as if she were waiting for God Almighty to come down and clear this mess up.

"Ma, sitting down isn't going to get your stuff up off the street. You need to get up, and start helping me load this stuff onto the truck," Estelle said with an impatient tone.

"Can you believe they did me like this?" Rubylee said, although in her mind there was a certain method to all of this madness and drama. She lit another cigarette. Estelle noticed the skin scrapes on Rubylee's arms and elbows.

"Two big grown men pulled me by my hair and wrestled me to the ground out here in front of all these people." Estelle knew it had to have taken two men to handle her mother; she was a big woman at five feet nine and two hundred sixty pounds. "Ma, I really don't have time for all of this. Let's get this stuff off the street and on the truck. I'm going to rent a storage place to put all of this stuff in."

"I don't want my shit in goddamn storage!" Rubylee roared

at Estelle with dissatisfaction. "My things will get fucked up sitting in storage!"

"Well, what do you want me to do?" Estelle fired back.

"Take my things to your house," Rubylee commanded Estelle.

"Momma, I don't have room for all of this stuff."

"I don't care; that's where I want it to go! I'm your mother. And the good Lord knows that I've tried to do right by you. Now I ask for a small favor, and you don't want to help me. I've been to your house enough times to know that my things can fit in there."

"Momma, I'm here with the truck, aren't I? Damn, why are you always placing a guilt trip on me?"

"Are you two going to load this shit up or stand out here and fight?" Justine walked around from the rear of the truck annoyed.

"She wants me to take her stuff to my house." Estelle's headache was growing by the second. It felt as if someone was hitting her head with a hammer.

"I don't want my things in storage!" Rubylee hollered at the top of her voice. She began flailing her arms around like a child throwing a temper tantrum. "You could have helped me with my rent. I told you when you went off and married that man that I couldn't afford this place. I told you that we needed to get us a big place. A nice six-flat. That way we could all live in there together. Had you listened to me, we could have avoided all of this here mess. This is all your fault, Estelle. You were supposed to take care of me; instead you ran off with that man and left me out there all by myself. You know that I don't work! You know that I ain't got no income! How was I supposed to take care of myself, take care of Keysha and Justine, pay the bills and buy food? I'm an old lady. I ain't got the strength that I used to have. I don't have long. I got one foot planted on the ground and the other one in the grave. When my mother was living I helped take care of her. I wasn't going to run off and leave her for your Daddy. We had plans for all of us to live together." Rubylee had now mustered up tears. "You don't love me no more. I'm just a burden to you. I ask you for a little help every now and again and you treat me like dirt. You and that husband of yours have plenty of money. I saw one of his check stubs one day while I was over there baby-sitting. I told you to convince him to buy a building but you won't do it. Life would be so much easier if you'd listen to me."

"Fuck it, Ma! I'll take your shit to my house," Estelle's head was killing her. She had grown tired of listening to her mother lay a major guilt trip on her. Every time things didn't go Ruby-lee's way it was her fault, never Justine's, who got away with so much without Ma ever chastising her.

"Well, I guess that means all of us are staying with you too."

"Fine, Ma. Let's just get this shit up off the street and loaded onto the truck. I don't have time for this, I'm supposed to be at work!" Estelle hadn't thought about what she'd just agreed to. She just wanted to load the truck, stop at a drug store to pick up some Extra Strength Tylenol, and get back to work ASAP!

It was three in the afternoon by the time everything was loaded off of the truck and placed in Richard and Estelle's high-class apartment with its beautiful view of Lake Michigan. The apartment was a corner unit on the eighteenth floor with two balconies. The one off the living room facing east boasted some of the most beautiful sunrises. The other balcony was in the bedroom and faced south, overlooking Lake Shore Drive. Richard had hired a colleague's wife who was an interior deco-rator to come and work her magic, which initially upset Estelle because she knew that she could do a good job on her own house. However, she and Richard had such different tastes. She loved hardwood floors and wooden cabinets, metal chairs and knick-knacks. But he loved a totally modern look. Glass tables instead of wooden ones. Extravagant centerpieces and cloth dining room chairs complete with skirts. He wanted things sim-ple and un-cluttered. Richard ended up having the apartment arranged to his satisfaction.

Now all of Rubylee's old worn-out and outdated furniture would clash with Richard's modern art-deco theme. Rubylee's

straight-back kitchen chairs were missing the backs to them and
weren't fit to sit in. Her wooden kitchen card table had deep
gashes and cigarette burns in it, and the surface had long lost its
gloss. The cushions on her dark brown sofa were badly soiled
and worn through. The drawer handles on her once white bedroom dresser were missing. The dresser mirror had a crack in it.
Rubylee's mattress had urine stains in it from when Keysha was
a baby and learning how to potty-train. The three-piece picture
set that Rubylee had picked up from the flea market, showing
John F. Kennedy, Martin Luther King Jr., and a white Jesus
Christ, would look completely out of place next to abstract art.
Estelle looked around at the bags of clothes, shoes, and dishes
and wondered where in the hell she was going to put all of it.
Richard was going to have a fit.

"Well, looks like I'm all moved into my new home now."
Rubylee plopped down on the tan leather sofa, kicked off her
shoes and placed her feet on the glass table. She lit a Winston
Salem and blew smoke in the air. Estelle noticed that the bot-
toms of her feet were black with dirt.

"Damn girl, I didn't know you were living like this!" Justine
had just come from the washroom down the hall. "Ma, they got
monogrammed bathroom towels, two face bowls, and a big-ass
tub. They got a huge mirror, marble surface tops, and those real
big light bulbs that you see in hotel bathrooms. And check this
out, Ma, the lid is on the toilet and the floor around the toilet
isn't ripped up. We'll probably never have to use a plunger
here," Justine commented in amazement. Estelle was about to
inform Justine that there was no way she would be staying here.
She was not going to go through the crap of her stealing from
this house. But just then Keysha figured out how to turn on the
stereo and cranked it all the way up as a popular hip hop song
began playing.

"Hey, that's my jam!" Keysha said, and started dancing.
Justine, who was just as silly and young at heart as Keysha,
joined her for a quick boogie session.

"Come on, Momma, get on up! Let's dance," Justine

shouted over the music, motioning for Rubylee to get up and join the two of them. Disgusted, Estelle rushed to the bathroom hoping to find some extra strength aspirin in the medicine cabinet. Rubylee rocked her round-as-a-barrel body onto its feet and made her way down the hall to find Estelle.

"Don't worry none." Rubylee inhaled on her smoke while she watched Estelle search frantically for the aspirin. Her voice had become husky and deep from all of the screaming she'd done earlier on the street. "If he's any kind of man, he'll understand how serious the situation is. You had to do what was right for family, and the Lord is going to bless you for the way you've been taking care of me, your niece, and your sister. I don't mean to bother you none, but we've got to get my things situated."

"Oh, Grandma, they got a fourth room that looks like an office. It's got a computer, a fax, and a copy machine." Keysha came bopping down the hall to the beat of the music.

"I know Keysha, I've been over here before," Rubylee replied.

"Keysha, that's Richard's office. Stay out of there, okay."

"Actually, we need to get that stuff out of that office so that I can put my things in there. I think that should be my room," said Rubylee.

Estelle didn't know what to do or think. She just knew that her head was killing her, her stomach was doing flips, and Rubylee's smoke was burning her eyes. She was about to snap at her mother and tell her not to get too comfortable because she'd only be here for a short time until they could locate another apartment for her. Estelle would take a couple of days off from work so that she and Rubylee could find something. The phone rang and she walked out of the bathroom and down the hall to the master bedroom to answer it.

"Hello?"

"Yes, is Mrs. Vincent home?" the voice asked.

"Yes, this is she."

"Hi, this is Little Heaven pre-school. We're calling because no one came to pick up your son at two-thirty. It's almost four, and we're wondering if there is a problem."

"Oh, shit! I'm sorry. I had a family emergency. I'm on my way to pick him up now." Estelle slammed down the phone and rushed out the door in tears. How could she have forgotten to pick up her baby? When she returned with Nathan a half hour later, Rubylee had already moved the majority of her things into Richard's home office. Nathan rushed over to Rubylee and gave her a big hug. Estelle just wanted to go in the room, shut the door, and lie down. She was about to do just that when Keysha came out of her room, informing her that Justine had been in her closet and taken a bunch of her clothes.

"Oh, yeah aunt-tee, some white man name William Holiday called from your job. He said that it was really urgent that you get back to him." Damn! She had the store visit today. She'd forgotten all about that too. In fact, she'd forgotten completely about work. She never even called to have someone open the store and here it was four-thirty in the afternoon and the store had been closed all day. Damn! She rushed out of the house.

Estelle parked the U-Haul between a police car and William Holiday's black BMW. When she walked into the store she saw that the place had been destroyed by looters. An officer was dusting for fingerprints and a few of her employees and two managers from other stores were there cleaning up the mess. All eyes were focused on Estelle when she walked through the door. Her shoulders tensed up so tightly that she couldn't turn her head right or left. She walked behind the front counter and into her office without saying a word. William Holiday was going over operations paperwork with Jackie, a young girl she'd just promoted from team leader to assistant manager. Estelle's stomach did a major flip when William's cold blue eyes met hers.

"Will you excuse us for a moment, Jackie?" William gave her the signal to leave. Jackie walked out and gently shut the door behind her.

"I can explain everything," Estelle began before William could say the first word. Estelle tried appealing to his sympathetic side as she explained the day's events. But it was no use. The store had been looted, the company had lost money and sustained damages, and it was because of her carelessness.

"As of this afternoon you were terminated, Mrs. Vincent. Hand over the store keys," William said without any sympathy. He almost looked as if he were enjoying himself. Estelle's stomach felt like it was coming out of her throat now. She opened her purse, not completely believing that she was being fired. This day was just screwed all up; she wished she could go back and start it over.

"William, I've worked here for six years, that has to—"

William cut her off sharply.

"I gave you nothing but praise, Estelle. I came to the store this afternoon with the regional manager to congratulate you because your promotion had just gone through. When we walked in this afternoon, the store wasn't open. It had been looted—four thousand dollars of company money was gone, and most of the merchandise was either destroyed or stolen. You made me look like a fool, Estelle, and now my ass is on the line. However, I will tell you this. I've reviewed the security tape. It shows you taking some money and running out of the store with it."

"I only took about fifty dollars to—"

Bill tossed his hand up, cutting her off midsentence. "I suggest that you obtain an attorney," he said, and waited for her to give him the keys. Estelle was shocked into speechlessness. A large boulder created by fear, frustration, and anger lodged itself in her throat. She handed over the keys, wanting to ask about her final paycheck, but the words just would not come out. She drove exactly one block before she had to pull over and stop. She swung open the door of the truck, leaned out and began vomiting.

8

Nina had just gotten out of the shower and toweled off after a very exhausting day at the office. She sat on the edge of the bed with a towel beneath her and put cocoa butter on her skin, which was feeling dry from the hard shower water. She'd planned on a nice quiet evening of sitting on the couch with a glass of wine, her throw, and a book by Brent Wade entitled *Company Man*. She heard Jay's car pulling into the garage and immediately sprung to her feet, marched over to her dresser, and pulled out her pajamas. The last thing she wanted tonight was to get him all excited by looking at her naked body. She just wasn't in the mood for any type of intimacy with Jay.

"Nina!" Jay howled out her name as he slammed the door behind him. *Why on earth was he yelling like that?* Nina grabbed her book from the nightstand and was about to head downstairs when Jay flung open the bedroom door, pushing so hard that the doorknob left a hole in the wall.

"What in the world is wrong with you? Look at the hole you just put in the wall!" Nina pinched her eyebrows into an expression of dissatisfaction.

"Who in the hell is this man you've been out slow dancing with?"

"What are you talking about, Jay?"

"You went out to After Thoughts last night and were out on the dance floor hugged up with some man. And I want to know what in the hell is going on! How could you make love to me one night and be with another man the next?"

"You'd better be careful what you say to me and how you say it, Jay." Nina fully understood that Jay was attempting to insinuate that she was some floozy running the streets. "How did you find out about that?" Nina wanted to know if he had the nerve to be spying on her, following her around. She wasn't about to deal with that type of behavior from Jay.

"One of the attorneys I work with saw you there. He came into my office today and told me all about it. Are you tipping around on me, Nina?"

"No! And it sounds as if your friend added a ton of fiction to his version of what took place. I went there after my class with a friend; we sat down and we talked. A song came on; he asked me to dance and I said sure." Nina was done with the conversation. There was really nothing more to tell. She'd introduced Richard to Rose; the three of them had talked for about another fifteen minutes and then Richard had gone home. She'd hung around and took Rose's steppers class so that she could learn how to dance. Nina moved around Jay to go downstairs and read her book, but he grabbed her by the arm just above her elbow and snatched her back in front him. He jerked her so hard, Nina thought he'd dislocated her shoulder.

"Nina, don't fuck with me! Do you have another goddamn man?" Jay was squeezing her arm so hard she could feel his fingernails digging into her skin. She looked into his eyes and saw the fury and anger there. His breathing was hard and heavy, which caused his chest to heave back and forth. But all of that didn't strike fear in her heart. She had enough anger and fury in her own heart from the years that she'd sat home not knowing where he was all night. Had he forgotten about that? Or the countless times she'd done laundry and found makeup stains on his shirts. Or times that he came home smelling like fresh soap, trying to hide the scent of another woman. Or the time he was supposedly at a buddy's house watching the Bulls game. She'd watched the highlights on the news and when he came home she asked his opinion about a questionable call the referee made, but he had no idea who won the game. Not to mention that slip-up he had a few months ago during their love-making session when he called out the wrong name. Oh, yes, he must have forgotten all about those things, but she hadn't. She'd told him time and time again that one day things would change. But apparently he didn't believe her.

"Let my arm go!" Nina growled through clenched teeth as she snatched her arm back with just as much force as Jay had applied when he grabbed her. She felt his fingernails tearing her skin open as she did so.

"I've been a faithful and devoted wife to you for twenty years. And I have my suspicions that you can't say the same." Nina could tell by the sudden expression of shock that formed on Jay's face that her reaction to him was not what he'd anticipated.

"Is this man the reason that you don't like making love with me anymore?"

"There is no other man, Jay! And you know exactly why I'm not turned on by you. Or have you forgotten that as well?" After Nina said that, she knew she was in for an ugly shouting match.

"I thought we talked about that, Nina, and put it behind us. It was a mistake, it could have happened to anyone."

"No, I don't believe that one, and by no means have I forgotten about it. In all our twenty years together, I've never called out another man's name while we were making love. If that's what you can even call what we do together, because it hasn't been good in quite sometime now!" Nina braced herself. Jay wasn't going to take an insult like that lying down.

"Watch what you say to me, Nina. Now is not the time to get smart with me."

Nina shifted her weight from one foot to the other and took a stance that sisters take when they're about to chew you up and spit you out. She pointed her index finger directly between his eyes. "I *know* your ass is not trying to threaten me! No, you better think about what you say to me." Nina again started to make her way around him toward the door, and once again he stopped her, this time by putting his hands on her shoulders and jerking her to a halt. Nina was so pissed that she snatched his hands off of her. Who in hell did he think he was? No one could put their hands on her like that! Jay included.

"Nina, it was a mistake, okay. That's all."

"You're damn right it was a mistake. Something like that doesn't fall from your lips unless you've been thinking about it all the time. I've put up with a lot of crap from you, Jay, and I'm just tired of it. I'm tired of you never having time for me. Hell, at this point I really don't care about you anymore."

"What are you saying to me? What do you mean, you don't care?" Jay took a step back from her, and at that moment the phone rang. Nina went to the nightstand and picked up the receiver.

"Hello" Nina answered, huffing.

"Hello, this is Dr. Nancy from Sanford Hospital in San Francisco. And I'm trying to reach Nina Epps."

"Who is that on the damn phone? Is that the man—"

Nina picked up a pillow from the bed and tossed it at him. She placed her index finger on her lips ordering him to be quiet. "This is Nina."

"Yes, I'm calling in reference to Gracie Howard. She was involved in a serious automobile accident this afternoon."

"Oh, my God! Is she okay?"

"Well, we're preparing her for surgery right now. The trauma from the accident has caused some complications with her pregnancy."

"Oh, Jesus," Nina suddenly felt lightheaded and weak. She sat down on the bed.

"What's wrong Nina? Who is that?"

Nina palmed the phone with her hand. "Gracie has been in a car accident. This is the hospital." She turned back to the phone. "Look, I'm going to get on the first plane out there," she said frantically, searching for something to write with. Jay handed her a pencil and a small notepad.

"Yes, that would be wise. It's just too soon to tell. We're doing everything we can."

"I understand. Where are you located?" Dr. Nancy gave Nina all of the information that she needed. As soon as she hung up the phone she explained to Jay what had happened. Nina fully expected Jay to fly out to San Francisco with her, but he bitched and moaned about how he had to be in court the following day for a critical antitrust case he'd been working on for months.

"Never mind, Jay! I'll handle it!" Nina cut him short.

The fact that Jay wasn't going should not have surprised her. Nina hustled down to the basement to pull out the large suitcase—she wasn't sure how long she'd have to stay with Gracie. Rose was right. She should have been communicating with her daughter instead of letting the walls of anger and disappointments separate them. Nina suddenly felt like she was going out of her mind as emotions of fear and sorrow started flooding her heart. Questions arose about Gracie's living situation that she didn't know the answers to. Like, where was her husband, for one? What kind of accident was it? Did they have to cut her out of the car? Was she paralyzed? Nina tried to push the horrible questions out of her mind. She told herself that Gracie was going to be just fine. She tossed the suitcase on the edge of the bed, flung open the sliding closet door and started pulling down clothes at random. She would call the travel agent first thing in the morning. Hopefully, she'd be able to get a direct flight from Chicago to San Francisco early enough to put her there by evening. Jay was on the phone, calling the hospital back to try and get more information. But all they were able to tell him was that she was in surgery.

9

It was such a crazy morning. Nina called the travel agent and booked a 10:30 A.M. direct flight to San Francisco. Then she called the office and canceled all of her meetings; she told her secretary to strike out the entire week and reschedule everything for the following week. She slept the entire five hours of the flight, but that was only because she hadn't gotten any sleep at all the night before. She was just thankful that the plane took off on time and that there were no delays. She woke up just as the stewardess was coming around telling everyone to raise their seats to the upright position. Nina damn near broke her neck rushing to get to the baggage claim area. She grabbed her things and hailed a cab. She arrived at her hotel, checked in, and tipped the bellboy generously to make sure that her bags made it to her room. She went outside and stood in front of the hotel. She hailed another cab and rushed over to the hospital. Nina burst through the doors of the emergency room and marched directly over to the nurses' station.

"Hi, I'm here to see Gracie Howard." Nina watched as the woman typed in Gracie's name, and waited for the computer to respond.

"Okay—she is in a private room on the other side of the hospital. Go down the hall through those double doors." The nurse stood up and pointed in the direction that Nina should go. *Damn,* thought Nina, *why is it that you're never in the right place when you walk through the door of a hospital?* "Then go all the way to the end of the hall. Take the elevator up to the fourth floor. When you get off, make a right and walk down to the nurses' station there, and they'll direct you to her room."

Nina quickly repeated the instructions back to the nurse and before she knew it she was off like a flash of lighting, running down the hall. When she reached the second nurses' station, they had her wait for Gracie's doctor before she entered the room. A moment later a slender, mature brown woman with salt-and-pepper hair, dressed in a white lab coat approached her.

"Hello, my name is Dr. Nancy. I'm Gracie's doctor. And you are?" Nina was caught off guard by the woman's thick Jamaican accent. She hadn't picked up on it when they spoke on the phone. More than likely because she was so upset with Jay.

"I'm her mother," Nina answered. She noticed how Dr. Nancy's eyebrows raised up as if she were surprised to hear that coming from her mouth.

"I thought you might have been her sister. You look absolutely wonderful, queen," Doctor Nancy said, then exhaled and began searching for the right words. She took Nina's hand into her own and led her down the hall. As she heard all of the beeps from the machines around her, Nina suddenly didn't feel rushed anymore. The smell of medicine and sick people choked the air around her but she was paying close attention to everything. They were making their way past the waiting room when she noticed a man comforting a woman who she assumed was his wife.

"I was unable to save the pregnancy. Your daughter lost the child," Doctor Nancy explained, as Nina felt the doctor's fingertips lightly brushing the back of her hand. "There were a few complications. When I did a final check of her uterus, after the miscarriage, I discovered that postpartum bleeding hadn't stopped.

Upon further examination I also saw that she had severe fibroid problems. The fibroid tumors were very large, about the size of a grapefruit. Gracie continued to bleed, and when the situation became life-threatening, I had to perform a hysterectomy and remove her uterus. She's so young, and I really didn't want to, but it was unavoidable. I'm afraid that she will never be able to have children of her own. The good news is that the lab report shows that the tumors were not cancerous."

Nina fought desperately to keep her tears of anguish under control. Thank God Gracie didn't have cancer. She had been upset that Gracie had gotten pregnant before she'd had a chance to really enjoy life. Now she was feeling awful that she would never be able to have children.

"Her head hit the windshield, so her face is pretty bruised and swollen. She has been heavily sedated and has been in and out of consciousness. However, she does not know about the surgery yet."

Nina cleared her throat. "If you don't mind, I'd like to talk with her about it."

"Sure, dear, I understand." Dr. Nancy sympathized.

"Do you know what kind of accident it was? Did someone hit her?"

"From the police report, it seems as if a child darted out into the street in front of her car. She swerved to avoid hitting the little boy and smashed into a tree. The steering wheel collapsed into her stomach and pinned her inside the vehicle. Then somehow the metal coils from the seat cushion ripped through the fabric of both the seat and her clothing, causing injury to the outer area of her womanhood."

Damn, Nina thought, then swallowed hard. "Where is Mark, her husband?" she asked.

"Well, the hospital doesn't know where he is. From the fragmented information that we were able to gather from your daughter when she came in, apparently he is in the middle of the Pacific Ocean somewhere on a navy ship." Nina felt her face drop. This was awful. How could she not have taken the time to find out more about Gracie's life and the things that she was going through? Why had she let her stubbornness interfere with their relationship?

"We are here. I want to prepare you before you go in. She is really bruised, but she will heal in time. The nurse has just given her a bath and an extra blanket because her skin was cold. What she needs is a lot of love to get her through this."

Nina walked into the room, looking at the curtain that surrounded Gracie's bed and feeling afraid to walk toward it or even to pull it back so she could see. *Damn you, Jay, for sending me out here alone!* She made her way around to the other side of the bed, which was next to a window, and gazed down at Gracie's swollen and bruised face. Nina instantly focused on the white gauze on Gracie's forehead. It had a large bloodstain on it.

"That's a rather nasty gash she sustained, but it will heal just fine," said Dr. Nancy, as she checked the heart monitor and then left. Nina lifted up the blankets to find her daughter's hand. Her fingers were so cold, and Nina rubbed them to try to get them warm. She stroked Gracie's matted hair, remembering the times that she had sat her between her legs and French-braided her hair for her. Dr. Nancy was kind enough to return with a chair so that Nina could sit down and a cup of water for her to drink. Nina noticed how dry and cracked Gracie's lips were, and picked up the clean folded face towel that was on the nightstand next to the bed. She took the tip of the towel, dipped it in the cup of water, and gently moistened her daughter's lips.

"Its okay," she whispered. "I'm here now, and you don't have to worry about a thing. Just rest up and get better. I will stay for as long as it takes." Nina felt a large boulder lodge itself in her throat. It was difficult for her to speak. Finally she allowed the floodgate to open and release her tears.

Nina had nodded off into a light sleep when Gracie awoke later that evening whispering, "Mom." Nina's eyes shot open as she instantly sat up in her chair.

"Yes, baby, it's me. How are you feeling?" Nina stood up so that Gracie would be able to see her better.

"I feel like crap," Gracie replied with a husky voice. "I'm cold."

"I'll have the nurse bring you another blanket."

"No, don't leave me," Gracie raised her hand slightly and Nina grabbed it quickly.

"Okay, sweetie, I won't leave you."

"Tell me what happened," begged Gracie.

"Baby, right now you need to concentrate on getting well," Nina said, rubbing her daughter's hair. Gracie tried to sit up, but the pain she felt in her stomach was paralyzing and forced her to lie back down.

"My God, what have they done to me!" Gracie began crying hysterical tears.

"Honey . . ." Nina began, frantically searching her mind for the right words. But they just were not there, and Gracie could see the pain in her mother's eyes.

"I didn't hit that little boy, did I?" Gracie asked.

"No, sugar, you didn't."

"But I lost the baby, didn't I?" Nina nodded her head yes. Words escaped her.

"It's okay," Gracie sniffled. "Mark and I will just have to try again."

"Honey—" Nina was finding courage from somewhere deep inside of herself. "There were complications, and they had to"—Nina paused—"remove the parts that allow you to have a baby."

"What exactly are you saying, Mom?" Gracie's tears began flowing faster.

Nina could only gaze at Gracie, unable to move or speak. Gracie released a tumultuous wail. Nina leaned over and held her daughter's face close to her heart.

10

The hospital released Gracie a week later with detailed instructions about diet and exercise. At Gracie's insistence, Nina checked out of her hotel and moved her belongings over to Gracie's two-bedroom apartment. It was a cozy place, although it screamed bachelor pad to Nina. All of the furniture was black—black leather sofa, black mini-blinds, black dinner table, black dishes, black bathroom towels with a matching black shower curtain. There was also a black TV, black stereo system, and black kitchen appliances. The entire place needed a woman's touch. Nina was curious as to why Gracie hadn't added her own special touches, but choose not to pry that deeply into her business. All Nina wanted was for her baby to get well and make a full recovery. Over the next few days Gracie voluntarily opened up to Nina and talked the way they used to. However, it was a little different now. Instead of directing Gracie, she listened. Gracie was a grown woman now, capable of making her own choices.

"When I married Mark, I didn't expect it to be like this." Gracie and Nina sat at the small black kitchen table near a window that had an obstructed view of the Golden Gate Bridge.

"He stays gone six months out of the year. The last time I heard from him was about two weeks ago when the ship docked in the Philippines." Gracie took an easy swallow from the glass of orange juice that was in front of her. "He claimed that he didn't know the navy was going to put him on a ship for six months. But in going through the house and cleaning up, I found the letter that accepted his application to do a tour of duty out in the islands of the Pacific. He knew he would be leaving for months before he even mentioned it to me."

Typical male, Nina thought. *They just have to lie about everything.*

"So that's why the hospital couldn't reach him," Gracie continued. "I was so stupid, Mom. I thought that he wanted to have babies so that we could raise a family together." Gracie started crying. Nina's heart sank. Until now, she had had no idea what Gracie was going through. "I thought he wanted to be with me, you know. Not on some damn ship! God, I hate it when I cry. It makes my stomach hurt when I do," Gracie collected herself. "It's difficult to function at times because I'm so bored, so afraid and lonely. Sometimes I find myself just sitting in here crying." It was almost haunting to Nina to hear Gracie say that. Gracie was going through the very same type of mess that she had.

"He wanted to load me up with a baby so that he wouldn't have too much to worry about while he was gone. You know, something to keep me busy? Or at least that's how I feel about it. The day I told him that I was pregnant, he decided to tell me about his tour of duty. I didn't know what to say or do, I was just in shock. He eventually charmed me into accepting it, but I still didn't feel right about it. When he left he said that he would call as often as he could, which as you can see is not very often. For all I know, he could have another family out there on an island somewhere." Gracie started crying again.

"Come on now, honey." Nina grabbed a Kleenex for her. "Stop crying, it's going to be okay."

"No, it's not, Mom. After he left, I got real depressed, I'm out here all alone with no family and no friends. Hell, I don't even have a job. I feel so useless. On the day of the accident I was on my way to Stanford University to see about completing my degree. Pregnant or not, I was going to see what it would take."

As Nina listened to Gracie she felt so sorry for her. The road that she'd taken was turning out to be the road of hard knocks. Gracie continued to spill out her soul about how Mark was the first man she'd slept with and how she had confused a screw with love. How he'd convinced her to drop out of school, marry him, and move out to California.

"Mom, I really did want to talk with you, but I was just so ashamed of how I treated you the last time we talked. I was too embarrassed by the fact that what you were trying to tell me all along was true. I am so sorry for that."

"Don't be, Gracie. I was wrong for not trying to communicate as well. I was just so hurt that you didn't follow through and realize your potential. But that was no reason for me to cut you off the way that I did. I'm sorry for that." Nina stood up and walked behind Gracie's chair and embraced her. They both let out large sighs. The two of them were glad that they'd finally torn down the wall that had been separating them and slowly eating away at their souls.

"So, how is Dad?"

"Well, you know your father. Mr. Workaholic. He's been calling for you, but he seems to always call around the time you're resting. He's trying to make partner at the firm and that's requiring him to put in long hours."

"Well, yes, Dad is going to be Dad. What about you? You look great. Like a world-class athlete or something. You're really keeping yourself together, I hope he appreciates all of your efforts."

"Well, like you said, your father is into his job and can't see anything else. But enough about me, honey. What are you going to do now?"

"I've been thinking about that. There are some things that I've come to realize, and whenever my husband decides to check on me, we're going to discuss them. I'm not going to just sit here anymore waiting on him to come around. I mean, this is not what I expected, Mom. As soon as I heal up from this, I think I'm going to make arrangements to fly back to D.C. and finish what I started."

"You don't want to stay here and check out Stanford?" Nina asked.

"No, it would be much easier for me to go back there, instead of having to deal with the possibility of losing credit hours. Besides, I have to do something. If I just sit here, I'm only going to get depressed about not being able to have children. Mark probably won't want me anymore because of it." Nina could hear Gracie's voice cracking, threatening to shed more tears. "I mean, I don't feel like a woman anymore, you know? I wanted to know what it felt like to have a baby growing inside of me. If not now, at least at some other point."

"Come on now, Gracie. There are other options available. There are plenty of children in this world who need a home."

"I know, Mom, but I wanted my own. Am I wrong for that? I mean, why is this happening to me?" At that moment the phone rang, and Gracie picked it up. It was Mark.

"His damn ears must have been burning," Nina muttered. Then she excused herself, saying she'd run out to the store to pick up some items that Gracie needed. Nina couldn't help but think that she, too, needed to make some changes.

By the time Nina returned she could see Gracie's spirits had been lifted a bit. Mark was on his way home that night and would be there by morning. Nina called the travel agent and booked her return flight home. Gracie insisted that there was no need for Nina to leave, but Nina realized that she couldn't interfere with their relationship. Nina knew that the moment she saw Mark, her anger would get the best of her; her motherly instinct would chew Mark up and spit him out. Gracie needed to iron out her own affairs, there was no need for Nina to be in the center of it. Whatever she and Mark decided would be fine by her. Just as long as Gracie was happy.

11

Richard thought long and hard about what Nina had proposed to him with regard to separating his joint bank account with Estelle. However, after thinking about it the following day at work he decided that once he got home he'd sit down and discuss everything with Estelle. He wanted to get their life back on track by working things out. But that evening when he arrived home, he opened the door and damn near had a heart attack. The entire house smelled like a burning ashtray. He spotted a pregnant cockroach speeding up the side of the wall looking for shelter. His entire office had been dismantled and was sitting in the corner. Some hideous-looking sofa was sitting in the center of the room, and there were bags of clothes all over the floor. He maneuvered his way through the clutter in the living room and made his way to the kitchen, where he found Rubylee hosing down the microwave with a fire extinguisher because it had caught fire due to the fact that she'd put aluminum foil inside of it. Rubylee peered over the top of her reading glasses at him with a blank expression. He refused to even speak to her, he just threw cold daggers at her with his eyes. He marched around the corner and down the hall into the master bedroom where he found Estelle sitting on the chaise looking out the window. Richard slammed the bedroom door shut.

"What the fuck is going on, Estelle?" Richard snarled like a madman.

"Don't talk to me like that! I've had a very fucked-up day, okay?"

"Oh, no, you haven't seen fucked-up yet! I'm about to show you fucked-up. I'm going to call the police and have these people removed from my house."

"Richard, please! My head is killing me. Can't we discuss this in the morning? Huh, baby? Please?"

"Hell, no, we can't discuss this in the morning. I want an explanation right now!" Richard heard the doorknob turn behind him and looked over his right shoulder at Rubylee, who was waddling her way into the room.

"Well, I figured I'd better come on in here before things get out of control," said Rubylee as she spun the wheel on her Bic lighter and fired up another Winston Salem. She took a long drag and let the smoke ease out of her nose.

Richard turned around with fire in his eyes and hate in his heart. He was only a breath away from becoming uncontrollably violent. "No shit!" he said, with his chest heaving forward full of anger.

Rubylee was no stranger to violent situations and had already prepared her speech for when Richard came home. She had specifically instructed Estelle to let her handle the situation, since she'd learned long ago from Stanback how to diffuse situations like this one. Rubylee showed absolutely no fear when she spoke.

"Let me explain something to you, Richard," she said with a heavy tone in her voice that made her sound like a man. "Blood is thicker than water. I taught that woman over there to always take care of family. I'm part of her family whether you like it or not. I'm her mother. And a black woman cherishes her mother dearly. A black woman will do just about anything for her momma. Life kicked all of us in the ass today, Richard, whether you know it or not. The Lord saw fit to put me outdoors today, and Estelle came to my rescue, just like any daughter would. If your mother was still alive, and she needed your help, you'd be right there, no questions asked. Unfortunately, when she came to my aid she forgot to do a few things and ended up losing her job." Rubylee thumbed the ashes off her cigarette and into an ashtray she was carrying. "My daughter has got a big heart, and you're a lucky man to have a person like her. Because you just never know. Life might kick you the wrong way and leave you afflicted with some disease. A woman like Estelle would never leave you because of misfortune like that."

"You know what, woman?" Richard did not appreciate Rubylee's intrusion or her explanation one bit. "One of us has got to go. Estelle, do you hear me? Either she goes or I go." Richard directed his attention to Estelle, who looked just as angry as he did.

"Hold on before you go and make such a harmful choice." Rubylee took another drag from her Winston Salem, dropped her jaw and let the smoke filter slowly out as she exhaled. Watching the smoke billow in the air reminded Richard of a gangster movie he once saw. Just before the villain would kill someone he'd drop his jaw and let smoke filter out of his mouth just as Rubylee was doing.

"Look at your situation. Your wife ain't working, I don't work, Justine doesn't work, and Keysha is too young to work. You got a little baby in there that's going to go hungry if you up and leave. Estelle won't be able to pay the rent and eventually, in this high-class place, they're going to put her out. Now, you got to ask yourself. Is that something that you really want to happen to your family? Seems like an awful big price to pay for just being angry. When you got married you said for better or for worse. Now at the first sign of trouble you're ready to jump ship. Think about it. I know that a man like you will do what's right. You're going to stay with this woman and help her handle all of her problems like man a should. Now, I don't want to hear any more talk about you leaving. This situation ain't no reason for you to get up and run off."

"Really, Richard." Estelle could see that he was being persuaded. "Once I find a new job, I will help Mom find a new place to live. Now come on, baby." Estelle slid her hand around his waist and hugged him. "Don't be like that. This is only temporary, I promise. In a few weeks all of this will be straightened out."

Richard watched Rubylee as she turned and walked out the door, not fully believing that this woman had actually given him pause and made him rethink his next course of action. Rubylee had missed her calling; she should have been a politician or a preacher. Richard had difficulty understanding why he suddenly felt guilty when a moment ago he was ready to rip off someone's head.

Rubylee removed Richard's clothes from the closets in his office and placed them on his bed for him to put somewhere else. As far as she was concerned, the room now belonged to her. Keysha and Justine took the guest room.

Over the next few weeks, Rubylee settled in like the roots of a tree settle into the earth. She placed her multicolored plastic cups in the cabinets along with her mason jars. Carryout boxes ordered from local restaurants littered his once perfectly set dinner table. In Rubylee's mind, she was living high on the hog.

Estelle wasn't able to find work as quickly as she thought she would, and gave up and settled down with Justine and Rubylee, whose asses had grown roots in Richard's sofa in front of his 48-inch large screen TV as they waited for the Jerry Springer Show to come on. When he returned home from work they'd still be sitting there as if they'd never moved, completely tuned into those trash TV talk shows. Rubylee even commented about how she'd like to be a guest on the show. Resentment and contempt toward Rubylee, Justine, and Estelle slowly took up residency in Richard's heart. A few weeks turned out to be the rest of the spring, the entire summer, and eventually the winter, by which time it was entirely too cold outside for any type of moving to be done. Richard sat back, feeling helpless as he watched his small slice of heaven turn into Rubylee's ghetto paradise.

12

During the flight home Nina did some thinking of her own. Jay had started putting his hands on her, which is something he'd never done in the past. She figured that was how things got started. First a grab, then a shove, and finally a hit. She was being honest and truthful with herself: She didn't really love Jay anymore. They'd become strangers who just happened to live with each other. And the suspicion of infidelity had slowly been ripping her apart. She had acknowledged the possibility of him having another woman within the first few years of their marriage, but she'd refused to accept that Jay would break her heart that way. Besides, he did marry her, that had to count for something, she recalled thinking at the time. It comforted her knowing that Gracie would grow up in a house with a father. That was one of the most important things to her at the time. So she closed her eyes, choosing to ignore Jay's suspicious behavior. Jay adopted the use of fear tactics and strict rules in order to assert his dominance and control over her. But now things were different for Nina. She didn't have to put up with that kind of treatment if she didn't want to. There was no need for her to walk around on eggshells praying that he wouldn't blow up about some trivial issue. She'd done her time, had finally become her own woman, and didn't want to live under the umbrella of Jay's dictatorship. In some ways she felt like the char-. acter Celie from the novel *The Color Purple*, written by Alice Walker. When Celie found her sister's letters after her husband had kicked her sister out of the house, she gained strength, and suddenly her husband didn't seem like the fire breathing dragon he held himself out to be. Even Rose didn't fully realize all of the emotional turmoil that Nina had silently endured. She'd kept so much of it private that Rose couldn't fully understand why she was so hellbent on making a change. Enough was enough; the rift between her and Jay had grown larger than the Grand Canyon. The timing of her decision was awful, but then again, is there ever a good time to tell your husband of twenty years that it's over?

By February, Nina had found an apartment that met her needs, even though it was difficult for her to go from living in a house to staying in an apartment. Her new home was a cozy two-bedroom in Schaumburg, Illinois, as far away from Hazel Crest, Illinois, as she could get. It was in an apartment complex that had excellent amenities: swimming pool, tennis courts, and state of the art exercise facilities. Once she signed the lease that sealed her fate for the next year, there was no way she was going to tell Jay that she was leaving when they were at home together and give him a chance to try and change her mind. Some time away from each other might be good, she rational- ized. Maybe after time passed she'd feel differently. Either way, she wanted to get away from her current situation. As the time drew near for her surprise announcement, she became an emo- tional wreck because she knew this would not be easy. She de- cided to take Jay to dinner at the Olive Garden, one of his favorite Italian restaurants. She sat down, really not all that hungry. The waitress, who resembled a waitress named Alice from a popular sitcom a few years back, came over chewing on a piece of gum.

"Can I get you folks something to drink?" she asked. Jay or- dered a beer, but Nina declined, water would be just fine for her. After a moment the waitress came back with bread sticks and a large bowl of salad for the two of them. Normally, the garlic-covered, butter-flavored breadsticks would have made Nina's mouth water, but now she couldn't stand the smell of them. The waitress placed Jay's beer in front of him and gave Nina her water. Jay already knew he wanted the chicken parmesan, while Nina ordered the lasagna, knowing that she wasn't going to eat it.

"Well, I'm glad to see that you're finally starting to come around," Jay said, taking a gulp of his beer. "It's been so long since you've taken me out to dinner. I was at work the other day thinking about how to get our lives back on track. I was thinking that maybe we should take us a vacation so that we could spend some time with each other. We could go somewhere a little different this time. One of my clients was just telling me that he and his wife travel to Nassau once a year. What do you think?"

Nina's stomach did a flip. She was suddenly finding it difficult to speak. She took a hard swallow, not fully wanting to believe what she'd just heard coming from his mouth. Was he trying to suggest taking a vacation to the Bahamas after all this time? For a fleeting moment she was considering it, but a vacation in paradise was not going to solve their problems.

"Okay, here you folks go." The waitress came back and placed their orders in front of them. "Is there anything else I can get you . . ." The waitress looked at Nina. "Are you okay honey? You don't look so good."

Nina collected herself as best as she could. "I'm fine thank you." At first she had thought that telling him this in public would be a good way to avoid a bitter argument. Now, she was of the mind that this should've stayed behind closed doors.

"Okay, let me know if I can get you anything else," replied the waitress as she walked away. Jay had his head bowed and was eagerly shoveling food into his mouth. He looked up for a quick moment and saw how Nina was gawking at him. She was searching to find the words she needed while desperately trying to keep her emotions in line.

"Jay, we have problems."

"No more than anyone else," he said, sitting up and scratching the back of his head.

"Jay, you're having an affair on me." Nina exhaled. The words were tough to get out. "You've been having an affair, or several affairs for all I know, over most of the years of our marriage."

"Nina, I told you that I was sorry for saying the wrong name and sorry for putting my hands on you. They were accidents, what more do you want me to say? I'm trying to make this up to you. Don't you want to go to the Caribbean?" That hurt her feelings. Was that the only reason that he wanted to go, so that she would forget about these little "accidents" in their relationship?

"No, Jay, I don't."

"Okay, so where do you want to go?"

"I'm leaving you." Jay set the fork down lightly on the plate, picked up the napkin from his lap and dabbed the corners of his mouth.

Jay leaned forward and spoke in a loud whisper. "What's this about, Nina? What are you trying to do?"

When he said that, Nina realized that the thought of her ever leaving him had never crossed his mind. Nina felt tears welling up to the surface. This was more painful to do than she had thought.

"I'm not putting up with your womanizing anymore. I've had enough of it. We need to be adults about this. I think you need your freedom. And I'm in the way. I don't want anything from you, Jay. You can pretty much have it all." Jay sat up with disbelief written all over his face.

"You see, Jay, I've been quiet about it over the years because I was thinking of Gracie. But your infidelities have ripped my heart to shreds." Nina felt a tear jumpstart and sprint down her cheek. "I know that you must be tired of trying to hide the evidence."

"Nina, listen to yourself." Jay spoke very calmly and directly. She recognized it as his lawyer's voice, the voice he used when he was trying to set his feelings aside. "Listen to what you are saying. You can't even prove that."

Nina chuckled a painful little laugh and quickly wiped tears away from her cheek and dabbed at the moisture that was forming on her upper lip from her running nose. "I did just prove it, Jay. Not once have you denied having an affair, but you want me to prove it, which means that the crime has been committed, it's just a matter of me building a strong case. Am I right?" Nina watched as Jay sat back in his seat, not believing that Nina had used his own words against him. It was now he who was at a loss for words. The pain of the truth quickly etched itself on his face.

"You can't leave me, Nina; we've been together too long. I mean, don't you think all we've built is worth fighting for?"

"At one point I did, Jay. And over the course of our lives together, I've tried to make you see that. I've tried talking to you, and I've tried to understand you. Lord knows that I have been righteous with you, Jay, but you've taken me for granted." Nina fully expected Jay to blow up, get all angry and begin huffing and puffing like she'd seen him during so many other stressful situations. Instead, he sat there with pain in his eyes, looking helpless and needy as an infant. This was a side of Jay she didn't recognize. During all of their years together she'd never seen him look so vulnerable. He bowed his head, hoping to conceal his shame. There was a long silence that seemed loud enough to wake the dead. When he looked back up, Nina saw that his eyes were glassy with sorrow and regret.

"I confess," he muttered. "I have not been the man to you that I should have been." His words were choppy and full of emotion. She watched him as he swallowed hard.

"She, uhm . . ."

"Jay, stop. I don't want to know the details." He bowed his head again. A confession was something that she had not expected to get. There was a difference between suspicion and reality. This awareness stabbed her in the chest and punctured her heart. Her pain intensified.

"I don't want you to leave me, Nina. We can get help. I can go to counseling. I'll do anything. Just—just give me a another chance." Tears flowed like water running downstream from Nina's eyes. There was no use for her to try and sweep away her sorrow now. She collected herself as best as she could in order to speak and say what needed to be said.

"Why Jay? Why did you do it to me?"

Jay shrugged his shoulders. "It's not one particular reason. I mean, there were many reasons, none of which gave me the right to do what I did. I'm confessing because I feel horrible. I should have gone with you to see about Gracie. But I didn't, and I lied to you. On the day you left for San Francisco, I didn't have a court case. I was with a—female all day. I felt like slime shit. I sat there thinking that my daughter was in a bad car accident and going into surgery and here I was with a woman who I'm not supposed to be with."

"Why, you heartless son-of-a-bitch!" Nina reacted immediately by grabbing a handful of salad and flinging it at him with as much power as she could. That wasn't enough to express her anger. So she picked up her fork and slung it at him, and then her butter knife. She didn't care if others noticed the tragedy that was unfolding. This entire situation had become too agonizing. "So I take it that all of the other times that you were with that jezebel you never felt one ounce of guilt, right?"

"Nina, it's a little more complicated than that. Yes, I had guilt, but not to this degree." No sooner had those words left his lips than Nina wished that he could take them back. She suddenly felt disorientated. She collected the thoughts in her mind as best as she could.

"You've hurt me, Jay. I don't believe you've hurt me like this." She popped open her purse in search of a tissue and money for the dinner. "I'm leaving now, Jay, I'm not going home." Nina's bottom lip quivered uncontrollably as she glared at him. She wanted to say good-bye but the words were stuck somewhere inside of her.

"Nina wait . . . I'm not going to give up on us. I—I made some bad choices and I want to explain myself to you. I want to try and make things right."

Nina didn't reply, she walked away as fast as her legs could take her. As she made her way out the front door the waitress noticed the distressed expression on her face. Nina bowed her head and rushed out of the door to her car. She ripped open her purse in search of her keys as she released her anguish and began sobbing uncontrollably. She opened the door, tossed her purse on the passenger seat, and started her car. She wiped the tears from her eyes, then sped off.

Jay sat at the table not knowing what to do. He'd tried to convince himself that none of this was happening. Whenever he thought of himself growing old, he'd always pictured Nina by his side. Now he'd destroyed that, but there was no way he was about to give up on his marriage and let her walk out of his life without a fight. He loved her; he could feel it in his aching heart. He made a silent pledge. He was going to change his ways and do everything in his power to mend the heart he'd so carelessly broken.

"Uhm—listen." The waitress had come back. "This one is on the house tonight, okay? Don't worry about a thing. Whatever the problem is, pray on it, and God will show you the way."

"Thanks," Jay replied as he got up, leaving the fifty anyway. The waitress was right; he needed to pray. The first thing Sunday morning, he'd go to church and beg to be forgiven for his sins. Right now he needed to call a cab. Nina had left him without a way of getting back.

13

Richard had started going through a metamorphosis that Estelle couldn't stop. The man he had changed into was not her Richard. This new man was a complete stranger to her. She knew that her relationship with him was under great stress, but she was hoping that he would adjust to having extended family living in the house. So far, though, Richard wasn't adjusting well at all. Estelle could feel the distance between them growing wide like the sea. Communicating with Richard had become impossible, and for the first time she began noticing the resentment in his comments to her and the contempt for her in his eyes. It hurt her so much, because she wanted him to understand how torn she was and how she couldn't just turn her back on her mother or any of her family, for that matter. That was a good quality to have, why couldn't he see that? Estelle tried to bring Richard around to her way of thinking through her persuasive ways, but he refused her every time she tried to touch him. The way he swatted her hand off of him, like she was a fly that had landed on his food, was difficult for her to accept. His sudden rejection of her was something that she wasn't accustomed to. She just needed time to get things back to normal, and she swore to herself that she would make all of this up to him. For now, she had to deal with Keysha and Justine. Keysha had just turned fourteen and was extremely rebellious and un-controllable, just like her mother. Keysha was only a freshman and already she was cutting classes and ditching school. Teachers called the house on a regular basis to discuss her disruptive behavior, stating that she seemed to be more interested in her social life than school. She'd been suspended three times. Once for fighting and once for bringing a butcher knife to school for protection. Then there was the issue of trying to find Keysha when school let out. She wouldn't come directly home like she was supposed to, and Estelle had to drive around for hours trying to find her. Then one night Keysha came waltzing in the door at one in the morning, which made Richard go off on her for coming back at such a late hour.

"You are not going to be sneaking into my home at this time of morning," Richard hollered at Keysha, who looked shocked that he'd even said anything to her. "There are rules in this house, and if you can't abide by them, you are free to leave."

"Tuh!" Keysha sucked her teeth and rolled her eyes in defiance, paying more attention to her manicured fingernails than to him.

"Oh, it's like that, huh?" Richard pulsed with anger. "Then don't come back here!" he said with a razor sharp tongue, and slammed the door in her face. Keysha began banging on the door as Richard turned the locks. The banging woke everyone in the house, and that's when all hell broke loose. Rubylee opened the door and found Keysha standing there in tears. Rubylee turned to Richard, who'd gone back to his bed on the sofa.

"You'd better not ever do something like this again, Richard!" Rubylee's eyes had become red with fire and her words full of fury. "In this house, we don't turn our backs on family." Richard flung the covers off and sprung to his feet. He stalked over to Rubylee and invaded her social space.

"Well, then she'd better learn how to respect my goddamn house! My doors aren't open all night!" Richard's ranting woke Justine and Estelle.

"What's going on, Richard, why are you shouting like that?" Estelle approached him, tying the strap to her robe around her waist.

"My house does not have an open-door policy, and I will not tolerate Keysha waltzing in here at one in the morning."

"Come here, baby." Justine placed her arm around her daughter. Both Rubylee and Justine ran to Keysha's defense, arguing that it wasn't Richard's place to discipline her because he wasn't her father. Estelle could see pure anger in both Richard and Rubylee's eyes as they ripped each other apart with bitter words. In all of their years together, Estelle had never seen Richard become that vocal. It was like her husband had switched from Dr. Jekyll to Mr. Hyde.

"You are just low down, Richard! The poor child has been through misery all of her life. As a doctor, I thought that you'd be more compassionate about that sort of thing. But I see that you're one of those self-centered bastards. The only thing you're concerned about are your feelings. That child isn't used to having doors slammed in her face like that!"

"That young woman hasn't been a child for some time now. And the only thing that's open at this time of night is her legs." Richard wasn't backing down.

"She went out to a party tonight, and I told her to be back by one!" Justine pointed her finger at Richard and began working her neck. "And I don't appreciate you insinuating that my baby is out there acting like some whore! So fuck you, Richard!" Once again, Richard felt as if he wasn't winning with words.

"Richard, baby, why don't you come on in the bedroom and lay down?" Estelle offered as a way to defuse the tension. She started pulling on his arm, but he snatched it back. "I don't want to go in the goddamn room with you!" Just then there was a thundering knock on the front door. Richard marched over to open the it. He flung it open with his tongue all set to rip apart whoever it was out there. What he found on the other side were two female Chicago police officers.

"We've received a complaint call from your neighbors claiming that there was a domestic disturbance. Is there a problem here?" asked one of the officers.

"No, there is no problem here," Richard answered with a sharp tone.

One of the officers stepped away and placed her hand on the butt of her revolver. "Sir, do you mind stepping out in the hallway for a moment?" Richard instantly noticed the posture of the officer and complied. The other officer clamped her handcuffs around Richard's wrists. "It's for your own safety, sir," the officer explained. Richard couldn't believe this shit was happening. One of the officers stepped inside and pulled the door shut behind her. The officer that was with him was a caramel sister who'd dyed her hair blond. She asked Richard what had happened, and he explained his situation to her. The other officer stayed inside for what seemed like an eternity but then finally emerged. She stepped down the hall a bit and consulted with her partner.

"Sir, we're going to recommend that you gather a few things and get yourself a hotel room for the remainder of the evening."

"What! You're putting me out of my own home! I haven't done a damn thing except raise my voice."

"See what I mean, officer?" Rubylee exclaimed from the doorway. "He has these anxiety attacks and just loses control of himself. I'm afraid that his mind may be going. I've already warned him about raising his voice at me in my house." Rubylee eyeballed Richard. She had total control over the situation.

"What the hell do you mean, anxiety attacks! I'm not crazy, you are! Officer, this old bitch is lying through her motherfucking teeth." Richard became belligerent and began shouting for Estelle.

"Estelle, you'd better come and get your damn Momma!"

"Hey!" The officer with the blond hair got his attention. "Women are not bitches! Either you get a hotel room for the night, or we'll detain you for twenty-four hours. It's up to you."

Richard was so angry he was shaking uncontrollably. He exhaled, then calmed himself down as best as he could as he agreed to get a hotel room. The blond officer uncuffed him, then escorted him back inside the house. Rubylee stood in the door gloating and blew smoke in his direction as he was escorted back out. Richard glimpsed Justine and Keysha in the kitchen, snacking and laughing. As he made his way down the hall to the master bedroom, he heard Estelle vomiting in the bathroom. Thank goodness Nathan was still asleep and didn't have to witness any of this.

The rift between Richard and Estelle grew even wider that night, and Estelle had no idea how to smooth things out. All she knew was that she felt caught between a rock and a hard place. Now, adding fuel to the fire, Rubylee once again tried to get Estelle to convince Richard to follow through with her proposal of purchasing real estate. Rubylee knew no boundaries, and although there had been high drama in the house on the previous evening, it was of no concern to her.

"I'm going to be frank with you. You better start screwing him," she said with conviction. "The man has got entirely too much tension pinned up inside of him. He reminds me of men who have been in prison. I'm telling you, Richard needs a release."

"Ma, please, I don't need that from you this morning."

"I know you don't want to hear me, but I'm going to tell you anyway. If you don't screw him, somebody else will." Rubylee unwrapped a fresh box of Winston Salems. She spun the wheel on her new blue lighter, placed it on the table and exhaled, letting smoke blow out of her nose. Rubylee collected her thoughts. "You see, baby, Richard is the type of man that's silent and easygoing, one of those men who doesn't like conflict too much. If you start a fight with him, nine times out of ten he'll back down, he's weak like that. Every now and again you have to let him blow up, like last night. Once you let him blow up, he'll calm right down. That's the perfect time to take him, screw his brains out, and get everything you want from him. They call that fighting and fucking. It's full of all that emotional anger and passion. Sometimes, that's when it's the best. Trust me, I know these things. When he gets back here you need to pull him in the room and take care of him. That should be the perfect time to ask him about buying a building."

"Ma, please! I'm in no condition right now to be with Richard, and your smoke is giving me a headache. I thought I told you that Richard didn't want you smoking in here."

"Yeah, you did. But this is my house too," Rubylee boldly stated. "Besides, he ain't here right now, is he?"

"Good morning, y'all." Justine shuffled into the kitchen wearing one of Estelle's red silk nightgowns that Richard had gotten for her on Valentine's Day a year ago. She opened up the refrigerator door, searching for something to eat. "Damn! Who ate the rest of the leftovers? I had my mouth all set for some greens and cornbread this morning."

"Don't you remember, fool? You and your daughter sat up last night and ate the rest of it. She's been eating an awful lot lately," Rubylee said, taking a sip of her black coffee.

"Heifer! If you don't take off my shit!" Estelle couldn't believe that Justine had the nerve to put on her underwear.

"What, this old thing? You don't wear it no more. Besides, my behind fills it out better that yours does." Justine bent square over just enough for the fabric to raise above her butt cheek. Estelle sprang to her feet, knocking the chair over, ready to wrestle Justine out of her clothes.

"Damn!" Estelle shouted, "Why do you take things that don't belong to you? Why are you so damn hardheaded? Every time I turn my back, you go and steal something."

"Shit! If you want this raggedy-ass thing that bad I'll take it off."

"Yes, I do, now go in there and take it off!"

"Estelle, sit down, I don't feel like that mess from you two this morning. You're both grown women now but still act like children."

"Ma, I shouldn't have to put up with with her thieving ass in my own house."

"Oh, you didn't seem to mind my thieving ass when I got you those Coach purses, the Seiko watches, or when I took you shopping after I found that woman's wallet full of money and charge cards! You didn't have a problem when you had me to charge one thousand dollars on that woman's Marshall Field's card for you," Justine snapped back, full of anger. "Or what about the time your ass didn't have shit to wear to that New Year's Eve party? I was the one who went down to Carson Pirie Scott and boosted an eight-hundred-dollar dress for you!"

"Justine, calm down. It's too early in the morning for you to be up fussing and cursing," Rubylee uttered.

"No, I'm sick of her judgmental ass always treating me like I ain't shit! But when she doesn't want to pay for something she comes crying to me about stealing it for her! Ever since she met that pretty motherfucker she's been walking around here like her shit doesn't stink," Justine barked as she slammed the refrigerator door shut. Justine began working her neck. "And Ma is right," Justine propped her hand on her hip, and then glared at Estelle with her facial expression full of attitude. "You'd better start screwing your husband because he's been walking around here looking at me. And I guarantee you, he don't want none of this, because I'll break his ass off!" Justine pulled the gown up over her head, balled it up, threw it at Estelle and stormed out of the kitchen naked.

"I *know* you ain't trying to threaten me!" Estelle hollered, noticing her sister's voluptuous shape. Although Justine was crazy as hell, she had a wonderful figure that would tempt any man if he were weak. "And if you ever think about spreading your legs for Richard, sister or not, I will kill your ass!" Justine could be so unpredictable at times, capable of doing anything or nothing at all. A truly complex sister, a real piece of work just like her damn father, emotionally unstable, living for the moment and nothing else.

"One of these days, Ma, I'm going to really hurt her."

"Now, you know how Justine is, she hasn't changed one bit. The girl is always looking for the next big thrill and refuses to be responsible for her actions. But she is right—if you don't start sleeping with your husband she just might. And you and I both know Justine is crazy enough to do it. I'm not saying that it's right. All I'm saying is, shit happens."

"I'm going to personally throw her ass up out of here if she crosses that line."

"And where is she supposed to go? Out there in the streets? You know that she's a little off in the head! That's your sister. You've got to love her no matter what. She's mentally off, you know that." Rubylee had been making excuses and saying that about Justine for so long that she'd actually started believing it to be the truth. "You've got to take the bad parts of her along with the good parts."

Estelle exhaled, slowly massaging her temples. She felt another migraine building.

"I need some money from you." Rubylee changed the subject.

"Ma, you know that I'm not working."

"Take it from Richard, money he's got plenty."

"I just can't keep taking money from our account like this."

"Listen to me and you listen good. Everything that he owns, you also own. I know that he's hiding a load of money somewhere but he's not telling you about it. He's a third generation doctor; I know his family has left him more money than what he's told you. I've been around too long, and I know that families like his always have money somewhere. I can just feel it. He's got it hidden from you and all we need to do is find it."

"Ma, I can assure you Richard doesn't have any hidden money. Besides, what business is it of yours if he does?" Rubylee was stifled and stunned by the question, realizing she'd said too much. Rubylee's primary reason for allowing herself to be evicted was to move in with Estelle so that she could hustle Richard out of his fortune. It was just that simple. Swindling was the only thing she was good at and was the only thing she'd known. If given the opportunity, she could con the remaining leg off of a one-legged man. All she wanted was a building of her own and a nice little stash of cash for a rainy day. A six-flat is what she had in mind and she didn't care how she went about getting it. "Are you going to give me some money or not?" Rubylee forced the issue. "There are some female things that I need to pick up. Now, if you feel more comfortable with me demanding these things from Richard, I'll most certainly speak to him about it."

Estelle released a depressing sigh. "How much do you need?"

Rubylee wanted to smile at how skillfully she'd gotten out of answering the question, but decided it would be in her best interest not to let her satisfaction show. "Why don't you give me about three hundred dollars. That should hold me for a little while."

"Ma, Richard is not Donald Trump. Three hundred dollars is a lot of money."

"You still have access to the bank account, right?"

"Yes. But—"

"Come on now, I know you're good for it," Rubylee interrupted. "Besides, once you find yourself a job, you'll be able to put the money back in no time at all. It's only three hundred dollars, it's not going to break the bank. Besides, that should hold me at least until the end of the month. On top of that, Richard is the kind of man who will always find a way to pay the bills. So I know nothing is going to get cut off because you gave me a measly three hundred dollars." Rubylee paused a moment and dropped her cigarette in the cup of coffee she'd been drinking.

"What you need to start doing is talking to Richard about getting us that six-flat."

"Ma, there is nothing that I can say or do that will make him want to invest in something like that. I need to concentrate on finding a job and then finding a place for the three of you to live." Rubylee rocked herself to her feet and shuffled over toward the refrigerator.

"Well, I guess I'll have to work on him myself," Rubylee muttered under her breath.

"What?" Estelle couldn't quite make out what her mother had said.

"I said, when will you have the money so that I can get myself some things?"

"Oh . . ." Estelle began massaging her temples. Her head felt as if it were about to explode. She made a mental note to herself to call her doctor and make an appointment to get herself checked out. The headaches were beginning to cripple her day-to-day functions. But first she had to get Richard to put her on his health insurance policy, since hers was terminated along with her employment. "I'll run out later this morning and get it for you."

Rubylee got up to go pour her leftover coffee and wet cigarette down the toilet when the phone rang. "Don't worry, sit down," Rubylee offered. "I'll get that." She walked into the front room and picked up the receiver. "Hello?"

"Hello, this is Seaway National Bank calling to confirm Dr. Richard Vincent's appointment at two o'clock on Monday."

"Oh, he's not here right now. Can I take a message?" Rubylee suggested.

"Uhm, that's okay," the woman on the phone said. "I've already left a message for him at his office. Thank you," she concluded, and hung up the phone.

Rubylee gently set the receiver back down on the cradle. Things were forming in her mind. Richard and Estelle's joint account was with First National Bank. Seaway National Bank was an entirely different institution. That's where Richard's family most likely had banked, and she had a strong suspicion that that's where his family's fortune was. Her mind began racing as she plotted up a scheme to confirm her notions.

"Who was that on the phone?" Estelle hollered from the kitchen.

"It was a wrong number," Rubylee shouted back.

Estelle got up to search the bathroom medicine cabinet for some more Tylenol. She snatched a wad of tissue from the roll and blew her nose, which made her head pound even more. Where was Richard? Why hadn't he phoned yet? She was silently stressing over his whereabouts. She balled up the tissue and searched for the wastebasket to toss it into. That's when she noticed the home pregnancy test box. She rummaged through the trash and found the applicator stick. She flipped it over and saw a pink plus sign on it. "Oh Shit!" she hissed, then slammed the bathroom door shut to collect her thoughts and figure out how she was going to handle this crisis.

14

Richard had just seen his last patient and was sitting in his office staring out the window at his view of Chicago's lake front. It was these quiet moments, sitting in his office undisturbed, that he'd come to cherish. Home just wasn't where he wanted to be anymore. He thought of his family and where they'd come from. He was the third-generation doctor in the family. His grandfather was one of the first black surgeons. He came from a small Negro town just outside Greenwood, Mississippi, and had been shipped off to Europe during World War II, just before Richard's father was born, to serve as a surgeon to the black units because the white doctors refused to treat black troops. When his grandfather returned home from the war, he couldn't live under the racially biased Jim Crow laws of the South. In 1946 his grandfather moved the family to Chicago and settled on the near Southside, which had become known as the Black Belt. Blacks with money and clout settled in that area, while rural and poor blacks settled in the slums just west of the city. His grandfather purchased a large gray stone house and opened up a family practice. During the late 1950s, Richard's father attended medical school and that was where he'd met Richard's mother. After the two of them graduated in 1957 they got married and had Richard the following year. After working for several years as associates under his grandfather, Richard's parents opened up their own practice and in 1975, they were some of the first blacks to make the transition from city living to suburban living. His parents were the first blacks who could afford to buy a home in the luxurious community known as Barrington Hills. It wasn't until 1984 that Richard finally decided to go into medicine at the request of his dying grandfather, with whom he was very close. His parents beamed with pride because he'd decided to continue a tradition. Richard regretted that they hadn't lived long enough to see him complete his education.

He recalled something that his mother once told him that he had never understood until recently. Although he had book and common sense, he lacked what she called street sense. After living with Rubylee, Justine, Estelle, and Keysha, he was becoming thoroughly educated in street sense. He remembered something his father told him as a young boy after some schoolyard bullies had taken his money.

"You must learn how to stand up for yourself and hold your ground. You can't let people run you over. And never settle for being someone's fool." Richard hadn't seen Nina in quite some time and never had a chance to get over to her office for her accounting expertise. When he thought about the missed opportunity for a little help, he got angry with himself, and decided to grow some damn balls. Now it was Monday, and he hadn't been home all weekend. He'd gone to Marshall Field's for a mini shopping spree and purchased a week's worth of clothing. He peeked at his watch, which said 12:15 P.M. He grabbed his suit jacket from the closet and left to head over to First National Bank. He'd made two appointments, one to meet with First National and one to meet with Seaway National Bank. When he sat down with the consultant at First National, he discovered that Estelle's so-called better management of money was a complete joke. There were large cash withdrawals, numerous bounced checks, overdraft fees, and late credit card payments. Their joint account had two hundred dollars left in it. Their savings account was down to one hundred dollars. Right then, Richard made immediate changes; there was no way that he would allow Estelle to place him in the poorhouse. He removed his name from their joint accounts. He thanked the consultant for his time and then left the bank. He hopped into his car and drove across town to Seaway National, which was a black-owned bank that his family had used for years. He'd made an appointment to see Ed Lawson, president of the bank and long time friend of the family. Ed Lawson had strikingly smooth cinnamon-colored skin and thinning gray hair. His distinguished features were only a glimmer of the way he had once looked. Still, time had aged him beautifully. Ed had come out of his office to greet him.

"Well, young Richard Vincent. It's always good to see you." They shook hands as Ed escorted him back to his office.

"How is the family?" he inquired.

"Well, that's sort of the reason why I'm here," Richard replied. Ed Lawson, who had known Richard since he was an infant, instantly picked up on the distressed tone in his voice. They entered his office and Ed shut the door behind them.

"Is everything okay?" he asked, offering him a seat at the conference table in his office. Richard explained his predicament to Ed's willing ear.

"That's just horrible, Richard."

"Yes, I know. However, I'm going to have to deal with it."

"Well, how can I help you?"

"I need access to the money my parents left behind. I need to open up a private checking account."

"I knew that you would eventually come for it. It's terrible how they had to make the transition from life to death, just terrible. I remember when they came to me for the loan on a home and a practice." Ed sighed. "Well, I've honored your wishes, Richard, I've left all of the money from their life insurance polices and the sale of the practice right here, safe and sound." Ed got up and moved over to the computer behind his desk and pulled up the account. "The money has earned some interest over the years and now you have one point eight million available. Are you sure you're not ready to branch out on your own and start your own practice?"

"No, Ed, I may be facing a divorce. I've got some major decisions to make before I make an investment like that."

"Oh, I'm so sorry to hear that things aren't going well, young Richard. Does your wife know about this account?"

"No, she doesn't know about it."

"Well, if your situation does indeed lead you to the courtroom, come back and see me. I have a close friend who is a great attorney who specializes in divorce. Maybe he could find a way for you to hold onto your inheritance," Ed offered, not only as a friend but also as a banker.

"Thanks Ed. But it looks as if I will have to take you up on that offer sooner than I'd like to admit. I'd like to transfer forty thousand over to a private checking account. Leave the rest where it is."

"No problem, Richard, I'll do it personally. I can get you some temporary checks and an ATM card in about forty-five minutes." Richard filled out the paperwork for the account and set things up so that his financial information would be sent to him at the office so that Estelle wouldn't know about it. After that he paid some outstanding bills and breathed a sigh of relief. He'd taken control of his situation and it felt wonderful. He walked out of the bank and bought a newspaper from the machine on the corner. He got in his car, not exactly sure of where he was going. He just knew that he wasn't ready to head home yet. He drove over to Western Avenue and stopped at Dicola's, a popular seafood restaurant, and ordered a half-pound of jumbo shrimp, some hush puppies, and a large drink. He decided to head over to the Dan Ryan Woods Forest Preserve and eat his meal in the car while he read the newspaper and collected his thoughts.

Both of his parents had half-a-million-dollar life insurance policies with a double indemnity clause in case of accidental death and Richard was named as secondary beneficiary. When they were both killed in the 1989 San Francisco earthquake, the insurance company paid him two million dollars. He paid off his undergraduate student loans, paid for dental school, then set the rest aside. Although it was a sizeable amount of money, he didn't want to squander it carelessly, which he could have easily done.

He thumbed through the newspaper and saw an ad that caught his eye. Come to the Bahamas, the ad read, and showed a picture of a couple holding hands and walking along the white sand beach. He sighed; maybe that's what he and Estelle needed. A vacation. Some time to get away from it all and fix the problems they were having, and he knew that Nathan would surely enjoy it. But the thought of leaving Rubylee, Justine, and Keysha in his house while they were away didn't appeal to him. His anger began to grow again as he thought about how he'd been escorted out of his own home by the police and how Estelle didn't seem to have the courage to stand by him when it came to challenging Rubylee. "No, screw her!" He shouted out loud. Screw her and the day he met her.

He thought about divorce again as bitterness settled into his heart. How could Estelle not see that Rubylee was a user? Humph, she wasn't going to use him anymore, that's for sure. Yeah, he could get her what she wanted but he wasn't in the business of giving handouts. Maybe he'd be willing to help if she had a part-time job or something, but this woman refused to work. What's that old saying about fishing? Why should I catch her a fish when she needs to learn how to fish. Hell, her mother is the reason Estelle's having those bad migraines. Estelle didn't have to work another day in her life, but something deep inside of him told him that he should keep the knowledge of his money to himself. He was glad that he wasn't a complete idiot.

Richard sighed, then took a sip of cola as he stared out of the car window at the gray March day. Although the wind was still biting, spring would be arriving soon. Another year was slipping away, and he'd grown weary of just existing in a marriage that was no longer laced with love and respect. He knew what he needed to do.

15

Rubylee parked her Chrysler Lebaron under the Lake Street el at the corner of Laramie. She turned the car off but the engine sputtered on, not wanting to shut down. She turned the ignition key again, then gave a few hard taps on the gas pedal, causing the engine to roar louder than the el train passing above her. She switched the key back to the off position which calmed the car down. She let the door swing all the way open, pivoted her round body and placed her feet firmly on the ground, noticing her swollen ankles. She placed one hand on each side of the doorframe, rocked a few times, and finally pulled herself up onto her feet. After slamming the door shut, she stepped up on the curb, praising the Lord, and walked a few steps over to the front door of a tavern that she and Stanback used to hang out at. The place still had the white Schlitz malt liquor bull sign swinging above the entrance. She pulled the door open then stepped inside inhaling the air which was clouded with cigarette smoke. A skinny woman in a red dress too large for her narrow hips and flat behind to fill out, stood hovering over the jukebox eyeing her choices. Rubylee watched her as she made her selection. The familiar guitar twang of B.B. King filled the room, followed by his soulful voice.

The thrill is gone. The thrill is gone away. Rubylee noticed how the woman snatched her beer bottle from the top of the juke box, covered the bottle neck with her lips, tossed her head back, and gulped down the liquor like water running down a kitchen drain. The woman danced with herself to B.B.'s guitar while Rubylee made her way over to the bar and took a seat on a red swivel bar stool. She spun around away from the bar to watch as two men played a game of pool under a low-hanging chandelier. The bartender who was at the other end made his way down to Rubylee.

"Well, I'll be damned. Look what the wind just blew in." Rubylee spun her seat back around and looked at her old friend, Red, who hadn't changed one bit. His skin was so dark it appeared black instead of brown. He was a huge, overweight giant who still possessed his signature red lips. "Woman, I haven't seen you in here in a long time." Whenever he spoke, it always sounded as if he needed to clear his throat. "What have you been doing with yourself?" he asked, then completed his thought. "I heard about the county sheriff's setting your things out on the curb."

"Well, you know me, Red. I've always got a plan."

"Yeah, Rubylee, I know. Boy, you and I go way back. Too many years to count and too many scams to remember, but man, back in those good old days we certainly made some money." Red pulled out a shot glass and filled it with Jack Daniels, one of Rubylee's favorite drinks. "Where are you living at now?"

"Well, I'm in high society now." Rubylee raised the glass up to her lips, jerked her head back and swallowed the entire shot. "Aaaah," she growled as the sting of the alcohol made its way down her throat. "I'm living on the Lake Front now."

"Lake Front! Damn, baby, how in the hell did you scheme up on that one?"

"I set my daughter up. I made her buy me a car, knowing that the following week I would be evicted for not paying my rent. I needed to make sure that she didn't have enough money of her own in the bank to pay my back rent. I set it up so that the only choice was to move me in the house with her. I played it beautifully, I could get an Oscar for my performance."

"Damn, Rubylee!" Red answered, stunned at how cold and calculating Rubylee was.

"Like I said Red, there's always a reason behind everything I do." Ruby pulled out her pack of Winston Salems. "I always got something in the works. That's why I'm here to see you. Do you still have all of those rental buildings that you stole from that church woman you were sleeping around with?" Red pulled out a white rag from behind the bar and began wiping down the counter. "Rubylee, to be honest, I just got out of jail this past summer. I've lost everything. Hell, I'm living back there in the storage room. I run the bar free of charge for a jack leg preacher in exchange for living back there. I've got to find me something better and quick."

"Well, that's why I'm here. I may have something for you. Can you still make a fake driver's license?"

"I can't. But I know somebody who can. What are you scheming up on woman? Who are you about to rob?"

"I'm not going to rob anybody. Well, not unless I have to. I'm living with my daughter and son-in-law now. He's a doctor, third-generation doctor to be exact. I got a feeling that the man has a fortune that he's inherited from his family. Now he's married to my daughter, and that makes me part of the family. But he doesn't see it that way. He wants to keep all the money to himself and not spread it around to others."

"You mean he doesn't want to give you any of his money."

"That's exactly what I'm saying, Red."

"How much money are we talking about, Rubylee?"

"I'm not sure yet."

"Well, how do you know that he has money?"

"I got a strange phone call for him at the house yesterday." Rubylee squinted her right eye and took a long deep drag off her cigarette. "It was from Seaway National Bank confirming an appointment for him. All of his money, according to my daughter, is at First National Bank. I'm betting cash money that he has an account at Seaway National Bank. I'm also guessing that it is a sizeable amount because I've been living with them for ten months now. He pays nineteen hundred dollars a month for rent and pays a four-hundred-dollar-a-month phone bill— Justine's ass has been calling the psychic hot line. He's got a one-hundred-and-fifty-dollar a month light bill, drives a Mercedes and hasn't missed a payment yet."

"Damn! Justine is staying with you too?"

"Yup. Keysha as well."

"Well, what does his house look like?"

"It's real nice. Four bedrooms. Its got all of that modern crap in it. The kind of shit that you don't even want to touch because you don't want to fuck around and break it."

"So where do I fit in?" asked Red.

"Well, I went through the house and got some important information of his." Rubylee stood up and reached into her back pocket and pulled out a small envelope and opened it. "I've got his driver's license number, social security card, date of birth and a recent check stub. What I need you to do is take this information and have a fake ID made up with your picture and his information. Then we'll go down to Seaway National Bank. You'll act like you're him, and we'll see how much money we're dealing with here." Rubylee passed Red the envelope.

"Rubylee, you would be stealing from your own family. I mean, wouldn't something like this upset your daughter Estelle?"

"Red, that's for me to deal with, not you. I know how to handle Estelle. I run her like Batman runs Robin. I've had control over her all of her life. Now, are you going to do this for me?" Red rubbed his chin and began contemplating the pros and cons.

"Well, it's going to take a little money." Rubylee reached into her huge bosom and removed some money. She counted out one hundred dollars. "I'm not giving you a penny more. Now, will you be able to handle this?"

Red quickly scooped up the one hundred dollars. "Come back

tomorrow at about one o' clock; I should have it by then." Red quickly stuffed the cash into his front pocket then poured them both a shot of Jack Daniels.

"Here's to our partnership." Rubylee held her glass up for a toast. Red smiled in agreement as he clicked her glass.

The following afternoon Rubylee pulled her car into a parking space outside of Seaway National Bank. Red was dressed in a navy blue pinstripe suit that he'd stolen from the jackleg preacher's closet. Rubylee began giving Red instructions, which he listened to carefully. He knew that Rubylee's plan would be as brilliant as her schemes had always been in the past. They stepped out of the car and walked across the middle of the street and into the bank. Inside there was a steady flow of lunchtime patrons but it wasn't too crowded, which meant there would not be a long wait. Red stood in line for his turn to see a teller. Rubylee milled around the counter at the rear of the bank busying herself with the deposit and withdrawal slips. She kept a close watch on Red, who didn't seem tense or uneasy. In fact, he looked completely comfortable and confident. She watched as the bank teller waved for the next person in line to step down. Rubylee casually made her way over to a counter that was closer to Red and the teller.

"Hello," Red greeted the teller then quickly cleared his throat.

"Hello, how can I assist you?" responded the teller.

"I'd like to make a withdrawal. Would you please look up my account and tell me what my balance is?"

"Sure," replied the teller. "May I see some ID?" Red causally slid the bogus driver's license with all of Richard's information and his picture on it in front of the teller. She picked up the license and typed in the information that she needed and handed it back to Red.

"Okay, Dr. Vincent, which account would you like to withdraw money from?" Red breathed a sigh of relief. He'd hoped that the teller wouldn't say that there was no account here under Richard's name. Now he was eager to see if Rubylee's hunch was right. She'd instructed him to withdraw five hundred dollars if the account had money in it.

"Tell me the balance on both of them," Red replied. The teller hit the keys a few times to pull up detailed information. "Okay, on your primary checking account you have thirty-seven thousand dollars." Red's heart started pumping faster with excitement. He'd hit the jackpot. "And in your savings account you have one million seven hundred and sixty thousand dollars." Red didn't think he'd heard the teller correctly.

"How much was the balance on that savings account again?"

"One million seven hundred and sixty thousand," the teller said slow and clear. "Is that the correct amount?"

"Oh, yes. That sounds about right," Red's eyes filled with greed. "Let me have ten thousand dollars from that account."

"Would you like me to put that in a cashiers check?" asked the teller.

"Uhm, no" replied Red. "I need that in cash."

"Okay, Dr. Vincent, I need you to fill out this withdrawal slip and sign here."

Rubylee watched as Red filled out the slip that the teller had handed him. Hot Damn! She thought to herself. She knew that Richard was hiding money from Estelle and she had his ass now. She couldn't wait to tell Estelle that Richard had been holding out on her. The teller returned with a labeled stack of money and began counting out the money in hundreds. Red's mouth watered as he watched the teller's pretty red manicured fingernails gently place the money down in front of him. He picked up the stack, said thank you, and walked out the door with Rubylee following close behind him. The two of them rushed across the street to Rubylee's car, got in, and sped off toward the Dan Ryan Expressway. Rubylee finally stopped on Maxwell Street in front of a green Polish sausage stand. The aroma of charred meat and grilled onions filled the air and made them hunger for a bite to eat.

"Okay, first things first." Rubylee turned her head to face Red. "Hand me those withdrawal receipts."

"Don't you want me to count out your money?"

"Red, I am no fool. That teller stood there counting a little too long. I know that she gave you more than five hundred dollars. From what I could gather it had to be a few thousand dollars, and since I know you, I know your immediate plan is to flash me some money so that I only see what's in front of me without looking at the big picture. I want to know how much he has."

"Now Rubylee, you know that I wouldn't try to hustle you, baby. We go back too far for that."

"Well, stop stalling, man and hand me the goddamn withdrawal slip!" Rubylee's temper flared up. Red reached into his suit pocket and handed her the slip. Rubylee unfolded the paper, looked at the amount of money Richard had, and folded the paper back up and placed it in her purse. She pushed her hand to the bottom of her purse and let her fingers touch the steel barrel of the gun she'd carried with her just in case Red decided to run off. It was the same gun Stanback had given her. She carried absolutely no fear about shooting Red. Rubylee was all business. There was no way that she was going to get excited and tip Red off to the fact that she hadn't realized just how much money her son-in-law had. Her face was stone, and very serious. "Count my money out for me," Rubylee demanded of him. Red was well aware that Rubylee was not the person to mess with. The way she kept her hand buried in her purse, he knew she was carrying a gun. He placed all of her money in her lap. Rubylee took the money, and gave Red one thousand dollars. Red wanted to argue but he held his tongue and gladly took what Rubylee offered him. To ease the tension in the air, he suggested that they both get something to eat.

After Estelle discovered the home pregnancy test, she stormed into the bedroom where both Keysha and Justine were and hauled them both off to a free clinic over on Sixty-Third Street. There was no way she was going to plunge into this discovery alone. No, she was going to make sure that Justine was there so that she would take on some of the responsibility of raising her daughter. She'd grown tired of Rubylee defending Justine's carefree attitude. Keysha swore on the Bible that the home pregnancy test wasn't hers but Estelle wasn't taking any chances. *She* damn sure wasn't pregnant and there was no way that Rubylee was. Justine couldn't possibly be that damn stupid, so that left Keysha as the only possible person. As she drove to the clinic Estelle attempted to have a rational conversation with Justine, but it was completely useless. Justine only wanted to talk about throwing a house party.

"Girl, with that place you and Richard have, you could throw a jamming party," Justine said as she bounced and jerked to the lyrics of Snoop Doggie Dog. "Just like Momma and Stanback used to throw. Remember how we used to hide up under the bed and listen to people having sex? And how Ma charged people one hundred dollars to use a bed? Oh, and what about the time I got drunk because I went around the room sipping from everyone's glass?"

"Yes, Justine, I remember. It wasn't so fun when you puked in the bed, now was it? I was Ma's personal damn maid. She had me cleaning up after all of those people. Motherfuckers were pissing on the floor instead of the toilet, blowing smoke in my face all night, and had me baby-sitting their bad-ass kids while they were in another room screwing, getting high, or in a back room gambling. So for me, I hated those damn parties. Now could you please get serious for once in your life."

"Girl, please! You take everything too damn hard; you let shit get to you. You freak out at the first sign of something gone wrong, and you're always trying to fix it and please everybody. You can't please every everybody you see. Shit, you're just way too sensitive. Ever since you married Richard you've been acting all goodie-two-shoes and shit. Like you come from a nice wholesome home." Justine chuckled. "Personally, I don't see how the two of you ever hooked up. You're nothing like him. You went to public school and had to fight every day. He was probably shipped off to some private school for the gifted. Ma threw a party every day of the week, and he's probably never partied at all. Your ass is from the ghetto and he's not. I just don't see it."

"I'm with you on that one," Keysha chimed in. "Sorry, Auntie, but I just don't see it either. I mean he seems all proper and straight-laced."

"Honestly, Estelle, does he fuck like a black man or a white man? Does he put his back, ass, and shoulders into it or does he do it jack-rabbit style? Or maybe it's you, Estelle. Are you sure you're satisfying him? I mean the brother acts as if he's never been fucked right. Hell, if he had some of my shit the brother would be walking around with a serious smile plastered on his face."

"You know what?" Estelle responded, "I don't want to talk about it anymore. And to answer your question, it's none of your damn business."

"Oops! Now I've hurt your feelings."

"Justine, you can't live like this the rest of your life," said Estelle, choosing to ignore most of what Justine had just said. "I want better things out of life for you, but you've got to get serious. If Keysha is pregnant, you've got a serious problem on your hands."

"Damn, Estelle! Why are you tripping? If she is, she'll get on public aid just like everyone else. What's the big deal? Hell, you know that your ass is from the ghetto, Estelle, so stop acting as if you're not. You know as well as I do, when you live in the ghetto, shit just happens," Justine snapped. She turned up the radio. Talking to Justine was impossible, just plain old impossible.

When the nurse came back with the results, Estelle was disappointed. Keysha was two months pregnant. When Justine heard the news that she was going to be a grandmother, a silly grin formed on her face and then she burst out into loud uncontrollable laughter. It pissed Estelle off to the point of wanting to shoot Justine where she stood.

"What's so goddamn funny, Justine? Your fourteen-year-old daughter is pregnant! She's too young to work, doesn't have health care insurance, and God only knows who the father is. So tell me, Justine, what's so goddamn funny?"

"I'm pregnant, too!" Justine found enormous humor in this awful situation. "That was my home pregnancy test," she continued to laugh.

Estelle felt a migraine of gigantic proportion building. Tension was forming everywhere: her neck, shoulders, and back. It was difficult for her to believe her ears. She didn't want to believe them. Both Justine and Keysha pregnant at the same time was just a little too much to deal with. Estelle massaged her temples vigorously in order to ward off the pain that was there. She was going to have to make an appointment to see the doctor about her massive headaches. Justine, being totally unpredictable as usual, placed her arms around Keysha and started laughing again.

"Who's your baby's daddy?"

"It belongs to this guy named Ronnie from around our old neighborhood. But he says that it's not his," Keysha began explaining.

"Baby, they all say that it's not theirs," Justine continued on as if none of this was an issue, problem, or concern.

"How old is Ronnie?" asked Estelle, although she really didn't want to know the answer.

"He's seventeen," Keysha replied cautiously. "Who is your baby's father, Momma?" Justine let out another obnoxious cackle.

"I have no damn idea! It could be Charles's or maybe it's Melvin's, although I hope not. I was high when I slept with him. Or it could be this dude named Mike I was messing around with, who just got out of jail."

Estelle suddenly felt light-headed and weak. Once again her stomach was turning sour and her ears couldn't stand to listen to another word coming out of Justine's mouth. The more Justine spoke the more upset Estelle became. She suddenly marched around the corner, up the stairs, and out of the door. Keysha and Justine followed close behind like pets following their owner.

The foul odor of Rubylee's pot of chitlins hit Richard's nose when he arrived home for the first time in a week. When Keysha saw him she ran into Nathan's room where he was playing while Estelle and Justine were standing in the center of the living room breaking the news of the pregnancies to Rubylee, who was sitting at the dining room table snapping green beans.

"Well, if the Lord has seen fit to bless me with another grandchild and my first great-grandchild I can only say that I'm glad he's going to let me live long enough to see them," Rubylee said.

"Grandchild?" Richard set his duffel bag of clothes down on the floor. "Somebody want to explain to me what's going on?"

Estelle quickly spun around. "I didn't hear you come in; how long have you been standing there?"

"Long enough to hear that someone is pregnant."

"Yes, Richard, the Lord has blessed me a thousand times today," Rubylee chuckled as she stood up to take her bowl of green beans into the kitchen. "I got another grandchild and a great-grandchild on the way."

Richard didn't know why he was shocked by the news that he was hearing. He'd come to the conclusion long ago that Estelle's family was one bad mistake after another.

"Well, Richard, it looks like you're going to have to buy that building now. This place isn't going to be big enough for all of us and two little babies."

"Excuse me!" Richard snapped, then howled at Rubylee. "Woman, I don't know what planet you're on, but you are going to get the hell out of my house! You, your crap, and your pregnant kids are going to get the fuck out!" Richard was already fighting and he hadn't even been home a good five minutes.

"Richard, baby." Estelle approached Richard, taking his

hand into her own before Rubylee could reply. "Baby, we can work this out. Don't get upset, okay?" Estelle was trying to get Richard to focus on her and not Rubylee. But his gaze upon her was locked and intense like an animal hunting its prey. Estelle was getting upset by the rage in Richard's eyes and feared that he was in a place were she was unable to reach him. Rubylee didn't appreciate the tone in Richard's voice. She hadn't raised her voice to him at all, and there was no way that she was going to let him start speaking to her any way he pleased.

"Wait one goddamn minute!" Rubylee waddled out of the kitchen with a large stirring spoon in her hand, shaking it at Richard. "You don't come in this house speaking to me like that."

"Oh, shit!" Justine said, and quickly scrambled to the sofa to watch what was about to happen.

Richard's rage suddenly consumed him. Had she forgotten who was footing all of the bills around this house? He was the one paying the rent, light bill, gas bill, phone bill, and grocery bill for three extra people. She was the one who had moved in on him without a dime to her name and two extra mouths to feed. He darted over to Rubylee and entered her personal space with the threat of a serious confrontation.

"Oh, you want to take this to that level!" Rubylee backed toward the kitchen table where her purse was. Son-in-law or not, if he laid a hand on her she was going to shoot his ass!

"Richard, baby, come on," Estelle began pleading as she tugged on his arm to come out of the kitchen.

"That's right, you'd better get him, Estelle! If you want to see him live another minute, you'd better get him!" Rubylee's hand was now deep in her purse and firmly on her pistol.

"Estelle, I'm drawing the line right here, right now! I am not going to stay another minute in this house with that woman, and I'm most certainly not going to stay here while your sister and her daughter give birth to two bastards. I will not be the chump who takes care of another man's responsibility."

"Don't you call my baby a bastard!" Justine sprung up from the couch.

"Estelle, either they go or I go!" Richard's voice thundered throughout the house.

"Get the hell out then!" Rubylee hollered from the kitchen. "We don't need your ass!"

"Richard, baby, don't make me choose, not like this. Can't we just sit down and talk?" Estelle pleaded.

"Don't beg that motherfucker to stay," Rubylee yelled from the kitchen.

"Yeah, Estelle," Justine chimed in. "You don't need no goddamn man giving you ultimatums."

"Estelle, either you get these two big heifers out of my house right now or I'm walking out on you, and if I walk out that door I'm not coming back!"

Estelle stood glaring at Richard, unable to find her thoughts. This situation had gotten completely out of hand. She felt her stomach doing flips and the urge to vomit was strong. On the one hand she had her mother who she could never turn her back on even though she knew that she was flawed and unconventional. Her mother, who had raised her and taken care of her. Her mother, who had made so many sacrifices for her. On the other hand, she had Richard, her husband who had the ability to provide her with so much more. It wasn't fair for him to carry the burden of Rubylee and her baggage but Estelle was torn and didn't know what to do.

"Baby, I can't put my mother out. Can't—" Richard tossed his hand up to cut her off. Estelle's words stabbed him in the chest. Richard built a wall around his emotions. He picked up his duffel bag and was about to walk out the door when Nathan ran out of his room.

"Daddy, you're leaving again?" Richard wasn't prepared for this response from his son. Nathan raised his arms high above his head for Richard to pick him up. He hadn't even thought about how Nathan must have been suffering through all of this. Ever since the change nine months ago, he hadn't spent any quality time with his son. Richard felt an enormous amount of guilt.

"Yes, Daddy has to leave again." Richard had to somehow tone down his anger and find an explanation for his little man. Richard picked Nathan up, feeling his son hug him so tightly that he was choking him.

"Are you going to leave forever? I want you to stay. I don't like it when you're mad all the time. You can't take me to the park when you're mad." All of Nathan's questions and comments sliced Richard apart on the inside.

"Nathan, I'll be back to see you. I promise." Richard wanted to say more but his words stuck in his throat. He set Nathan down, but Nathan refused to let his neck go.

"I'll be back, okay?" Richard hugged him tightly once more before Nathan ran back to his room crying.

"Richard, stay," Estelle pleaded.

"I can't do that, Estelle. I will never again be escorted out of my own home by the police."

"Richard, baby, I'm sorry about—" Richard cut her off by turning his back and walking out.

"Estelle, you don't need him." Rubylee shuffled out of the kitchen. "I've gotten along all of these years without a man. Believe me when I say that you don't need him."

Estelle looked at her mother and for the first time realized that she wanted to be nothing like her. She didn't want to turn out to be some frustrated old lonely woman who nagged and complained all the time. She wanted her husband.

"Baby, don't you worry about a thing." Rubylee put her arm around Estelle. "Haven't I always taken care of things?" Estelle gazed at the floor feeling tears welling up to the surface.

"You don't have to worry about a thing, I've got plenty of—" Rubylee caught herself. At that moment it dawned on her that she never got the bogus identification back from Red. No wonder he didn't say shit about her only giving him one thousand dollars. He still has access to one point seven million dollars. *Damn!* She wanted to kick herself in the ass. Now she would have to track Red's ass down. She prayed that he hadn't taken a ton of money and left town. Estelle charged out the door to try and catch Richard but he was already gone.

Richard drove directly to O'Hare Airport. He parked his car and took the shuttle to the United Airlines terminal and walked directly up to a ticket agent.

"Good evening," said the ticket agent. "What can I do for you?"

"Yes, uhm, I'm looking to get away for a while." Richard had no idea of where he wanted to go. He quickly glanced around the airport and noticed a man getting off a plane wearing a straw hat that said "Bahamas." He turned back to the ticket agent. "Do you have a flight leaving for the Bahamas tonight?"

"Yes, we do," replied the agent.

"Put me on the next flight out of here," Richard said, and handed the agent his personal credit card, driver's license, and passport.

"Do you have any luggage Dr. Vincent?" asked the agent.

"No, I don't," replied Richard.

"Do you need a hotel?"

"Yes, put me someplace nice, price doesn't matter."

The agent handed him his ticket and hotel confirmation. Richard went over to the bar, sat down and ordered himself a drink. There was so much on his mind that he had to sort out. He would call the office in the morning and get one of the other associates to cover his schedule. Richard wasn't exactly sure when he would return. Right now all he wanted was an exit, and the Bahamas was a perfect get-away destination.

16

Several weeks had passed since Nina left Jay. They'd spoken a few times, and Nina discovered that he was adamant about going to counseling to try and work things out. Although it ripped her heart apart, Nina stuck to her guns. She'd been telling Jay for years that one day she would leave him, but as her grandmother used to say, "some people just have trouble believing that fat meat is greasy." And that was Jay's biggest issue: accepting the fact that she was fed-up.

"Nina, come on now, we can work this out. I'll do whatever it takes," he pleaded with her one day when she agreed to meet with him. "All of these years we've spent together have to mean something."

Nina was determined not to break down and cry. The years *had* meant something. She'd spent a good portion of her life with him. It hadn't been all bad, but Jay just wasn't the man for her anymore. She'd questioned for years whether or not she would have married him had she not gotten pregnant. Although it was painful to admit, the answer was no.

"Jay, I need some time," Nina explained. "None of this is easy and it's not all your fault. I've had my suspicions about you for quite some time. I should have spoken up sooner, but I didn't."

"Nina, baby, I know that I was wrong, I'm man enough to admit that, but I don't want to lose you over it. I mean, let's be realistic here, I don't want to be alone anymore than you do."

"Then why don't you go and stay with that tramp you were sleeping with!" Nina snapped at Jay so quickly he flinched with surprise.

"Nina, I'm not here to argue with you; I just want to have a rational adult conversation."

"Humph! Jay, I can't even count the number of times I've tried to sit down and discuss our problems with you. Whenever I did, you were always too busy or had to rush off before you were late for a meeting. Hell, now that I think about it, you were probably running off to be with whoever she is."

"Nina, I know you're angry and you have every right to be, but I'm not going to give up on us. I've come to realize that you're the best thing in my life and I'm not going to let this situation tear us apart."

Nina began to gather her things. Once again she felt as if he wasn't listening to her. Couldn't he see that their marriage was already torn apart and beyond repair? Couldn't he see that she was dead serious? In her mind there was really nothing more to discuss so she excused herself.

"Nina, wait." Jay stood up and tossed some money on the table. "Let me walk you to your car."

"Fine, that's up to you, but I'm done talking." Jay didn't say much as he followed her. Nina assumed that he was trying to collect his thoughts. She opened the door and tossed her purse on the passenger seat. She got in and was about to close the door but Jay was in the way.

"I want you to know that I love you, Nina. I know that I don't say it much, but I do."

Nina exhaled. Why was he doing this? Why couldn't he just let her go? She didn't want anything from him. Not the house or any of his money. There was no real debt between them, with the exception of the house, and he was the one who paid the mortgage. They didn't have any small children, there would be no child support or emotional custody battles to deal with. Hell, this was the dream divorce, if there was such a thing.

"Nina?" Jay paused, "I want you to come back home; you've made your point now. I want us to go to church and pray. We could sit down with the pastor and get guidance on how to make things right."

Nina didn't know how to respond to that. She looked up into Jay's eyes and saw the sincerity in them, but it wasn't enough for her to change her mind. She was ready to get on with her life and let the past go.

"Jay, I've taken a few days off work. I'm going to come by while you're at work and gather the rest of my belongings. I will put the keys in an envelope and slide them under door when I'm done." Nina could tell by the expression on Jay's face that he didn't believe what he was hearing. She pulled on the car door, forcing Jay to move out of the way. Nina was shocked when Jay pounded on the car window with the side of his fist. He was again the bully that she knew him to be.

"What! You have another man or something? Huh? Is that why you're not coming home?" No, he doesn't have the nerve to accuse me of cheating on him, Nina thought as she rolled her eyes, started the car, and pulled off.

Nina loved her new apartment in Schaumburg. She had a second-floor two-bedroom unit with a washer and dryer, a balcony, and a fairly decent-sized kitchen. Closet space was a bit tight, but she would get closet organizers in order to create the space that she needed. Apartment living took a little getting used to at first; the first few nights she couldn't sleep very well. But once she was settled in, it wasn't so bad and she was so happy the building was quiet.

It was now early Sunday morning. Nina unplugged the boom box from her bedroom and carried it into the kitchen where she sat it on the counter and plugged it in. She tuned the dial to WNUA, the smooth jazz station that was broadcasting live from the Hilton Towers Hotel downtown. She listened to the jazz guitar and George Benson's voice crooning the smooth melody. He was singing one of her favorite songs, called "Masquerade." How she loved that song. *Are we really happy here . . . with the lonely games we play . . . looking for words to say . . .* George serenaded her as she grabbed a plastic cup, opened the refrigerator, and poured herself a glass of orange juice. She leaned back against the counter and began thinking about the things that she still needed to buy, like drapes, furniture, microwave oven, dishes and a TV. Just to name a few. She was starting from scratch. Nina's thoughts were interrupted by the ringing of the phone.

"Hello," she answered, hearing a ton of static in the background.

"What's up, girl?" It was Rose on her cellular phone. "I'm almost there, are you ready yet?"

"You are not almost here, Rose, so stop lying. You're never on time and no, I'm not ready yet." The two of them were planning to spend the day at Gurnee Mills Shopping Mall.

"Well, girlfriend, I'm about to surprise the hell out of you."

"Rose, what are you talking about?" Nina smiled. Then the doorbell rang.

"You hear that, girl!" Rose shouted into the phone. "I'm not only on time but I'm early! Now, buzz me in."

"You are so damn silly," Nina laughed as she placed the phone back on its cradle. She walked over to the door and buzzed Rose into the building, opened the door, and stood in the hallway and watched as Rose made her way up the stairs. Rose had just gotten her hair done in a French Roll style with curls placed on the top of her head. Nina shut the door as Rose walked in and made her way to the bedroom for a seat at the foot of Nina's bed.

"Girl, who did your hair?" Nina inquired, noticing how nice it looked.

"I had to get a new hairstylist, honey. That little heifer from that other salon had me with split ends and she cut my hair too short. I asked her to just clip the ends and the heifer made like a lawnmower and started cutting everything."

"Really!"

"Yeah, it took the longest time for it to grow back out." Nina began scratching her own head. "Yeah, I have an appointment for tomorrow evening to get something done with this mess on my head."

"I really like the blond wood bedroom set you picked out."

"Honey, I was just happy to catch it on sale, and glad as hell that it all fit in this room."

"Have you heard from Jay?" Rose asked.

"God, yes. I heard from his crazy ass last night. He just got the divorce papers and is vowing never to sign them because he still feels that there is hope for us. Girl, I don't know what to do. I want to close this chapter of my life and move on but Jay is holding on. I'm a little worried that he's going to have trouble coping without me."

"Well, no matter how you look at it, Nina, divorce isn't easy."

"Believe me, I know. My emotions have been driving me crazy but I still feel that it's best. I will always have feelings for Jay, I can't just turn them off. I told him that we can be friends, but that's not what he wants. Anyway, enough about that; let me hop in the shower and get dressed. There's some food in the fridge if you want to eat something before we drive up there."

"That's okay. I'm saving my appetite for that cinnamon bun place. I've got a sweet tooth that's out of this world. I swear, I'm going to have to question God as to why we have to go through all of these changes when our cycle comes around. One minute it's a salty taste, the next it's a sweet tooth. One minute you're mad, and the next you feel like you're about to fall apart."

"Oh, and let's not forget that bloating, cramping, and sour stomach shit!" Nina offered.

Rose chuckled. "You too, huh? Hurry up, woman. We've got some highway to eat up."

As soon as they arrived at Gurnee Mills, Rose hustled directly over to the cinnamon bun stand. Nina had a taste for ice cream so they stopped at Baskin Robbins and purchased a scoop of rainbow sherbet. As they ate they made their way through the crowd of shoppers.

"How is my goddaughter, Gracie, doing?" Rose inquired.

"She's okay. I spoke with her a few days ago, and I told her about the separation and divorce. She didn't quite understand why I didn't want to stay and work things out. But then again, I wouldn't expect her to understand. Other than that, she's doing okay because Mark took her back with him, and now she's staying with him on the military base."

"Well, is she happy? I mean, after the loss and everything?"

"She still has her moments, but overall I think she's coping well. I asked her what she thought about adoption, but she wasn't ready to discuss her options yet."

"Well, is she going to go back and finish her degree?"

"That's still up in the air, I guess. But to tell you the truth, Rose, I'm just glad she's okay, you know what I mean? I was so angry about little things and now I realize that her well-being means more to me than a piece of paper. I'd be proud of her if she did, but she's got to make a commitment to complete a program."

"Well, good for you. I'm so happy that you two are working things out. So, where do you want to go first?"

"I need to stop at Bed, Bath & Beyond," Nina replied.

"Okay," Rose agreed, and the two of them headed there first. They spent the entire day at Gurnee Mills roaming in and out of stores trying to locate good sales. Rose pulled Nina into a lingerie shop and examined a bin full of underwear that said three pair for a dollar.

"See if you see any extra-large underwear over there, Nina," requested Rose.

"Here you go." Nina handed a few pairs to Rose, then went to look at the matching underwear and bra sets. Nina was eyeing a green formfitting raceback bra and matching bikini panties when Rose walked up to her.

"That would look nice on you," Rose said as she began sifting through the rack at the other end. "Hey, what ever happened to that guy you were dancing with that one night? What was his name?"

"Who, Richard?" Nina replied, picking up a plum-colored set from the bin.

"I'm not sure. I haven't seen or heard from him in a while."

"That was one fine brother there, with that sexy ass walk of his. Wow, its enough to make a girl salivate."

Nina laughed. "Come on, woman." Nina grabbed Rose by the wrist. "Looking at underwear has started to mess with your brain." They exited the store and stepped back out into the crowd of people. They walked two doors down and were about to pass a travel agency when they noted a sign that said, SIX NIGHTS AND SEVEN DAYS IN PARADISE FOR ONLY THREE HUNDRED AND NINETY-NINE DOLLARS.

"Come, girl, and look over here with me." Nina followed Rose inside. Funjet vacations was offering a deal on a vacation to the Bahamas. After listening to the travel agent, who was a vanilla sister who looked like she was in her early thirties, Rose was sold on the idea of getting away. The only catch was, you had to travel within the next three weeks.

"Come on, Nina, what do you say? Why don't we get away for a while. Lord knows that I could use a vacation, and I know that you most certainly could, with all of the drama that's been going on with you."

"I don't know, Rose, I've always wanted to go with a male companion, not my girlfriend."

"Girl, please, we could go down there and relax, party, and shop."

"She's right, you know," offered the sales rep. "It's not uncommon for girlfriends to make travel plans for a place like the Bahamas."

"Oh, really," Nina replied.

"Yeah, girl," Rose responded, wanting to convince Nina.

"I'll tell you what. If you don't have enough cash, I'll spot you a loan."

"You're serious, aren't you?"

"Yes. Why not? I mean, what else have we got to do?"

"I don't know how I let you talk me into things, Rose," Nina said, digging into her purse for her wallet and credit card. "I knew that I shouldn't have eaten that damn ice cream cone. Now I've got to workout extra hard to get back in shape."

"Tuh! Don't even go there, Olive Oil," said Rose. Nina and the travel agent laughed. "I may go down there and find me a man who loves big women."

"Oh, I see now. You want to go down there so that you can cut up."

"I'm just going down there for some fun. If romance happens to come my way, so be it. You never know, my future husband may be down there. Besides, you're about to get on the market yourself. It's not going to hurt for a sister to take a peek at what's out there." Both Nina and Rose handed the travel agent their charge cards and the woman excused herself to complete the transaction.

"Let's not go there, Rose. I'm not really looking for anyone."

"I know that, love," Rose leaned into Nina and whispered, "but a little d-i-c-k would do the both of us a world of good."

"Get away from me." Nina laughed as she pushed Rose away from her. "Old silly butt . . ."

Two weeks later they were on a plane that was slated to arrive in Freeport/Lucaya, Grand Bahama Island, at midnight. Nina still couldn't believe that she'd let Rose talk her into coming, but she was thankful that she had, and was beaming with excitement. The change of pace and scenery was just what she needed. Although she had damn near missed the plane screwing around with a slow sales clerk at Woodfield Mall who had trouble ringing up the five swimming suits that she purchased at the last minute. Why does it never fail that whenever you're in a hurry, something or someone always slows you down? The two ladies got their luggage, moved through customs, and took a taxi over to the Princess Hotel, Resort, and Casino. They were greeted in the lobby, and the hotel staff served them Bahama Mommas to quench their thirst. The bellman took their luggage and names and assured them that their belongings would make it to their rooms. They went to the front desk to check in and get their individual room keys. Nina's clerk was a bit faster so she milled around the tropical theme lobby sipping on her drink, which was very sweet but still had an alcoholic taste to it.

"Okay, the front desk clerk said that there is a pool party going on, and that we could get more free drinks and food around there," Rose said, pushing her wallet back into her purse.

"Don't you want to see the room first?"

"Girl, if you've seen one hotel room, you've seen them all. Now, come on, let's go around here and see what's happening." The two of them followed a couple dressed in their swimming suits around the hotel and out to the pool deck. There was a party going on all right. There was a poolside bar and grill complete with a dance floor full of people dancing to the latest hit by Zhane called, "Hey, Mr. DJ." There was a huge swimming pool with water bridges that you could swim under and a hot tub gigantic enough for at least fifty people.

"Oh, yeah, now this is what I'm talking about." Rose began swaying her shoulders to the beat of the music. "Come on, Nina, loosen up and let's go have some fun." Rose rushed over to the bar and found the two of them a seat in the corner with a view of the pool and the dance floor. The pool was beautifully lit with green and red lights. Nina noticed a few couples in the water taking a romantic midnight swim.

"May I bring you ladies a drink?" A tall, heavyset, handsome, and very chocolate man came up to Rose. "They're on the house tonight," he offered.

"Yeah, baby." Nina knew that Rose was about to start. She'd crossed her legs, flashing her thick calves, and then she leaned forward just enough to watch this man's eyes fall and focus on her ample bosom. "Would you bring me back a Sex on the Beach, and my friend here, she'll have another Bahama Momma." The man smiled, then asked Rose if she would dance with him once he returned with their drinks.

"Yes, baby. Now you go on and hurry back." The man walked off toward the bar.

"You are a mess."

"Girl, I told you. I need to get me some. I've packed myself a box of condoms. I'm going to have myself a damn good time down here." The man seemed to return within seconds. He set the drinks down on the table and acknowledged Nina as he did.

"May I have this dance?" he asked Rose.

"Why yes," Rose said, following the man out to the dance floor. Nina observed as Rose moved to the rhythm of CeCe Peniston singing "Finally." She had to give it to Rose. The girl hadn't lost a thing in the dancing department. Rose possessed some beautifully shaped legs, and she knew just how to strut her stuff. Nina removed the straw from her first drink and placed it into her second one. She turned her attention to the swimming pool. She noticed a brother who was lifting himself out of the pool. She watched as he stood up and stepped over to a lawn chair where he picked up a towel and began drying himself off. He had on a sexy pair of black Speedo swimming trunks. Nina took great interest as she observed his beautiful brown skin, thighs, and a tight ass that was made for squeezing. She prayed that he would turn around so that she could catch a glimpse of all that he had to offer. Rose was right; she needed some action, but not the kind of mess she'd been used to with Jay. No, she was looking for one of those all-night sessions. She caught herself ogling the man. It must be the alcohol, she reasoned, then realized that maybe this man wasn't here alone; there was probably some woman waiting in the shadows to come wrap her arms around him. The man started walking away in the opposite direction, and his stroll reminded her of Richard's stroll. She turned her attention back to Rose, who winked at her as she slid the palms of her hands onto her chocolate friend's behind.

17

Nina got up early Saturday morning, put on her lavender nylon jogging shorts and matching sports top that left her well-defined abdomen exposed, and headed out the door for a morning workout in the weight room. She was making her way past the swimming pool and bar area where they'd been last night and momentarily closing her eyes to enjoy the warmth of the Caribbean sun and breeze on her skin when she collided with a man who carried his morning orange juice and a newspaper. The juice spilled all over both of them.

"I am so sorry," said Richard. He'd been reading the paper and not paying attention to where he was walking. Nina recognized Richard's voice instantly.

"Richard?"

"Nina?"

"What are you doing here?" They both asked simultaneously.

"Okay, one at a time," said Richard.

"When did you get here?"

"I arrived last night around midnight, and you?"

"I've been here for about three weeks now."

"Really?" Nina replied, then began trying to wipe the orange juice off of Richard's white linen shirt. "I'm afraid I've ruined your clothes."

"Don't worry about it. It was my fault. I should have been paying attention to what I was doing. So, where is your husband?"

"Uhm, well, I sort of left him. I have my own apartment now, and my girlfriend dragged me down here because she felt that I needed a break. A lot has happened since we last sat down and talked. What about you? I know that your wife must be lurking around here somewhere."

Richard took a deep breath and exhaled.

"Well, like you, I've left my wife. I'm down here sorting out my thoughts about what I'm going to do next. I haven't gotten an apartment or anything yet. I've just been living down here in a suite for the past three weeks."

"Is that right?" Nina didn't want to express it, but she was damn happy that his wife wasn't with him.

"So that means that you haven't been around the place yet—the casino, the beach, or shopping at the international bazaar—right?"

"Nope, I haven't seen any of it yet."

"Well, I'll tell you what, don't pay for all of these expensive bus tours. I've rented a car and I'll take you where ever you want to go. Call me anytime; I'm in room 1501," Richard offered. He was damn sure excited about running into Nina. He was trying hard not to be obvious, but his eyes betrayed him, marveling at her beauty.

"That is so nice of you, Richard," Nina replied as she watched Richard's eyes falling down all over her. God, the way he was looking at her was igniting her fire. She couldn't recall the last time that anyone had looked at her with such hunger. "Uh . . . okay. Room 1501, right?"

"Yes," said Richard. He adored the pleasant tone of her voice.

"Can I call you later this morning after my workout?"

"Please do. I'll be looking forward to hearing from you."

"Okay, well then, let me go workout, so that I can get back to you."

"All right then, you have yourself a nice workout." They began walking in opposite directions. Richard stepped far enough away to turn around and take a peek at her from behind. When he turned, he saw her undressing him with her eyes. They both laughed.

Richard hustled back to his room, stripped out of his clothes, and searched the drawers and his closet for something to wear. When he arrived three weeks ago, he went on a shopping spree and purchased everything that he'd need. He had clothes in the closet that still had the tags on them. He settled on his navy blue shorts which complemented his muscular thighs, and a matching navy blue spandex-blend shirt. He hopped in the shower, washed his hair and trimmed his mustache. As he stepped out of the shower, he looked at his naked body in the mirror and slapped the palm of his hand on his stomach a few times, pleased to see the results of his efforts in the weight room for the past three weeks. He decided to trim the hair around his private area. He preferred to keep the hair short in that area. He splashed on some Joop, the cologne that Nina had seemed to like the last time they were together.

Nina skipped the weight room and rushed back to her hotel room. She couldn't believe that she'd actually bumped into Richard down here. *It really is a small world, Mr. Jiminy Cricket,* she thought to herself. Nina kicked off her gym shoes and searched her suitcase for her makeup bag. She couldn't stand digging through the suitcase, so she picked it up and turned it upside down, dumping everything out on the bed. The maid was going to have a fit, but Nina didn't care. Richard was there in Freeport. She turned on the shower, picked up her makeup bag and set it on the counter. She went back to the bed, dug through her belongings, and pulled out her white sundress. She searched the room for an iron but couldn't find one, so she called the maid service and had them deliver one. She jumped in the shower and when she got out she felt like a million bucks. She wrapped the towel around her body then went over to the nightstand where the phone was.

"Hello, Rose? It's me, Nina. Did I wake you?"

"Woman, do you know what time it is?"

Nina glanced over at the alarm clock. "It's six forty-five A.M."

"Nina, it is too damn early in the morning. Call me back later." Nina listened as Rose's voice began to trail off. "I've got a hangover." Then she heard Rose hang up the phone. *Humph, well I'll just leave her a voice mail message and let her know that I'll catch up with her later. After all, she was the very person who told me to loosen up and enjoy myself.* Nina went back to the bathroom, plugged up her curling irons and began fixing her hair.

Richard had just finished trimming his toenails when he got the phone call from Nina. They agreed to meet down by the pool where they bumped into each other. Richard hung up the phone, put on his sunglasses and headed out the door.

Nina approached Richard as he stood next to the pool towel pick-up counter, the Caribbean breeze carried the scent of his cologne in her direction. If she recalled correctly, it was the very same scent that she had enjoyed when they danced together several months before. Richard stood in awe as Nina approached him in her white sundress. She looked absolutely stunning.

"Are you ready?" he asked.

"As ready as I'll ever be," she replied, feeling butterflies dancing in her stomach. They headed out toward the front of the hotel where the parking lot was. When Richard said that he'd rented a car, she was thinking Ford or Chevy, not a hot red Corvette.

"Hey, I'm only going to live once, Nina. So I figure that I might as well enjoy it to the fullest."

"Is that so?" Nina responded, thrilled at his way of thinking. Nina sat in the car and felt as if she were sitting on the ground. Richard turned the key and fired up the motor and Nina felt a thrill that she'd never experienced before. The live-in-concert version of "Distant Lover" by Marvin Gaye came blaring out of the speakers. Nina listened as Marvin's lips hugged the microphone and women screamed his name. "See there, you planned to have that song playing, didn't you?" Nina asked, as Marvin's voice sent a chill down her spine and forced her to pop her fingers and sway to the music.

Richard smiled at her and then winked his eye. Before she could stop herself she started stroking the nape of his neck.

Nina was beside herself. How could she possibly go from not wanting anything to do with any man to wanting Richard so badly that her center was soaking wet, throbbing, and begging to be pleased? She couldn't understand that one, the only thing that she did understand was how she was feeling. Absolutely wonderful. It was difficult to even imagine a time that she'd felt this wonderful in the company of Jay. Here she was with a drop-dead handsome man who listened to her, paid attention to her, and complimented her on her efforts to look nice for him. Richard was the type of man who talked *to* her instead of at her. Having Richard in her life was something she could certainly get accustomed to, but she had to keep things in order here. Although they were both separated, they were still married, and that meant hands off, the last time she checked the rule book. Nina caught herself doing what she always did, thinking too damn much, instead of enjoying the fact that she was happy as hell to see Richard.

Richard was all too willing to run from store to store with Nina and observe her as she modeled clothes for him. Nina tried on a beige straw sun hat that Richard thought looked absolutely beautiful on her, so he purchased it for her and asked that she wear it for him while they were together. Richard made her feel so beautiful in the hat that it was difficult for her to keep from tossing her arms around him to express her gratitude.

"Are you hungry, Richard? I'll treat you to lunch if you'd like."

"No, I'm fine," Richard replied as they left the store.

"Where to now?" Nina asked, wondering what other shops Richard was going to take her to.

"Come on." He took her by the hand and led her down the sidewalk toward a jewelry store. He'd noticed that she wasn't wearing any earrings. If she was going to be his doll, he wanted her to be fully accessorized.

"May I help you locate something stunning for your wife?" asked the sales clerk, assuming that Richard and Nina were a married couple.

"Yes," Richard continued without correcting the woman. "I'd like to see some diamond earrings."

"This way." The clerk directed him to a glass case. Richard leaned on the glass, looking at his choices.

"Let me see this set here," he pointed, "and the larger set over here."

"Richard, what are you doing?" Nina questioned, feeling twinges of excitement rush through her.

"I want to do something special for you while we are here." Richard turned to meet her gaze so that she could see that he was not joking. "I want to see what you'd look like with a set of diamond earrings."

"Both of these are beautiful," said the clerk, who set them on the countertop.

"Which set do you like?" Richard asked Nina.

"Richard I can't let you—"

Richard cut her off. "Let me do this for you. I may never get another chance to express how truly happy I am to see you." Nina sighed, completely thrilled in one breath and uncertain the next. She chose the earrings that she liked, which were the half-carat ones with the eighteen-karat gold mounts. She gasped as she studied herself in a mirror with large diamonds in her ears. Richard walked to the end of the counter with the clerk to pay for them. Nina was completely stunned by Richard's generosity.

By the time they arrived back at the hotel, the sun was setting. They were walking past the pool area loaded down with shopping bags when Nina eyed Rose on the dance floor directing a serious crowd of dancers doing the electric slide.

"Come on, honey . . . I mean, Richard. Let's drop these bags off and come right back down." Nina couldn't believe her tongue had betrayed her like that. Richard adored her for calling him honey.

A short time later they both came back down, and the party was just beginning to jump. Nina thought that Rose would be pissed at her for disappearing all day, but when she saw that heavyset chocolate man from the night before with his hands squarely placed on Rose's hips while she worked them around in a circle, she knew that whatever it was Rose and that man were doing, they were both having a great time at it. Rose took a break from all of the dancing as night finally settled in. Both Rose and Nina excused themselves and went to freshen up.

"All right, heifer, why didn't you tell me you called him and had him to come down here?" Rose asked as she dabbed at the sweat around her neck with a towel. "And when did you get those diamond stud earrings? I've never seen you with those on before."

"Whether you believe it or not, I did not call him. He's been down here for the past three weeks. And the earrings are a gift from him."

"Girl, stop lying," Nina just smiled at Rose. "Get out of here; you're serious, aren't you?" Rose moved closer to Nina to inspect the earrings. "Damn, these had to cost a small fortune."

"How do you like my hat? It's a gift as well." Nina modeled the hat for her by turning her head from side to side.

"Girl, what did you do to the man?"

"Nothing, Rose. He said that he wanted to do something special for me, so I decided not to look a gift horse in the mouth."

"Uh-huh, yeah, okay. A man just doesn't spend money like that for the hell of it. I take it you've been with him all day."

"And what if I have?" Nina replied playfully, batting her eyes and showing all thirty-twos.

"Girl, if he's spending money like that, I'm not mad at you. You should see yourself, you're just glowing with happiness. I'm glad you're having a good time."

"Yes, I am. I haven't felt this good in a long time. Now what about you and your new friend?"

"His name is John. He's a real nice guy. He's a firemen from Atlanta."

"Oh, really?" Nina said, adjusting the straps on her dress. "Has he put out your flame yet?" The two of them exploded with loud laughter.

"Girl, don't worry; before it's all over I'm going to get me some of that. Now, come on, let's go before some hoochie momma grabs him." Rose grabbed Nina and rushed her out of the washroom.

Nina located Richard sitting at a table waiting for her.

"I've ordered you a Bahama Momma. I hope its something you like."

"Goodness, yes, a drink is just what I need after a busy day of shopping."

"You look gorgeous, Nina," Richard said as he noticed the sparkle of the earrings and how beautiful and smooth her skin was.

"Why, thank you, Dr. Vincent. You don't look too bad yourself." Just then, as if it were fate, the DJ slowed the pace down and played, "The Secret Garden" by various artists, the first of which was Barry White. The man's deep and very distinctive voice filled the air around them.

Tell me a secret, I don't just wanna know about any secret. I wanna know about one special secret. Because tonight I want to learn about all the secrets in your garden. Richard listened as Barry White sang seductively, taking the words right out of his mouth.

"May I have this dance?" he asked.

"Why, yes, you may." The two of them made their way into

the center of the dance floor and embraced each other as if their very survival depended upon not letting go. Neither one of them fully understood what the chemistry between them was. They only knew that it was working and the temptations they were feeling felt oh so right. Richard placed his hand at the small of her back and pulled Nina close to him.

Nina felt herself melting on the inside as the stiffness of his manhood pressed against her stomach. They both slipped into a rhythmic groove that neither one of them wanted to end. Richard exhaled as Barry crooned.

I'll take good care of you. That's what a man is suppose' to do. And I'll be there for you all the time. Let your hair down, let me get in the mood. . . . In Richard's mind, Barry was saying everything that he couldn't or was hesitant to say. After the music ended it was difficult for either one of them to pull away from each other and deny their passions. But once again, Nina placed her hand on his chest and pushed him away from her. She gazed up into his brown eyes, seeing his desire for her. He took her face in his hands and kissed her softly on the lips.

"Richard," she whispered as she pulled back. "What are you doing to me? Why do you have me feeling this way?"

"Do you want me to stop?"

"Yes . . . I mean no . . . I mean I don't know. I'm just kind of confused."

"Shhh." Richard put his fingers to his lips then kissed her on the forehead. "Just keep dancing with me." Nina allowed herself to slip back into the comfort of his arms. How could she possibly deny her feelings?

Richard's suite was as big as her apartment. He had a fully equipped kitchen, a dining room with a fireplace and entertainment center. The master bedroom had a super-king-sized bed with blue satin bed linen, and a private balcony complete with patio furniture and a breathtaking view of the beach and the Atlantic Ocean. There was a sitting room and an oversized whirlpool, as well.

"What is that scent I'm smelling?" she asked as she stood in the doorway of the balcony and watched the white-capped waves of the ocean as they came ashore.

"It's my green tea aromatherapy candles that I've been burning while relaxing in the whirlpool." That's when Nina noticed all of the candles placed on the tile around the whirlpool. At first glance she estimated that he had about thirty candles. "The scent is supposed to help relieve stress," Richard continued.

"Oh, I see."

"I hear some doubt in your voice. Tell you what, why don't you have a seat here on the balcony for a moment while I set things up." Nina noticed a book of poetry sitting on the patio table with a page turned down.

"I see that you've been reading a little poetry. I didn't realize that you liked it. Do you write any?"

Richard came back to the balcony. "No, I'm afraid that I'm not that talented. But hey, let me see the book for a second. I marked off a poem called "Nina's Paradise." It reminded me of you. Here it is. Listen to this." Richard cleared his throat.

" 'Nina possesses a beauty rivaled only by the setting of the sun on an island paradise. Her honey skin can only have been produced in heaven's sweets and goodies factory. When I strum her honey surface, her body serenades my thirst with captivating lyrics. The flow of her strut and the mystery of her stride cause my eyes to seek for her hidden paradise. Nina is my potion of choice. She hypnotizes me with sensuality. She teases my yearnings, feeds my hunger, and excites my imagination with the promise of endless possibilities. She pours words of temptation in my right ear. Understanding fully that her expressions will only overflow then seep out down the side of my neck leaving a moist trail of obscene intentions.' "

"Ooo, baby. I really like that," Nina replied, enjoying the feeling of how the words had ignited her passion.

"Isn't that a hot little poem?"

"Yes, it says just enough. Go on and finish what you were doing while I look through the book."

Richard moved about the place, running water in the whirlpool, getting additional towels and lighting the candles. Finally, he turned off all the lights, leaving only the romantic yellow glow of the candles to illuminate their surroundings.

"Nina," Richard called for her with a deep soothing tone. She stepped back inside the romantic surroundings of the love nest he'd set up for her. Richard placed his hands on her shoulders. Delighted with the fact that she was allowing him to caress her, Nina allowed him to slip his fingers under the straps of her sundress. His very touch was sending shivers down her spine. Richard's eyes fell all over her as he deliberately let her dress fall to the floor. Richard slipped his hands around her back and unclasped her bra then gently placed moist kisses on her shoulders as he removed it. His hands traveled down the length of her spine, around to the side of her hips and under her lace bikini underwear. Richard caressed her bottom; he stopped when his hands were full, feeling her muscles flexing and noticing that her hips were thrusting slightly.

Nina took a step back from him and carefully pulled her panties down. She then approached him and began pulling his shirt up in order to get it out of his shorts and over his head. She undid his belt buckle then unsnapped the button on his shorts, allowing them to fall to the floor. He stepped out of the shorts one foot at a time.

"Hurry up and get out of those briefs," Nina suddenly ordered him, a bit surprised at her own tone. But she loved being the aggressor. Richard was obedient. She surveyed his body from head to toe. Baby-fine hair covered his broad muscular chest and ran down his well-defined abdomen and his powerful thighs. His deliciously sexy cock was dark brown with a red underglow. It was silky to the touch and full of pulsating veins that were increasing the size of his erection, causing it to throb like a light switch being flicked on and off. She gripped his huge erection and ran her hand the length of his shaft, enjoying the soft smoothness of his skin. When she squeezed his erection the tip of it became moist with his nectar. She rubbed the head of his member with her index finger, enjoying the sight of him quivering. Then she turned and led him by his manhood over to the candlelit whirlpool where she'd surely be able to relax and get more comfortable. She slipped into the warm water, feeling the tension exit her body from every place imaginable. She sat down near one of the water jets and let the jetting pressure massage her lower back. Sitting in a bubble-filled whirlpool, inhaling an intoxicating scent with Richard, was the last place Nina thought she'd end up. But she couldn't ignore the fact that she was deliciously delighted to be with him. She placed a towel at the edge of the whirlpool and relaxed her head.

"I have got to get me one of these," she mentioned, as she released a large sigh.

"I know what you mean," Richard replied, as he lowered himself into the water right next to her. She gripped his cock again, which was wickedly stiff, even under water. He felt so marvelous in the palm of her hand and she felt his throbs intensify. For a fleeting moment she considered protection, but quickly dismissed the thought. This was a chance that she was going to take. Nina didn't want anything between them while she devoured him.

"Richard," she echoed his name because her passions had complete control over her now. Her body was aching for him. She stood up, letting the soapy water run off of her glistening, honey-colored skin. She positioned herself directly in front of him so that her mound was before him. Nina gazed down at Richard as she ran her fingers through his hair. "I want to feel your hot tongue." Nina parted her legs for him. Richard was more than willing to follow her lead. "That's a good boy," she moaned, tossing her head back as his warm wet tongue swept across her womanhood. She felt him as he gently parted her lips and let his tongue find the center of her honey pot. She began thrusting her hips, feeling his tongue probe deep inside of her. A loud moan escaped her lips as the tip of his tongue found her swollen love bead. She cradled the back of his head and held him to the spot that he was at. There was no way she was going to allow him to alter the circular motions of his tongue on her hard love bead. Richard began sucking it and she felt a shiver of pure ecstasy run the length of her spine.

"Suck it hard, baby! Oh, yes!" She felt herself reaching the point of no return. "Right there, baby, suck harder!" She ordered him, and began frantically thrusting her hips. "Yeah, baby, I'm almost there, yes, that's my spot!" She exploded with an intensity that she'd never experienced before, feeling her nectar run out of her juicy love tunnel and onto Richard's eager lips and tongue. She needed him; she needed to feel him inside of her. "Sit back!" She commanded him, then lowered herself down on his cock, guiding it into her, inch by inch. She quivered as his wood flexed inside of her, as she pushed herself all the way down him. He filled her to the hilt. She rocked slowly, feeling nothing but pure ecstasy made all the more pleasurable by the thrilling sound of swirling water.

After their intense session the two of them got out of the whirlpool and toweled off. Nina crawled into the super-king-sized bed and lay on her stomach, ready to drift off and enjoy the euphoric state that she was in. But Richard was intent on making love to Nina in a way that she would always treasure. He withheld his own pleasure in order to make sure that she was thoroughly and completely satisfied. Richard placed a small dish with some massage oil into the microwave and heated it slightly. He returned to the bedroom and stood over Nina, who had melted into the mattress. He walked around to the other side of the bed and stood at her head. Dipping his fingertips in the warm oil, he leaned forward and placed his fingers at the base of her neck, then ran his fingers along the length of her spine. Nina cooed with pleasure, stirring Richard's passions. He took his time as he strummed her skin like a harp player strumming a beautiful melody. The sight of Nina drifting off into the blissful unknown was his confirmation that this kind of attention was not something she was accustomed to receiving. He asked her to turn over so that he could continue with his work. He started with her round succulent breasts. He caressed them, enjoying the feel of her erect brown nipples. He just had to know what they tasted like so he tickled them with his tongue. Richard lubricated his fingers and began exploring every nook and cranny of her womanhood. He ran the length of her vagina lips using his thumb and forefinger moving at a leisurely pace, slowly awakening her from her coma-like state. He deliberately slid his fingers inside of her deliciously warm pink tunnel, feeling her wetness increase with every stroke. He gracefully parted her lips with his thumbs, slowly pulled back the pillowy flesh that concealed her love bead, then placed a warm moist kiss on her. That brought her completely back to him, ready to savor the feel of his manhood inside of her. The head of his cock met her lips as she gripped his ass and pushed his stiff poker inside of her. She began thrusting her hips hard. Her womanhood was alive in a way that she'd never known before. Richard plunged inside of her so deeply that she got a sensation of both pain and pleasure.

"Oh, yes, baby, that's it—pull me into you," Richard urged her as his thrusts became more vigorous and his sounds became more audible. His movements were fast-paced and frantic.

"Yes, Richard, fill my pussy up with your big dick." Nina screamed with pleasure as she locked her legs around his back, feeling the energy of both of their orgasms beginning to stir. Richard responded by extending his manhood to even greater lengths and pumping with all of the energy he had left. Nina clawed at his back.

"Yes, baby, that's it, you're going to make me shoot." She felt Richard's warm breath enter her ear as she nibbled on his neck, drinking the sweet sweat from his body. She unlocked her legs and spread them wide as Richard unleashed his nectar inside of her.

Richard had no idea how long they'd been asleep, glued together by sweat and nectar. He was still inside of her warm love cave feeling her light contractions against his cock that was still semi-erect. "You are so beautiful," he whispered in her ear, then slowly pulled himself out of her, listening to the sucking sound of her womanhood begging him to stay put. She released a tranquil gasp as her source of pleasure left its spot.

"Stay there, don't move," he said with a loud whisper.

"Don't worry, Honey. I'm not going anywhere," said Nina, half asleep.

Richard grabbed another towel and soaked it with warm water. He wrung the excess water out of the cloth then went back and sat on the bed beside Nina. He slowly began washing the sticky sweat from her succulent body. Richard studied her wet skin as he went about his task, noticing how goose bumps formed on her skin and how her back arched at certain spots, which until then he had not discovered.

"My goodness, baby, that feels so good. You have totally drained me. I'm so weak with pleasure, I can barely speak," she mumbled.

"Just relax, baby, and let me make you feel wonderful." Richard continued washing her entire body from head to toe. It didn't take long for Nina to drift off into a coma-like sleep. Satisfied that he'd thoroughly pleased her, he showered, turned off the whirlpool, then slid into the bed with her. He pulled her back into his chest, inhaled the scent of her hair. Holding her tightly, he drifted off to sleep.

Nina awoke to the sound of rain slapping against the window. As she slowly became fully aware of her surroundings, she smelled fresh coffee, eggs, sausage, and buttermilk biscuits. With her hand, she began searching the bed for Richard, and when she couldn't locate him she opened up her eyes and saw him leaning in the doorway of the patio naked. She took a long morning stretch and yawn then focused her attention back on his wonderfully tight chocolate ass. She savored the thought of sinking her teeth into him once again.

"It sounds as if that storm is pretty nasty," Nina said as she tossed back the covers.

"Yes, it is." Richard replied as he stepped out of the doorway. "I had room service bring us up some food. I know that after that wonderful event last night, I'm hungry as hell."

Nina laughed. "Oh, yes. I'm very hungry as well." Nina walked out of the bedroom, stepping over her underwear and into the bathroom to freshen up. Then she made her way to the kitchen where there was a beautiful spread of fresh fruit, juices, bagels, muffins, and pastries. Under the covers of the silver warmers she found eggs, bacon, sausage, and the buttermilk pancakes she'd smelled earlier. "Richard baby, there is enough food here to feed ten people."

"Well, I wasn't sure of what you liked so I just got everything." Nina picked up a strip of bacon and began eating it.

"Now, you do realize that this is going to ruin my diet. God, this is so good, all of this food must have cost you a small fortune."

Richard replied with a smile, thinking only of how much he enjoyed romancing her. Looking at her round behind as she plucked grapes from a vine in the fruit section of the spread was certainly the most delicious delight he'd ever had the pleasure of experiencing. He approached her from the rear and slid his hands around her body and rested them on her tummy. She tilted her head to the side and he began landing sweet kisses on her neck.

"Now, hold on a minute," Nina chuckled as she placed a grape up to his lips. "Let a sister eat something first before we start that up again." She playfully pushed him away from her with her rump.

Later the two of them headed over to the casino to play the slot machines. Richard wasn't much of a gambler, but every now and again Nina had indulged herself by driving over to Gary, Indiana, to play the slot machines on the Riverboat. When they stepped inside of the casino, they were greeted and offered a beverage of their choice. Nina chose to have a glass of wine while Richard settled for a rum and coke.

"Okay, baby, which machine do you think I should play?" Nina asked as she gazed into Richard's almond eyes.

"Humm, let's move toward the back," Richard answered. "I'll find you the perfect machine." Nina stood on the tip of her toes and gave Richard a quick kiss on the lips then quickly rubbed her lipstick away from his bottom lip with her thumb. They maneuvered their way through the crowded casino in search of one of those plastic buckets to place your winnings in, then found a dollar slot machine. Nina sat in the seat in front of the machine and read the different combinations that she needed in order to win money.

"Okay, baby, let's see what happens," Nina said as she slid a dollar chip into the slot. Richard gave her a quick peck on the cheek before she pulled the handle. A cherry, a lemon, and another cherry popped up. Nina plopped in another dollar and felt a chill run down her back as Richard nibbled on her ear.

"Baby, stop that before I take you back into the room and . . ." Nina was interrupted by the sound of the whistle going off on the machine. Three sevens were lined up and the machine was spitting out money.

"Aaaah!" Nina screamed with delight. "I won!" Nina immediately checked the board and discovered that she'd just won three thousand dollars. "Baby, tonight is on me." She clapped her hands and bounced in her seat.

There was a small wait to be seated in the hotel's seafood restaurant. Richard stood with his back against the wall while Nina pressed herself against him, enjoying the feel of his erection in the small of her back.

"Well, speaking of the devil. We were just talking about you, Miss Thang!" It was Rose walking in to have dinner with her friend. Nina burst out laughing.

"Girl, I'm so sorry. I forgot to call you today."

"Uh-huh, tell me anything," Rose said laughing, then formally introduced her friend John, the fireman, to both Nina and Richard. They exchanged greetings and agreed on having dinner together. Before dinner arrived, the ladies excused themselves to go freshen up. Both Richard and John behaved like true gentlemen and stood as the ladies walked away.

"All right, heifer, I want details," Nina said, pushing the door open. "Every last curl on your head is gone."

"Uhm, excuse me, Miss Gel Queen!" Rose quickly responded, noticing Nina's head as well. They both laughed.

"So are you having a good time, Rose?"

"Girl, I'm having the time of my life. John makes me feel absolutely wonderful. He's single, owns a home, and loves to read as much as I do. Girl, it's been so long since I've been able to hold a decent conversation with a brother. Oh, and get this. He told me that he loves my size, and he expressed how he thought that full-figured women were a delicacy."

"Hey, now!" Nina chimed.

"And let me tell you. The man definitely knows how to put out a raging fire."

They both laughed. "Today, we were shopping all day long. The man didn't complain once about being dragged from store to store toting all of my bags. We're talking about going to the beach in the morning. You guys should come with us."

"I'll mention it to Richard. I'm sure he'll be up for it. And girl, you won't believe this one. I won three thousand dollars today over at the casino."

"No, you didn't!" Rose responded with disbelief.

"Girl, on the second pull the machine went crazy. So since you suggested that I come down here, I figured that I would reimburse you for your airfare."

"Really?" Rose flung her arms around Nina and gave her a gigantic hug. "Girlfriend, you're the best. I love you so much."

"I love you too. Now, let's hurry up and take care of our business in here before some hoochie momma takes both of our friends."

18

Richard was the first person waiting in the lobby the following morning. A short time later Rose and John approached with their arms locked around each other's waist. Rose wore a one-piece lime green bathing suit with a matching wrap tied around her waist. John was sporting blue swimming trunks that met his knees and an oversized Atlanta Braves T-shirt camouflaging his round belly.

"Good morning," Richard greeted the two of them.

"Good morning to you," they both replied in unison.

"Where is my girl at?" Rose inquired.

"She went to her room to change. I'm waiting just like you," Richard responded. No sooner had he finished his sentence than Nina approached wearing a bright-yellow bikini bathing suit with a matching wrap carefully tied around her waist and looking strikingly stylish. Richard instantly thought of the poem he'd read to her yesterday called "Nina's Paradise." *The rhythm of her strut and the mystery of her stride made his eyes search for her hidden paradise,* he thought.

"Good morning," they all greeted her as she came up and slid her arm around Richard.

"Good morning," she replied. "Well, damn near afternoon now, but are we about set?"

"Yes," John chimed. "Let's get out to the beach." Richard and John picked up large duffel bags full of beach necessities and followed Rose and Nina.

The beach had everything they could possibly want: food, drinks, lawn chairs, showers, shopping, snorkeling, parasailing, and jet skiing. They stepped out onto the hot white sand in search of a semi-private area where they would be able to set their picnic. They all sat down on lawn chairs that John and Richard had picked up and stared out into the clear blue Caribbean water. Nina handed Richard some suntan oil which he gladly applied to her body.

"This is the good stuff," Richard mentioned as he read the label. "It doesn't come off while you're in the water."

"Only the best for you, baby," Nina chimed, then thought about going for a swim. "Come on, let's go get in the water."

"Okay, let me grab my camera. I want to get some pictures of you in that sexy-ass bathing suit."

"I've got to hand it to you, Nina girl. You're wearing the hell out of that bathing suit," Rose complimented her as John pulled her close and began nibbling on her ear.

"Stop that! You're making me feel self-conscious," Nina responded, pleased with the fact that everyone had taken notice of how hard she worked to keep herself together.

"Yeah, girl, whatever." Rose giggled as she felt a twinge of delightful pleasure run the length of her body from John's playful tongue.

Richard urged Nina to come into the water and pose for him. Nina quickly dashed to the shore's edge as the hot sand stung the soles of her feet. She expected the water to have a slight chill to it but to her amazement it was very warm. The water felt as warm and relaxing as the whirlpool in Richard's room.

"Now, this feels heavenly." Nina exhaled as the warmth of the water began working its mystical magic on her. She waded in the water until it swallowed her thighs, the surface of water stopped just below her womanhood, which all of a sudden began throbbing, informing her that it was in need of some attention. Richard observed her every movement, proud of the fact that she was his woman.

"Stop right there," Richard requested of her. "You look so beautiful." Richard raised his camera up to his eye and adjusted the focus. Nina struck a pose. She raised her elbows and locked her fingers behind her neck. Viewing Nina through the camera lens Richard noticed how the yellow sun highlighted her honey skin. How her chiseled jawline complemented the most kissable lips he'd ever had the pleasure of tasting. She ignited his desire for her with the way she lowered her eyes and gazed directly at him through the camera lens. Her eyes were full of sensuality, telling him things that her lips dared not say. Richard snapped a photograph, then quickly snapped another, then another, and yet another.

"Richard, baby, what are you doing?" Nina laughed, feeling a bit embarrassed and shy. She submerged her body in the water up to her shoulders then slowly stood back up, feeling the excess water cascade off of her body. To Richard, Nina looked like a goddess. Maybe it was the way she never took her eyes off of him, letting him know that he had all of her attention. Or maybe it was the radiant glow that seemed to surround her, or the way the fabric of her swimsuit clung to her wet skin. Whatever the reason, Richard had never felt this way about a woman before. His emotions were suddenly stronger than any he'd ever felt. The buzzing sound of jet skis caught their attention.

"My goodness, look at them go," Nina said as a couple went skipping across the water on the craft.

"Would you like to try it?" Richard asked. Nina smiled, feeling the adrenaline run through her body at the thought of Richard's exciting and adventurous proposal.

"Yes," she responded. "Let's go back and tell Rose and John so they will keep an eye on things while we're out there."

The jet ski attendant explained how to operate the watercraft as he handed Nina a life jacket. "This is a very big jet ski, it's large enough to seat three people," explained the attendant, then asked a completely unrelated question. "Excuse me," he said with his thick accent, "but are you a model?" Richard noticed him undressing his woman with his eyes. "I noticed you taking photos." Nina smiled showing all thirty-twos, delighted at what he'd just asked her. She'd considered modeling before, but for the most part it was just a crazy idea.

"Yeah, man, she's my model." Richard stared the attendant down with a reply that carried a tone filled with jealousy and confrontation.

"Come on, baby. I've got a surprise for you," Nina laughed as she boarded the craft. Richard continued to glare at the attendant.

"You must return within thirty minutes," mumbled the attendant as he moved away from them. Richard boarded the craft, locking his hands around Nina's waist.

"What's wrong, baby? Did he make you jealous looking at me like that?" Nina asked, tickled to death. Richard grumbled. Nina pressed the throttle, which caused the nose of the craft to rise up high out of the water. The power of the motor humming beneath her was exhilarating. The engine roared as the craft zoomed and skipped across the water. Nina was heading far away from the shore toward a secluded area.

"Baby, where are you taking me?" Richard inquired as water splashed all around them.

"Why? Are you scared?" Richard looked back. He could barely see the shoreline of the beach. They were out in the middle of the Atlantic Ocean, and the only thing surrounding them now was clear blue water. Nina slowly released the throttle and calmed the craft down as it coasted to a stop. Then she shut the motor off. The ocean gently rocked the craft from side to side. Suddenly Richard felt as if he were marooned on a raft.

"Baby, what are we doing way out here?"

"It's a surprise," she said as she unsnapped her life jacket and tied it around the bars of the jet ski. She turned around in the saddle to face Richard, carefully balancing herself as she did.

"What kind of surprise is it?"

"It's called coochie surprise." Nina slowly and carefully lay back on the bars. She ran her index finger around the trim of her bikini and pulled the fabric back exposing her tight neatly trimmed little crotch. She slowly and carefully raised her legs toward the heavens, pleased that she was as limber as she was, and wiggled out of her bikini. "Now, scoot back all the way on the seat," she ordered him. "Lie on your stomach and bring me that sweet tongue of yours."

Richard let the tip of his tongue brush across her delicious little lips as she raised her hips in the air and locked her feet at the ankles around his neck. Nina felt the warm sun heat up the bottom of her feet. He penetrated her with his smooth long tongue. She gasped then moaned as he scooped out her nectar, savoring her slightly salty taste.

"Damn, baby, you do that so fucking well." Nina slowly began thrusting her hips against his face, feeling water splash on her skin as her movements grew frantic. His tongue moved up and down her valley, causing more of her wetness to come forth. Her orgasm began to build quickly as he found her spot and began rotating his tongue in circular motions around it.

"Oh, baby, damn!" She cooed as she used one hand to cradle his head, holding him to the spot she wanted him to focus on. She could feel her juices running out of her into the crease of her bottom as he began sucking her clit hard, the way she liked it. Shivers began running through her body as she approached the point of no return.

"Yes, baby, that's my spot," she cried as she felt the walls of her womanhood contracting, begging to be filled with Richard's long hard silky wood.

"Baby, I need to feel you inside of me." Nina's voice was pleading with him. Richard sat upright then carefully maneuvered himself out of his life jacket and Speedo bathing suit.

Richard sat still as Nina squatted, then skillfully steered herself down on the delicious hot shaft. Richard grabbed the handlebars of the craft for stability. Nina was soaking wet and slid down on him without any resistance. She was savoring his warm cock as it went all the way to the back of her passion tunnel. Nina slowly circled her hips being mindful of not rocking the watercraft too hard. She felt the head of his manhood beginning to swell as he took one hand and squeezed her ass.

"Yes, baby, work that ass!" Richard urged her as she twitched and squirmed, slithering around in a figure-eight motion.

"Come on baby!" Richard slapped her ass as his own hips began thrusting, pushing deeper and deeper inside of her.

"Baby you're about to make me come," Nina shouted. She started biting on his neck, quickly approaching the point of her passion spilling out all over him. Suddenly her orgasm burst and her tight cunt gripped Richard's penis and squeezed it with an intensity she'd never felt before.

"Oh Nina, I'm about to shoot it all up in you." Richard's breathing was spastic and uncontrolled as Nina pounded down hard on his penis feeling the warm shots of his nectar shooting over her walls and making her gasp and claw at his back, feeling the strength of her orgasm consume her entire body. Richard was so deep inside of her that he felt the fast-paced thudding of her heart pounding against the mushroom head of his cock through her warm wet juices. They held onto each other, waiting for their hard breathing to return to normal. Neither one wanted to let go as they drifted into a light, euphoric nap.

A while later, Richard opened his eyes, noticing that they had drifted further out into the Atlantic Ocean. He quickly searched his surroundings looking for land, noticing only the blue horizon.

"Nina, baby."

"Humm," she replied, not wanting to come out of the blissful state that she was in. It felt so good feeling the aftershocks of her orgasm as her pussy contracted against his delicious dick.

"Can you see land?"

Nina quickly popped her eyes open. "Yes, I think that's it way over there. My God, we're really out here," Nina replied, rising up. She studied Richard's eyes, searching for how he was feeling. Then saw it. A beautiful gleam in his eyes that could only have been for her. She passionately kissed him, cradling the back of his head and sucking on his warm tongue. She began to feel his warm cock extending inside of her, wanting to go another round. She pried herself away from his delicious lips.

"Baby, we'd better head back before they end up sending a rescue team out here for us," Nina explained as she skillfully raised her body off of him.

"Where in the hell have you two been?" Rose asked with a puzzled tone as she stood up and brushed the white sand off her behind. "I've been standing out in the water trying to figure out where you went. One minute you were there and the next minute you were gone."

"Girl, I was just out there riding with Richard," Nina responded as both she and Richard conked out on their lawn chairs.

"Well shit! Let a sister know something if you're going to disappear like that; you had me here all worried about y'all. I thought that maybe the both of you fell off the damn thing and drowned."

Richard and Nina laughed as they gazed at one another still feeling the exciting twinges of their hot little adventure. *The things that your passions will make you do are amazing,* Richard pondered to himself. He had been out in the middle of nowhere without a life jacket on, floating naked on a watercraft, and he didn't know how to swim a lick.

"What have you two been doing?" Richard asked.

"Man, just sitting here having a ball," replied John, who was lying flat on his back with his black sunglasses on. "We were talking about our childhoods and the things that we loved growing up."

"Oh, really?" responded Richard. "Like what?"

"Well, when I was a kid I used to love going over to my aunt's house in the summer. She had a huge white house with a front porch that had a swing on it. All around her property were apple trees. When I came over I'd go out there and pick the apples and she'd make me a homemade apple pie." John licked his lips. "Boy, nobody made apple pies like she did."

"Was it good, baby?" Rose responded as she kneeled down then stretched out next to him.

"Oh, yes. Nobody could cook like my Aunt Tee Tee, my mother included. She would get up on a Sunday morning, go down to the kitchen, and cook a colossal breakfast: grits, bacon, eggs, hash browns, buttermilk pancakes with homemade strawberry jam."

"Now, that's cool," Richard smiled. "I can see you sitting at the kitchen table just waiting for your plate."

"Man, you just don't know. When I became an adult and went over there for the holidays, I took home at least four plates of food." They all laughed. "Boy, I sure miss her. She passed a few years back. Died in her sleep."

"Aw, man, that's too bad," Richard responded.

"Yeah, but she lived a long life. She was eighty-six when she died."

"When I was a kid," Richard began reminiscing, "there was this old tree with a tree house in our backyard. There was a ladder that hung down, and I'd have to climb it in order to get up to my wooden box home. That was my little slice of heaven. I used to love camping out in that tree. At night I could hear the crickets singing as I gazed out of the square window at the stars in the sky. Man, they were so beautiful and bright. I would hold my hand out wishing that I could pluck one from the night sky and put it in my sleeping bag."

"That sounds so peaceful, baby." Nina took his every word to heart as she pictured a tiny hand trying to catch a star. "When I was a little girl, I grew up on a farm. There was a large tree in our yard as well, but there was a creek that ran through our yard too. My father had tied a rope and an old tractor tire around one of the branches of the old tree, and I would go swinging on that rope and tire. I used to love going back there to play in the water on a hot day. I would take my dolls down there and spread out a blanket. Have myself a little tea party and take my dolls for a swim. I did that every Saturday morning." Nina smiled as she noticed the beautiful orange and red colors of the setting sun.

"Well, I wasn't like y'all," Rose blurted out, "all beautiful and shit. I grew up in the city, the ghetto where crazy-ass black folks live. I know y'all have heard of it. The thing that I remember most about growing up was my momma's Friday night card parties. People were all up in the house drinking, smoking, and dancing. I loved it because I got to hang out in the front of the building all night long, selling flavored ice cones and jumping double-Dutch rope. And let me tell you I could jump some rope! I'd have my nappy-headed ass out there under the streetlights singing mess like *Engine Engine number nine. Going down the Chicago line.* Or *Bubble gum, bubble gum in the dish. How many pieces do you wish?* Or my favorite, *Yo momma don't wear no drawers—A ding dong—I seen her when she took them off—A ding dong—She put them in the garbage can—A ding dong—And blew up the garbage man.*" Everyone burst out with laughter.

"I remember that!" Nina hollered with excitement. "The next verse went something like: *She threw them up in the sky— A ding dong—And Superman refused to fly.*"

"Now that shit is funny," John said in between laughs. "No matter where you go, black folks always have something to say about each other's momma."

"Lord have mercy," Nina chimed. "Rose, you've got me sitting out here with tears in my eyes."

"Girl, like I've told you a thousand times before, I like to keep shit real."

"I like that in you, baby," John replied, giving Rose a sweet kiss on the lips.

"All right, Nina." John looked at her. "Who is your favorite singer?"

"Gosh, that's a hard one, but the person that comes to mind right away is Teddy Pendergrass."

"Ooo, girl, yes!" Rose was in agreement. "Now there's a man who knows how to sing a woman out of her panties."

"Well, that's what he was known for," Richard responded.

"I know." Rose replied. "I threw mine at him." Another round of loud laughter filled the air.

"Okay, since we're doing favorites. John, what's your favorite movie?" asked Richard.

"Oh, that's easy," John replied. *"One Flew Over the Cuckoo's Nest* with Jack Nicholson."

"Ooo, yes," Rose said. "That was an excellent movie."

"What about you, Richard, what's your favorite movie?" asked John.

"Humm, I really can't say that I have a favorite. But the first movie that comes to my mind is a *A Soldier's Story."*

"I can agree with that one," Nina responded. "That movie has my baby Denzel Washington in it."

"Girl, please, I like a man who's a little rough around the edges, give me Laurence Fishburne."

"Okay, I see that this is getting a little deep," Richard laughed. "Who wants a drink? It's on me."

"Now you're talking, brother," Rose bellowed as Richard got to his feet.

"Hang on, Richard, I'll come with you," John said. "You're going to need more than two hands. And Rose," John said, looking down at her, "don't let no sugar daddy come over here while I'm away. I've got all of the sweets you'll ever need."

"Get on out of here with your silly self," Rose said, as she pinched John's behind.

The days had run into each other and before Nina realized it, time had run out. She and Richard had been making passionate love all week long, and it was difficult to face reality. She felt like she was on Fantasy Island. Just when she wanted to completely lose herself in her fantasy, reality hit hard. Showing up at a real screwed-up time out of nowhere to tell her that it was time to come home. On the eve of her last day, she was snuggled up next to Richard in the comfortable love nest he'd created for her, realizing that this was it. The last night that she'd get to be in the room with him. The last night that she'd be able to feel his arms around her or smell the scent of their intensely delicious lovemaking. Nina felt her emotions getting out of hand so she skillfully escaped Richard's embrace. She put on her blue bathing suit and headed out the door toward the beach. She needed to think of how to handle this mess she'd gotten herself into. How would she possibly find the words that wouldn't hurt, insult, or offend?

Richard had become so comfortable with Nina sleeping in his bed that he instantly flipped his eyes open when he could no longer feel the warmth of her body against his chest.

"Nina?" he called out, but got no answer. He tossed back the covers and frantically searched the house. "Nina?" he called again. As he made his way past the balcony he glanced down below and saw her walking across the street toward the beach. He jumped into his swimming trunks, then rushed out the door.

Nina kicked off her sandals and left them sitting on the sand. The water felt so warm and Nina enjoyed the feel of her feet slowly sinking into the sand. Seating herself in the shallow waves, she spread her legs and allowed the water to soothe her womanhood, which was very tender.

Richard approached Nina from behind, noticing the magnificent sunset about to dip down behind the horizon. He paid attention to how beautiful she looked sitting in the water in her blue bathing suit and the straw hat that he'd purchased for her earlier that week. He admired her brown tanned back and defined arms, which he'd had the pleasure of being embraced by. As he drew near, his heart suddenly began racing. There was a strangeness in the air around him that he could feel.

"Good evening, stranger." Richard greeted Nina as he sat down beside her.

"How did you know I was here?" Nina asked.

"I saw you from the balcony."

Nina sighed and listened to the water as it came rushing toward the shore. "My flight leaves at three o' clock tomorrow afternoon," she mentioned, trying to prevent a tear from falling. Richard heard the trembling in her voice and put his arm around her to comfort and soothe her.

"I know," he responded.

"I never even bothered to ask you what happened between you and your wife and to tell you the truth, I really didn't care. I was just so damn happy you were here by yourself."

"A lot has happened between Estelle and me, and I needed to get away. Well, run away would be more accurate."

"So, what does that mean? Are you going back to her?" Nina asked, not really wanting to know the answer to her question. But she needed to bring closure to this thing that they had. She had to protect her feelings before they got the best of her. Richard sighed. The only thing he knew was that he needed to get away and that there was no way he would go back into that house as long as Rubylee was still there. Then again, after reconsidering, he really didn't want to ever go back to Estelle. Things had been said and done that couldn't be taken back.

"I see, I understand," Nina responded dryly, taking Richard's silence to mean that yes, he would be going back to Estelle.

"No," Richard replied. "It's about time I either shit or get off the toilet. My marriage to Estelle died years ago; I've just been waiting for the burial. I've been doing some critical thinking while I've been down here, and well, I guess that I've just been avoiding the inevitable. I need to go back and bring closure to my situation."

"Richard, don't say things like that for my sake. Everything that we've shared, I wanted. I don't have any regrets about that or at least none that I feel at this moment." Nina paused, choosing her words carefully. "I'm not some husband-stealing home wrecking—whatever. I mean, if you want to work things out, I'm not going to be in your way. Everything that has happened between us can remain right here on this island." Richard understood that Nina was offering him an uncomplicated way out of their relationship. Although he adored and respected her for that, he didn't want to let her go. He wanted Nina, and wanted to continue to build on what they'd started.

"When I handle what needs to be taken care of back home, will you have room for me in your life?" Richard asked.

"What are you saying, Richard?"

"I'm saying that I don't want our relationship to end."

"Richard, I'm still married to Jay. Although I've moved out and gotten my own place, he refuses to sign the divorce papers because he feels we can work this thing out. On top of that, you have a child to take into consideration." Richard released a defeated sigh. Nina watched his body sag as he pondered the situation.

"I know. It's going to be difficult for Nathan to understand what's going on, but I'm leaving a marriage, not my son. I'll always be available for him. I feel that in the long run, things would be harder on him if Estelle and I were to remain together."

"Richard, leaving is a huge decision. You have to make sure that divorce is something that you really want."

"Do you still have feelings for Jay?"

"I'll always have feelings for him, I can't just shut them off. I feel as if I still love Jay. But I'm no longer in love with him. I care about his well-being, but that's as far as it goes. Do you understand what I'm trying to say?"

"Yes, I do, in a strange sort of way." Richard gathered his thoughts. "Well, I know that I can't run forever. I have to turn and face reality at some point. However, I refuse to set foot back in that house. Do you think it would be possible for me to stay at your place for a short while? Just until I get things squared away?"

Nina chuckled a bit. "Sugar, the last thing that you need is to be staying at my place while you're in divorce court. The judge would eat your ass alive if it were discovered that you were living with a lover. Besides, there would be entirely too many complications involved if you lived with me. Lord knows that I don't want or need any complications."

"Yeah, I can understand that."

"Look, Richard, you're a wonderful man. And if our situations were any different, I'd come after you with both barrels loaded. I don't want to be nor do I plan to be alone for the rest of my life. I would love to remarry and settle down with someone who makes me happy."

"Do I make you happy, Nina?"

"Yes, you do. And believe me when I say that I want you, baby. I want you more than a fish wants water. I feel so comfortable with you, I can talk to you and tell you anything. You're a good listener and that's a wonderful quality to have. I've been married to Jay for twenty years and let me tell you, I don't think that the man ever really listened to me. He heard what I was saying, but to him I was just being a nagging wife." Nina paused. "I just don't want you to make any major decisions on my behalf. You need the space and time to think clearly. If it's meant for us to be with each other, we will."

"Understand this, Nina." Richard pulled her closer to him so that he could deliberately speak in her ear. "You mean a great deal to me. I like the way that you respect and treat me. It feels so good to have a person in my life who doesn't take me for granted. I've grown tired of being used and manipulated. I'm going to make some major changes in my life and when I do I want to know that you will be there waiting for me."

Nina felt her heart sink. Why was he doing this to her? She was trying to make things simple and uncomplicated. Why was he playing with her heart like this? Did he really want her? Or did he only think that he wanted her?

"I am not one to play with anyone's emotions, Nina. I'm dead serious. I want a relationship with you. So where does that leave us?"

"Confused, Richard. It leaves the both of us completely confused."

"Well, well, well, look at what the tide washed ashore this evening. Two black people from the sea," Rose said, laughing and beaming like moonlight as she and John walked up barefoot, hand in hand.

"Good evening," Richard replied in unison with Nina.

"Girl, what has gotten you out of bed on this beautiful evening?" Nina asked.

"Probably the same thing that has you out," Rose replied as John squeezed her closer to him.

"Well, I certainly hope that we'll all get together again before we leave tomorrow," John offered.

"Absolutely," Richard chimed. Last night after the sunset he and John laughed it up like two old college buddies who hadn't seen each other in years. Richard stood up, then helped Nina to her feet.

"Turn around Richard," Nina directed him, then began brushing the white sand off of his behind. Rose unlatched herself from John so that she could walk alone on the beach with Nina. The ladies walked along the shoreline with Richard and John behind them at a respectable distance, laughing loudly.

"Girl, I'm flying back to Atlanta with John for a few days."

"Really?"

"Honey, I think he is the one for me. He suggested it, I didn't. He's offered to cover my expenses. He wants me to see this house that he has built. And . . ."

"And what?" Nina was on edge.

"Well, we've been discussing the idea of making our relationship more than just an island fling. He wants to continue to see me and Lord knows, I want to continue to see him. So far he's everything that I could have asked for in a man. He's mature, kind and considerate, compassionate, single, and has no small children."

"Are you sure, Rose?"

"Girl, I know. It seems like I'm moving at the speed of light, but he makes me happy. Alone is not something that I want to be for the rest of my life. He's the first man I've met in years who doesn't seem to be playing games. He's a very serious person who doesn't use excuses for failures, setbacks, or disappointments. My God, Nina, John gives me chills when we talk." Rose smiled. "Girl, I know that love does some strange shit to you."

"Humph!" Nina quacked. "You don't have to tell me that one."

"It's making me do things that I thought I'd never do, but I feel something with John. There is something different about him. When I look into those teddy-bear eyes, I see something that I've never seen before."

"Really? What do you see?"

Rose released an exaggerated sigh. "Honesty. I believe that I see honesty."

"Hey, what are you two talking about up there?" John hollered from behind. Rose looked over her shoulder and smiled at him.

"You, baby," she teasingly replied.

Rose and John boarded their flight for Atlanta at two-thirty the following afternoon. Nina and Richard said their good-byes and watched the plane as it taxied down the runway and took off toward Atlanta. Nina had another thirty minutes before her flight left so she and Richard went over and sat at a table in front of a donut shop until it was time for her to board.

"So, when are you coming back?" Nina inquired.

"I should be back early next week. I'm lucky to be working in an office where the other associates are understanding of my need to get away. They've covered my patients for me until the end of the month."

"Oh, I see. Do you have any other thoughts about how you're going to handle your situation yet?"

"Well, there is no easy way to handle this. However, my strategy is to speak with an attorney first and find out what my options are. After that, I'll sit down with Estelle and let her know how I feel."

"Do you think there is any hope for your marriage?"

"It's difficult to say. Since I've been away I've been asking myself critical questions. All of the answers that I come up with point toward separation. I've been pushed to the point of wanting to physically harm her, and that's not good. I've enjoyed being free, so to speak, these last few weeks, but I know that I have responsibilities back home that I can't ignore. Well—one, actually, and that's Nathan." Richard paused. "It's going to be a rough ordeal and I'm not looking forward to this mess at all. I know that the emotional stress is going to kill me."

"Yes, I know what you mean, and chances are she'll try to use Nathan against you."

"Naaa, I don't think she'll do that."

"Trust me, I'm a woman and I know. Eventually she will." Nina felt a bit sad for Richard as she watched him exhale and ponder over his thoughts. She reached into her purse and grabbed a pen and a scrap piece of paper. "Here is my home number and address if you need someone to talk to. Don't hesitate to call me, okay? Although I want you to be able to think clearly without input from me, I also realize that you may just need someone who will listen to you." Nina gazed into Richard's eyes as she handed him the piece of paper. Like Rose, she could see so much in his eyes, so much uncertainty and pain, that she sympathized with him, longing to remove all that was troubling him. Richard hugged her, then kissed her on the ear, then on the cheek, and finally gave her a passionate kiss on the mouth. Both of them had powerful emotions that were difficult to contain.

"Well, it looks as if they've started boarding the passengers on your flight. You'd better go. I'll call you as soon as I get settled into a hotel room back in Chicago."

"You do understand why I don't feel comfortable with you staying with me, don't you?"

"Of course, I do, and you're right. It's best that I don't."

Nina stood up and gathered her two carry-on bags. Richard escorted her over to the stewardess who was checking tickets. Nina embraced Richard once more and spoke deliberately in his ear.

"I care about you, Richard. I care about you a great deal." Her emotions had won. She spoke from her heart even though she tried not to. She kissed him on the cheek, then quickly turned to board her flight.

19

Richard returned to Chicago during the early morning hours on a Sunday. He got himself a room at the Marriott Hotel near O'Hare Airport, grabbed himself a bite to eat, then settled into his new room. The following day, in between patients, he called his bank to make a payment on his charge card before the expenses from that monthlong vacation posted to his account. The bank's automated voice system picked up and Richard followed the instructions that would put him in contact with someone.

"Good afternoon, Seaway National Bank, how can I help you," said the teller. Richard gave her his account information and credit card number. Once she completed the transaction for him, he asked what his adjusted balance was on both accounts.

"On your primary savings you have a balance of thirteen thousand, two hundred dollars, and fifty-four cents. On your secondary savings account you have one million, five hundred and ninety-nine thousand."

"That's impossible," Richard said. "Two hundred thousand dollars of my money is missing. Are you sure that's the correct balance?"

"Hang on, sir." He heard the teller punching the keyboard hard. "Well, according to our records, you've made withdrawals

of ten thousand dollars every day for the past twenty days."
Richard almost wanted to laugh.

"That can't be. I've been in the Caribbean for the past
month."

"Well, that's not what our records show."

"Well, I couldn't have been two places at once, now, could
I?" Richard snapped at the teller. "Connect me with Edward
Lawson. Tell him Dr. Richard Vincent is on the phone."

"Dr. Vincent, I can connect you to my immediate supervisor
but not the president."

"Never mind, I have his direct number!" Richard slammed
down the phone, then picked it up and dialed Ed. The phone
rang a few times and Richard heard someone pick up the line.

"Ed Lawson speaking."

"Ed, this is Richard, how are you?"

"Young Richard Vincent. It's always good to hear from you.
What can I do for you today?"

"Well, there seems to be a problem with your bank records."

"Oh, how so?"

"According to—"

"Hang on Richard, my assistant is setting some information
down in front of me." There was a short pause, then Ed spoke
again. "Richard, I've just been handed a summary of your account. It seems you've withdrawn a very large amount of
money this past month."

"Well, that's what I've been trying to tell you, Ed. That's impossible, because I've been out of the country for the past
month. I just returned from the Bahamas yesterday, and I have
airline tickets and a hotel bill to prove it."

"Well, that means that there is a thief around here! Richard,
how soon can you get here?"

"My last patient is at three o'clock. I can be there by, let's
say, four o'clock."

"Good, I'm going to pull the surveillance tapes and call the
authorities. No one from my staff will be going home tonight
until I get to the bottom of this. I will not tolerate stealing in my

bank! It's a federal offense, and I aim to see that someone answers for this." Ed spoke with an angry edge in his voice.

"I'll see you at four, Ed." Richard hung up the phone.

Rubylee had been kicking herself in the ass for an entire month. She couldn't believe that she'd forgotten to get the bogus identification back from Red. Every day for the past month she'd been out in the streets searching for him. She pushed down the thought that maybe he had withdrawn the money and skipped town. Then she reasoned that that was not a possibility. Although Red loved money, he did not have good sense. She knew that he was around the damn city somewhere, boasting as if he were a high roller who'd made it to the big time. It was just a matter of finding his ass, and when she did, he'd better pray that she didn't put a bullet in it. The one thing she knew about Red was that he loved to gamble, and it was just a matter of finding out which back-alley poker game he'd slipped off to or which casino he was spending all of her money at.

It was approaching three o'clock, and Rubylee was making her way across the parking lot of Sportsman's Park Horse Racing Track in Maywood. She'd hung around the betting booths all day hoping to catch Red there, but he never showed up. She fired up her Chrysler, which was blowing blue smoke, and sped off down North Avenue toward Central Street. There was a barbershop back that way that had a small gambling room in the rear. When Rubylee arrived she parked her car, opened her purse, and pulled out her pistol. She stuck the weapon between her belt and blue jeans, then covered it up with her over-sized Bulls T-shirt. Rubylee shuffled into the shop, focusing on a barber sitting in the center chair with a white coat on, thumbing through a newspaper. Luckily for Rubylee, she was vaguely familiar with him so he allowed her access to the back room. A tall burly man opened a steel door, allowing her to enter. As she walked in she saw three men sitting under a ceiling fan at a small green card table with a stack of money and a small black radio in the center. "For a small piece of paper it carries a lot of weight." The O'Jays were harmonizing one of their hit songs called "For The Love of Money." Rubylee's trained eye estimated that there was about ten thousand big ones on the table. She pulled her cigarette from behind her ear and asked the burly man for a light. He spun the wheel of his lighter a few times until the flame finally shot up. Rubylee took a long drag, then dropped her jaw, allowing smoke to filter out.

"You know a dude name Red?" Rubylee questioned.

"Why, are you his wife?"

"Nope. You might say that I'm his business partner."

"Yeah, I know him," the burly man replied. Rubylee reached into her pants pocket and pulled out a fifty dollar bill.

"Do you know where I can find him?" The man took the fifty then smiled, showing a mouth full of gold teeth.

"He's around that corner in the washroom. But, uhm, he's taking care of a little business back there right now." Rubylee took another long drag.

"That's all right. He won't mind me interrupting him at all." Rubylee went around the corner and down the dark corridor. She pushed open the door of the washroom, letting her eyes focus on the back of Red. His pants were down around his ankles and his head was bowed down observing some man on his knees, tugging on his privates and making loud slurping sounds. Most likely paying off a debt to Red.

"Yeah, man, I'll be done in a minute," Red said, releasing sighs of pleasure. Rubylee flicked her cigarette on the ground then squished it out with her foot. She lifted up her T-shirt, pulled out her pistol, approached Red, slipped her arm around his waist, placed the cold steel barrel of her gun on his erect penis, and spoke purposely in his ear.

"The party is over, motherfucker," she whispered as she cocked the hammer back. "I told you not to fuck with me, didn't I!" The man on his knees sprung up and rushed out of the room.

"Now, Ruby baby, hold on. Let me explain." Red began begging. "Why don't you put that away so that we can talk?" Rubylee aimed the pistol at the wall and fired.

"Damn, baby! Can't we talk about this?" Red squealed with fear.

"Pull your clothes up." Rubylee commanded him. "You and I are about to take a ride."

"Rubylee? I've got about ten thousand dollars in there on the table; why don't you take that? I mean, damn baby! I wasn't going to run away with your money."

"Motherfucker, you must think I'm a damn fool! Ten thousand is chump change. Where is that damn ID?"

"It's right here, baby, in my pants pocket." Red reached down to pull his pants up from around his ankles.

"Stop right there!" Rubylee shouted.

"What? Can't I pull up my pants?" Red pleaded.

"Not just yet. Sit down on your ass and lay flat on your back."

"But—" Rubylee cocked the hammer back, which silenced Red. He did as she told him to.

"Open your mouth." Rubylee demanded. "Wider, Red. You know the drill." Rubylee kneeled down and stuck the barrel of her gun in his mouth and pushed it back into his throat to the point that he started gagging. "Don't make any sudden moves, Red. My finger might slip and pull the trigger back." Now that she had him where she wanted him, she checked his pants pockets for a gun but instead found a barber's straight razor that was dangerously sharp.

"You weren't planning on trying to cut me, now, were you, Red?" Red muttered no as best as he could. Rubylee moved to his back pocket and found his wallet with the ID she'd been looking for. She removed the barrel from his mouth.

"Now put your clothes on. We've got to go and handle some business."

"Rubylee, at least let me go in there and get my money off of the table."

"Fool, don't you realize that those men in there are gone

with that money? That trick you had back here sucking on your shit has probably run off with them. If they were any real friends of yours, they would have been back here by now to see if you were all right."

"Where are we going, Rubylee?" Red asked with the tone of a frightened child.

"To the bank. We're going to get all of my money today!"

Richard arrived at the bank at exactly four o'clock. He marched over to Ed's office where he was greeted by an assistant who escorted him down the corridor and into a conference room where he found Ed Lawson, two Chicago detectives, the head of the bank's security team, and a female teller who had a look of desperation, fear, and nervousness written all over her face.

"Richard, I'm glad you're here." Ed sprang out of his seat to greet him. "Come on in and have a seat." Ed led him to a seat across from the teller and the two detectives.

"That's not Dr. Richard Vincent," uttered the teller. Richard noticed she was sweating.

"Richard, we've been discussing your account with Miss Ivy Spears, here." Ed motioned his hand toward the teller. "After reviewing your account it was discovered that this impostor chose only to go to Ivy for services."

"So, Miss Spears, what you're telling us is that this gentleman here was not the person who came to your window on all of these occasions," said one of the detectives, holding up Richard's account history sheet.

"No, that's not him."

"And you have no idea of who this impostor is?" the detective asked.

"Right. I told you. I have no idea who that man was. He presented me with ID that said he was Dr. Richard Vincent." Miss Spears was visibly distressed.

"Dr. Vincent," the second detective spoke, "have you recently lost your identification?"

"No, I've been out of the country, and it's been in my possession the entire time," Richard answered.

"Frank, why don't you play the surveillance tape of one of the times this incident took place," Ed requested of the security guard.

"Sure thing Mr. Lawson." Frank the security guard picked up a remote control and pressed play. Richard watched as a large black man with red lips approached the teller then handed her the bogus ID. The security guard froze the tape so that Richard could get a good look at the man.

"Dr. Vincent, have you ever seen this man before?" asked the first detective.

"No, I have no idea who he is."

"Do you have any idea how he got hold of your personal information?" the detective questioned.

"No." Richard gawked at the screen in shock and disbelief.

"Well, sometimes these lowlifes go around and rummage through trash cans for valuable pieces of mail that have your account information on it."

"Well, this person wouldn't have been able to get my information that way either," Richard said. "I requested that no information about this account be sent to my home address. Initially, it was just a basic savings account. There was no money being deposited or withdrawn until last month. Besides, the address that the bank has is for my office."

"Well, then, someone from inside this bank must have supplied that man with Dr. Vincent's information," said the detective, as he pointed at Red on the video screen.

It was four-thirty when Rubylee and Red pulled up in front of Seaway National Bank. Rubylee had a strong desire to shoot Red and kill his ass when she listened to how he'd returned to the bank every day for a month and withdrawn ten thousand dollars each time. He'd blown nearly two hundred thousand dollars in a month on gambling, prostitutes, and drugs. But she still needed him. She was forcing him to enter the bank and make a withdrawal of a quarter million dollars. Her plan was to take the money and get out of town that night. She'd deal with Estelle, Justine, and Keysha once she got down to Mississippi and settled in somewhere. She grabbed a large duffel bag from the back seat of her car.

"Get your dumb ass out of the car!" Rubylee growled at him. "And you better not run or I'll pop you," she said as she flashed her pistol.

There was a loud knock on the conference room door.

"Come in," said Ed. It was another bank security guard. He walked directly over to Frank, who Richard assumed was his supervisor, and spoke in his ear. Shortly after that, the second security guard left and Frank spoke.

"You're not going to believe this, but the man on the tape has just entered the bank with a woman."

The two detectives sprang to their feet and immediately began giving out instructions. "We're going to treat this like a bank robbery," said the first detective, who instantly picked up the telephone to make a call. The second detective instructed the teller to go out to her window and let him make a withdrawal and then hit the silent alarm.

"Frank, I need you to discreetly go around and get everyone out of the bank lobby," said the second detective.

Richard listened as the first detective called for all types of back-up and gave orders to block off Eighty-seventh Street to both traffic and pedestrians. Richard's heart was thumping so loudly he could hear it. The first detective hung up the phone.

"Dr. Vincent and Mr. Lawson, I need you to stick around. I'm going to need statements from both of you."

"Come on, Ivy," said Frank, who was escorting her out of the office. "Are you up to this?"

Ivy nodded her head.

"You know the procedure, right?" Frank asked as he escorted Ivy out of the room.

"Richard, we can watch everything from here," said Ed, who picked up the remote and clicked on the cameras.

Rubylee and Red had been waiting in line and knew it was their turn.

"Come on, let's go." Rubylee shoved Red. "Wait a minute! I always go to the sister down at the end. Let somebody else go." Rubylee let the woman standing behind them cut in front.

"Next in line, please." Ivy motioned for Red and Rubylee to step down.

"How are you doing today?" asked Red.

"I'm pretty good, and yourself?" Ivy replied.

"I'm okay," Red answered.

"Good. What can I do for you today?"

"I'd like to withdraw two hundred and fifty thousand dollars," Red requested. Rubylee stood next to him, making sure that Red didn't screw this up for her.

"Wow, that's a rather large sum. May I see your identification?" Ivy requested like she'd always done. As she pulled up his account information she triggered the silent alarm. "For that amount of money, we'll need to go into a private area. Are you sure you wouldn't rather have a cashier's check instead?" offered Ivy.

"Listen, just take us to the damn room so that we can count the money and leave," Rubylee snapped. She had grown impatient. She wanted her money, and she wanted it now.

Richard sat in the room, reacting with horror and disbelief when he saw Rubylee standing with Red at the teller window. Now he knew how this person got hold of all of his information. Rubylee! He felt violated and his stomach was turning. He suddenly felt sick.

"Richard, I hope this incident doesn't cause you to remove your money from this bank. I assure you, you're going to be reimbursed all that was stolen from your account, and I'm giving you my personal guarantee that our current policy on identification verification will be changed."

"No, Ed," Richard replied. "You still have my business."

Rubylee stepped out of the counting room with Red and made their way across the bank lobby.

"Wait a minute, Red, something ain't right." Rubylee stopped in the middle of the lobby, noticing how empty it had gotten. It felt like a ghost town to her. "Where did everybody go?"

"Come on, Rubylee, it's after five o' clock, everyone probably went home," said Red as he continued on toward the front door.

"Yeah, you're probably right."

Rubylee caught up with him as he stepped outside. No sooner had Rubylee slung the bag over her shoulder than she heard voices shouting at her.

"Lie down on the ground!" Panic set in quickly as Rubylee suddenly saw a small army of police officers with rifles and guns pointed at her and Red. Shouting seemed to be coming from every direction.

"Drop the bag of money and lie down on the ground!"

Red tossed both of his hands high up in the air. "Don't shoot!" he begged. Rubylee tried to quickly turn around and head back inside the bank, but she ran into an officer who was sneaking up behind her and got into a struggle with him.

"Get down on the ground!" he growled at her as he grabbed her by the collar and tried to sling her down. But Rubylee was too large a woman to throw off balance. She ended up slinging him down. She quickly pulled out her revolver as another officer jumped on her back and another grabbed her by the neck, while yet another one grabbed her pants at the waist. Rubylee fought. There was no way that they were going to throw her down on the ground the way they had when she was evicted.

"She's got a gun!" An officer grabbed her arm and tried to get her to drop it. The officer who had been slung to the ground quickly got to his feet and began pulling her down by her hair. Now there were five grown men attempting to bring her down. Eventually Rubylee's knees gave way to the weight of the men pulling her down. As she fell to the ground her weapon discharged and shot Red in the back of his head.

20

Nina had been busting her ass attempting to catch up on her workload since she came back from her trip. Then, unexpectedly, she was pulled into the office of Mr. Stein, her boss. When she stepped inside, Kay, the director of human resources, was sitting there with him.

"What's going on?" Nina asked as she sat down.

"Nina, I'm going to cut to the chase." Mr. Stein sat down behind his desk. Nina felt tension enter her body from every possible angle.

"The company is doing some restructuring and your department is being phased out. I'm being forced to handle the staffing overages."

"So, what are you saying?" Nina wasn't sure if he meant that she would have to work without an assistant or that she was being transferred.

"We are going to have to terminate our business relationship with you."

"What!" Nina was completely shocked and instantly felt anger rushing through her blood.

"I'm sorry, there was nothing that I could do. These changes are coming directly from the CEO's office. You're a valuable asset, and I hate to lose you."

"Nina, we're offering you a very nice severance package," Kay added.

Nina didn't care about that right then. She was distraught about the reality of being canned. Anger was leaving and depression began settling in fast. What was she going to do now? This was not in her plans.

It was now six-thirty, and Nina sat on her sofa with her legs tucked under her. She'd purchased the sofa with the money she'd won in the Bahamas. She had on her leopard-print boxer pajama shorts and a matching cropped camisole. She was reading *Their Eyes Were Watching God* by Zora Neale Hurston when her door buzzer rang. By no means was she in the mood for company but she figured that it was probably Rose, whom she hadn't seen or heard from since she returned from Atlanta.

"Who is it?" she said into the intercom.

"It's me, Jay. We need to talk."

"Damn!" Nina mumbled. She buzzed him in and he walked into her apartment and shut the door behind him. Nina sat back down and got comfortable on her sofa.

"What happened? I called your office and they said that you no longer worked there."

"I got canned, Jay. Six years of busting my ass and this is the gratitude that I get."

"I'm sorry to hear that." He came over to where she was on the sofa and slipped his arms around her, hoping that she still felt something for him.

"Yeah, well, so was I. But that's not why you came here, is it?"

"No, I came to try to talk some sense into you about this." He removed the divorce papers from the inside pocket of his suit.

"You need me, you know that you can't make it on your own. Especially now that you've lost your job." Jay scooted closer to her. Nina watched his arm as it landed around her shoulder. Jay was attempting to cuddle her tightly. "You need to come back home. I miss you and I need you. Don't you miss me?"

"Of course I miss you, Jay." Nina huffed. "But—"

"Shhhhh." Jay kissed her lightly on the forehead. "Think about it, Nina. It's going to take a little while before you're able to find another job. How are you going to survive? You've never been out on your own."

Nina was already feeling low, and what little bit of hope she had left, Jay was taking from her. Maybe he was right, she began to ponder. Her apartment was expensive as hell and she barely had furniture to sit on. She had no job leads, and between her high car note and high rent, her savings account wouldn't last long. She felt defeated.

"Come on, now." Jay began kissing her on the cheek, then the neck. She felt his hand running up and down her back. "This little independence thing of yours has got to stop. I'm not going to tolerate it. I'm your husband, and it's my job to take care of you." Nina sat silently, at a loss for words. Jay slipped his hand under the elastic of her boxer shorts and skillfully attempted to remove them. Nina allowed Jay to move her hand down to his erect manhood. She listened as Jay's breathing became frantic with anticipation.

"Come on now, baby. We haven't been together in so long. I need you, don't you know that?" Nina turned her head away from him, not wanting to hear his words. Jay began placing kisses on her neck. She fought as her body began to deceive her. In her mind she really didn't want Jay. Only her body was responding to Jay's familiar and routine attempts at intimacy.

"Haven't I taken good care of you?" Nina felt his breath on her ear as she closed her eyes, attempting to stop the tears that were building. Jay was waiting for an answer. "Anything you've ever wanted I've always gotten for you," Jay cooed as he began thrusting his hips. Nina knew that he wanted her to squeeze his throbbing cock but she couldn't. She had to stop.

"Jay, taking care of me and loving me are two different things." The words Nina was searching for were coming to her now. "I really don't believe that you ever loved me. I was too young and dumb to know any better when I got pregnant. I admit, you did your job. You took care of things, but I was more like a pet to you. You just enjoyed the idea of having someone depending on you. And now you just want me back because I'm like a pair of comfortable shoes that you don't want to get rid of."

"Nina!" Jay quickly sat up. Nina, looked into his eyes and saw fire in them. For the first time she felt afraid of him. "We're too old to be starting over. Now, you're going to pack your things and come home right now or else!"

"Or else what?"

"Don't push me, woman!" Jay's tone was threatening violent action against her. At that moment the door buzzer rang.

"Are you expecting company tonight, Nina?" Jay quickly snapped at her. Nina could hear the suspicion and jealousy in Jay's tone .

"Jay, please! You're the one who's been having the affair, or have you forgotten about your little confession?" Nina got up and walked over to the intercom. "Who is it?"

"Nina, baby, it's me, Richard." Nina couldn't believe this. Why hadn't Richard called before he came and why on earth did he have to call her baby. Although the intercom didn't produce the best sound quality, it was clear enough for Jay to hear it well.

"Oh, so you've got another man!"

"Jay, it's not what you think. He's just a friend." Nina was attempting to defuse what was quickly growing into an intense situation. She buzzed Richard in, then stepped out into the hallway to greet him. She pulled the door closed behind her.

"Richard, what are you doing here?"

"I needed your comforting," he replied. "I had no place else to go, baby. I need you so badly." Richard embraced her. At that moment Nina forgot about everything and exhaled. She felt so safe and loved in his arms. She wanted to give herself completely to Richard. She wanted to hear how much he cared about her and wanted to tell him that this past week had been miserable without him. She wanted to tell him that she herself was happy to see him because she needed his comforting as well.

"Who in the fuck are you?" Jay flung the door open. Nina's heart quickly raced as she detached herself from Richard.

"Who the fuck are you?" Richard answered with the same question.

"I'm her motherfucking husband!" Jay's chest quickly swelled with anger as a confrontation seemed inevitable.

"Jay, please, we haven't been together in months and I hardly still refer to you as my husband." Jay grabbed Nina's arm and snatched her over to him.

"So, it's like that now! You're just going to throw away twenty years of marriage and not try to salvage anything."

"Don't grab me like that!" Nina jerked herself away from him. "Jay, when I left I told you that it was over."

"Nina, what are you doing? A minute ago, you looked like you were ready to come crawling back to me." Jay shouted at her like she was filth on his shoe.

"Man, I think that you need to leave!" Richard barked like an angry dog ready to attack. Richard was harboring anger and frustration of his own and a physical confrontation with Jay would be a welcome outlet. "It doesn't take a genius to see that she doesn't want you." Nina observed Richard's chest heaving. My God, what was she going to do? This situation was about to explode and get ugly.

"You know what Nina, fuck you!" Jay pointed an angry finger at her. "FUCK HIM and FUCK YOU!" He stepped out of the doorway and shoved Richard out of his path. "I don't want your whorish ass anyway!" he shouted as he walked out of the building.

"Richard, I don't know what to say. I'm sorry that you had to see that."

"No, its not your fault. I should have phoned first," Richard apoligized. "Maybe I should just leave and give you some space."

"No, there is no need for you to leave. Come on in," Nina offered. "I could use a good tonic after that little charade."

Richard sat and explained the day's events to Nina, and what had happened once he went down to the police station. Red had died on the scene, and Rubylee was being charged with murder and bank robbery offenses. She would most likely be placed behind bars for the rest of her life.

"Does your wife know about all of this yet?" Nina asked, completely shocked.

"No, I don't believe that she does. I'll have to go over there sometime soon. Tomorrow, most likely."

"Oh, you poor thing. I feel so sorry that you have to go through all of this," Nina said as she began stroking the back of his head.

"This entire situation is pretty screwed up. I just hope that it doesn't get any worse than this."

"Yes, me too," Nina replied in agreement. "But I don't see how it possibly could."

21

Estelle had not had a good night's sleep since Richard had left a month ago. Dark circles and puffy bags had formed under her eyes. Her hair had started falling out in large clumps and she'd lost about fifteen pounds. She took up the habit of smoking to calm her nerves but it wasn't helping much. She worried constantly about everything; where was Richard and why hadn't he called? This was so unlike him. She'd lost him and didn't know how to get him back. On top of that, she was stressing about not being able to find a job and pay the bills. Then there was the issue of Justine and Keysha and the two new children that were on the way. Neither her sister nor her niece was thinking about or was even considering pre-natal care.

Now she lay in bed gawking at the ceiling as another morning arrived. She hadn't slept all night. Rubylee hadn't come home either, which was so completely unlike her. Estelle covered up Nathan, who had been sleeping in her bed since all of the drama of Richard leaving had taken place. She sighed as she stroked his hair. He was growing up so quickly. He'd be five soon. The house had a horrifying silence to it, which was unusual, especially with Justine and Keysha living there. However, Estelle was enjoying the private time with her thoughts. When Richard finally did return, she'd make things up to him. She'd cook for him, be more attentive and loving. She would listen to him this time instead of forcing him to deal with situations that by right he should have been consulted about from the beginning. And she was most definitely going to get her family out of the house. One way or the other. Estelle tossed back the covers, sat up, and slipped her feet into her house shoes. She walked down the corridor toward the dining area, stopping at Rubylee's room to peep in on Keysha and Justine, who were sprawled out and snoring loudly. She quickly shut the door; a rank odor filtered out from the room. Most likely from the bags of clothes and musty sneakers that Rubylee had let go unwashed for too long. Estelle walked into the dining area, which was a mess. Music CD's were all over and videotapes were lying around everywhere. Daily newspapers had not been picked up and Nathan's toys were sprawled all over the floor. The kitchen was a complete disaster area. Garbage had stacked up and was overflowing. Dishes were piled in the sink and her once white stove had become an unrecognizable grease counter. Estelle exhaled as depression, reality, and truth placed their hands on her shoulders and pushed her down into a seat. She held her head in her hands, then began scratching her head trying to make some sense out of all of this. Another one of those migraines had started building and suddenly she felt as if she couldn't function. The phone rang and scared her half to death. It rang a second time. She stood up and walked over toward the dishwasher to pick up the receiver that was hanging above it. She leaned on the dishwasher.

"Hello."

"I have a collect call from Rubylee. Will you accept the charges?"

"Yes," Estelle muttered. A moment or two went by, then Rubylee was on the line.

"Ma, why are you calling collect?"

"Estelle!"

"Yeah, I'm here."

"You need to come down here and get me out of this place."

"Get you out of where? What are you talking about?"

"Jail, Estelle! I'm in Cook County Jail!" Rubylee barked.

"Jail! What in the hell are you doing in jail?" Estelle questioned, rubbing her temples, feeling that migraine maturing. Rubylee was a true drama queen.

"Don't worry about that. Just get down here so that I can tell you how to get me out!" Rubylee howled, then suddenly they were disconnected.

Estelle went into Rubylee's bedroom and shook Justine's shoulder.

"What?" She mumbled still half asleep.

"Ma is in trouble. I have to run out of here to see about her. Keep an eye on Nathan for me until I return."

"All right," Justine replied, pulling the covers back over her shoulder.

"Justine." Estelle shook her again, wanting to make sure she'd heard her.

"What!" Justine was now fully awake.

"Do you hear what I said?"

"Yes. Damn! Can I get some sleep now?" Estelle didn't say anything, she just turned and walked out of the room.

When she arrived at the correctional facility at Twenty-second Street and California, Estelle felt as if she were a criminal. She was forced to go through metal detectors and fill out paperwork in order to see her own mother. She was asked to dump everything out of her purse and pockets. After waiting for nearly three hours, they finally called her name. She was escorted by an officer into a long narrow room that was partitioned by bulletproof glass. There were people sitting down and talking through the glass on black phones. The officer informed her that she had twenty minutes and that all phone conversations were recorded and monitored. Rubylee was already sitting down, dressed in a bright orange correctional facility uniform. Estelle didn't know what to think. Her mother's hair was a mess and the expression on her face was one she'd never seen before.

Estelle slowly picked up the phone, not knowing what to expect.

"We don't have much time, and we've got to work quick," Rubylee began.

"Why are you in here?"

"Because they're trying to frame me! That's why."

"Frame you for what?"

"Estelle, pay attention. Ask Richard for some money to get me out of here."

"Ma, I don't even know where Richard is."

"Find him, goddamn it!" Rubylee roared like a lion trapped in a cage. "He has the money that I need to get out of here with."

"Ma, Richard doesn't—"

"Damn it, Estelle, shut up and listen!" Rubylee became visibly agitated. Estelle sat in silence and gazed into her red eyes.

"Richard has over a million dollars at Seaway National Bank. Don't ask me how he got it, I just know it's there. They have me in here for bank robbery and murder. I didn't rob the bank; Red did, I was just going along for a ride," Rubylee lied, sticking to the story she'd told the police. "I know that I can beat this one. My fingers never touched the trigger of my gun. When the police were wrestling with me, one of them must have pulled the trigger on the gun and shot Red. I'm scheduled to go in front of a judge today in about an hour. They gave me this court-appointed attorney named McKinney. He's a short white boy with brown hair, bad breath, and a cheap suit. He doesn't know much. Looks like he just graduated from law school yesterday. Once I get out of here, I'll make a few phone calls."

"Your time is up." A female officer stood behind Rubylee.

"Give me one goddamn minute!" Rubylee snapped. The guard signaled for another guard to come down and assist her.

"Do what you have to do in order to get that money from Richard, Estelle!" The two officers snatched Rubylee out of her seat. Rubylee resisted and ended up being wrestled to the floor once again. One officer had her knee on Rubylee's neck and her arm twisted behind her back in order to place the handcuffs on her. They pulled her to her feet and escorted her out of the room. Rubylee was yelling something, but Estelle couldn't hear her. Her heart was pounding furiously as the entire event unfolded in front of her. Estelle was completely confused. She had a ton of questions for Rubylee. Why did she walk into a bank with a gun? Did Richard really have an account like she said? And if he did, why was she trying to take the money? Estelle barely had enough strength to stand up and walk out of the room. She collected her belongings and made her way over to the courtroom. She found a place to sit down in the back of the courtroom near the door. A moment later a short white man with brown hair and a cheap suit stood at the door, searching the courtroom.

"Are you Mr. McKinney?" Estelle asked.

"Yes, are you Estelle?" he replied.

"Yes."

"Great, I've been looking for you." Estelle scooted over on her bench seat in order to make room for him to sit down.

"Do you know what's happening?"

Estelle waved her head in the no motion. She felt as if she were about to faint. The attorney explained in detail the events that had placed Rubylee behind bars. Estelle had difficulty digesting the shocking truth.

"Do you think she has a chance? I mean, she said that she thinks she can beat the charges," Estelle said with a hopeful tone.

"I'm going to be honest with you. It doesn't look good. According to the statement from your husband, Rubylee has been living with you for several months. She had access to sensitive documents which she supplied to Redmond Jones, aka Red. So that proves intent to commit the crime. On top of that, she has a record of drugs, theft, and prostitution. And she's also about to step in front of a very tough judge."

"Wait a minute. Richard is aware of all of this?"

"Yes, he was at the bank when the arrest and murder took place."

"Well, where is he now?"

"I don't know."

Estelle felt the room spinning around her. Why hadn't Richard come home to tell her all of this? She needed him. She didn't have any money in the bank, and bills were due. He was so right about Rubylee, and she regretted not standing by him when she should have. He probably hated her for that.

"Excuse me. I see that they're bringing her out now. I'll try to get the judge to set a reasonable bail."

Estelle attempted to listen but found the proceedings difficult to hear because she was so far back. However, she did catch the part when the judge said that bail was denied and slammed down the gavel. The corrections officer escorted Rubylee out of the room. Mr. McKinney headed back toward her.

"The judge denied bail. She'll have to remain behind bars until the trial. Here's my card. Call me in about a month and I'll let you know if there have been any updates." He tapped Estelle lightly on the shoulder, opened up a folder that he was carrying, and walked out into the hall shouting out the name of another client.

When Estelle walked out of the courthouse the wind was blowing hard and large pellets of rain were falling fast and furiously. People raced up the steps of the courthouse in search of shelter. Estelle stepped out into the cold rain, feeling the pellets sting her skin as she wandered toward her car like a zombie without a purpose. She opened the car door, got in and slammed it shut. The only sound she heard was the rain tapping on the roof of the car, begging to get in. Water dripped from Estelle's hair onto her lap as she stared blankly at the dashboard. Her emotions were building like a tide rushing to shore. She opened her mouth and released a pain-filled wail. Why was this happening to her? How had things gotten so out of control? She no longer wanted to deal with any of this. She desperately wished that she was someone else, someone who didn't have the problems she had. She sat in the car for hours, gawking at the dashboard and feeling her mind slip into the comforting arms of insanity.

It was nightfall when she finally started the car and drove back home. She parked the car and wandered into the lobby of her building.

"Are you Estelle Vincent?" Estelle stared blankly at a man dressed in the uniform of a sheriff's deputy. She mustered up enough strength to nod her head in the yes motion.

"Here you go. I need you to sign here." He handed her a clipboard and a pen. She scribbled her name as best she could without a clue as to what she was signing.

"You have just been served. You are to appear in court on the date indicated in the letter." He spoke with a military-type tone and then left. Estelle stepped inside the elevator and pressed the button for her floor. She opened the envelope, read it and suddenly found herself gasping for air. Bill Holiday was following through with the lawsuit from her job. The company had actually pressed formal charges against her. When the door opened on her floor she felt stunned, weak and hopeless. Estelle walked down the hall and stood in front of her apartment door listening to loud voices and thumping music. She turned her key in the door and pushed it open. James Brown was shouting, *What's that? Body heat. What's that? Body heat. Iiiiii* . . . Her living room was filled with people shouting, dancing and stomping their feet to the beat of the music. Estelle stood there bewildered.

"What's happening?" she screamed, but no one seemed to hear her, or care for that matter. The apartment was hot and muggy and people were packed tightly together, gyrating and groping each other as the James Brown record continued to play.

"Get out!" she screamed again, but no one heard her. The

music was too loud. Justine came bouncing up to her full of excitement.

"Hey, girl, it's a party going on in here!"

Estelle was thunderstruck, her eyes were wide with confusion as she stumbled through the mob of people and into her room where she slammed the door and lay on the bed in the fetal position with her ears covered. A moment later, Nathan entered the room.

"I can't sleep, Mamma. Its too noisy. Can I sleep with you?" Estelle didn't say a word, she just gazed at the clock on the nightstand. Nathan crawled into the bed beside her and assumed the same position.

The following afternoon, Richard turned the key in the door of the place he once had called home. He'd finally come over to discuss the problems of his marriage with Estelle. But when he walked into the apartment he found it difficult to believe that he'd once lived there. There were beer bottles and cans tossed about the apartment. Trash was on the floor, the once tan carpeting was completely black and riddled with stains. In the dining area, he found Justine passed out on the sofa with some dude sleeping behind her with his hand firmly placed on her breast. They were so out of it, neither one of them heard Richard come in. Richard maneuvered through the mess that was on the floor and walked past the washroom, where his nose was assaulted by a rank odor. He pushed the door open, peeped inside, and noticed that the toilet was clogged. He moved down a bit further and pushed the door of Rubylee's room open. He found Keysha asleep on top of some young boy. Suddenly he heard faint sniffling and crying from his bedroom. He marched to the end of the corridor and flung the door open. Nathan was sitting at the foot of the bed crying.

"Hey, little man." Richard kneeled down. "Come here." Nathan ran to him and locked his arms around his father's neck. Richard stood up with him, hugging him tightly.

"What's wrong?" he asked Nathan, who was sobbing uncontrollably.

"Mommy's eyes are open but she won't wake up and she's cold. I tried to keep her warm but she's still cold." Richard looked down at the bed but Nathan had covered Estelle up from head to toe. He gently set Nathan down and called to Estelle. When she didn't answer he pulled the sheets back and was horrified when he saw Estelle staring blankly at the alarm clock.

"Estelle!" Richard shouted, then touched the skin on her face, which was cold and felt like hard wood.

"Oh, no!" Richard wailed. "Oh, God, no!"

22

Nina buzzed her door to allow Rose inside the building.

"What's the major emergency that you had me run over here for?" Rose came in and closed the door, then took a seat beside Nina on the sofa.

"She died, girl," Nina muttered.

"Who? Who died?"

"Richard's wife."

"Girl, you're kidding me!" Rose blurted out in complete disbelief.

"No, he went home the other day to tell her about how her mother had gotten caught robbing a bank and—"

"Wait a minute." Rose was trying to put things in order. "Back up and start over. What was her mother doing trying to rob a bank?"

"Girl, I'm sorry, we haven't talked since you've been back. It's a long complicated story."

Rose kicked off her shoes, folded her arms and rested them on her bosom. "I ain't got nothing but time." Nina recounted the entire saga, presenting it to Rose the way Richard had told it the other night. When Nina was done, Rose sat with her mouth gaping open with disbelief.

"Damn! That's just plain old fucked-up."

"Tell me about it." Nina released a depressed sigh. "On top of that, Jay finally signed the divorce papers and has vowed to never speak to me again. He called me all kinds of horrible names. I told him that it didn't have to be that way, but he hung up on me. So I guess that makes me a free woman now," Nina said, feeling an emotional breakdown about to occur.

"Girl, I am so sorry that I wasn't here for you."

"Tuh, girl please. You've got to learn how to roll with the punches." Nina quickly wiped a tear from her eye.

"So, do you have any leads on a job yet?" Rose asked.

"Nope, not a damn one. I'm going to update my résumé and start pounding the pavement sometime next week. How are things with you and John the fireman?"

"They couldn't be better. We've been discussing the idea of me moving down there."

"Really?"

"Yes, it's a big step, I know. I told him that I needed to think about it. He said fine and that he would wait for as long as it took."

"He seems like a really nice man." Nina said.

"I must admit he is my sweetie pie. Have you heard from my Gracie lately?"

"Actually, I just spoke with her a little while ago. She was a bit upset about the divorce, but I explained to her that her father and I have been having problems for a long time. She didn't understand why I wasn't willing to give Jay another chance and was very upset with me about choosing Richard over Jay. But that's the way it goes, you know. After we got over that hump, we had a pretty good conversation. She's going back to school now and plans to be done with her undergraduate degree by spring next year. Then after that, she and Mark are going to look into adopting a child."

"Good for her. I'm glad that she's doing well."

"Rose, I need to ask you a difficult question."

"What is it?"

"I feel so strange about this. I'm not sure if what I did was right. When Richard came by to tell me about Estelle, he . . . Well, he was looking for some comforting. I told him that he needed time to grieve and that I felt as if I was in the way. I mean I know that I was wrong to act on my passions because I knew that he was married and that making love to him was forbidden."

"Now, Nina, don't go beating yourself up," Rose interrupted. "You were both consenting adults, and what happened between you . . . well, shit! It just happened. Don't go crying over spilled milk."

"I know, Rose, I just feel bad. You know, just plain old bad."

Rubylee was being escorted into the visiting room once more. She figured that Estelle had at least found Richard and she could now move on to Plan B since the judge denied her bail. She knew of a good lawyer who would take her case, but he was going to cost and would have to be paid a certain amount up front. Rubylee was a bit puzzled when she saw Justine sitting in the seat on the opposite side of the glass waiting on her. She sat down and picked up the black phone, noticing how upset Justine looked.

"Hey," she said. "What's wrong with you?"

"Momma, Estelle is gone. Richard told me where to find you." Justine was near hysterics.

"Gone? Gone where?" Rubylee wasn't understanding what Justine was telling her.

"Gone, Momma! She's dead!"

"DEAD! She was just in here the day before last. That's impossible."

"Richard came home yesterday and found her dead in her sleep." Justine began sobbing uncontrollably. "They said that she had a blood clot in her brain. Momma, I was having a party when she came home. I didn't know she was feeling that bad. She wanted me to put everybody out, but I didn't." Rubylee sat back in her chair as a blank stare filled with bewilderment and disbelief covered her face.

"Momma, what am I supposed to do?" Justine shouted into the phone. "When are you getting out?"

Rubylee allowed the phone to fall from her hand. She wasn't getting out. She was going to have to face this shit. Estelle was gone. Her baby was gone. Rubylee felt the tears rushing up from deep inside of her. She clutched her chest as her emotions began taking control of her. She glanced back at Justine, who was shouting into the phone. There was nothing Rubylee could do for her. Nothing that she could even do for herself. Something inside of her had just broken, like shattered glass on the pavement. She picked up the phone and placed her hand against the glass.

"Momma, why are you looking like that?" Justine asked confused.

"Live your life, Justine. I can't do anything for you." After that Rubylee entered a hypnotic state. She stood up, turned her back on Justine and wandered away like a ghost.

Richard was kneeling down, lacing Nathan's shoes and explaining to him that none of the recent events were his fault and that Estelle was in a much better place. Nathan nodded his head with understanding, then locked his arms around Richard's neck. Richard stood up and carried Nathan down to the limousine that was taking them to Estelle's funeral service. It was difficult to believe that Estelle was gone. The hole in Richard's heart was large. The judge allowed Rubylee to attend Estelle's funeral under heavy guard. Two officers brought her into the funeral home dressed in a bright orange correctional facility outfit. They sat down in the front row across the aisle from Richard. Rubylee looked defeated, lost, and pitiful. Although Richard didn't care for her personality much, it was sad to see the fire gone from her. Rubylee had died on the inside. There seemed to only be a shell housing her remains. The preacher spoke kind words and offered his condolences. Before Richard knew it, the service was over and they were off to the cemetery to bury her. Rubylee wasn't allowed to attend the burial. She was promptly escorted back to jail. How sad, Richard thought, that this would probably be the last time she saw the outside world. After the burial services were over, Richard headed back home to deal with the task of cleaning up and making plans for the future. He was not going to stay in that apartment. Over the past few days he'd decided what he wanted to do. He was going to break the lease, buy the home he'd always wanted, and purchase a practice of his own.

"Richard, what's going to happen to us?" Justine humbly asked once they were back at the apartment after the wake. "What are Keysha and I going to do?"

Richard sighed. It was sad that this poor woman had never been taught how to be independent. She'd never been taught how to be responsible. She only knew how to sponge, use, and leech off of others for her survival.

"Its time to grow up, Justine. It's time to learn how to be an adult."

"Why can't we just stay here with you? Aren't you going to need help with Nathan? I mean, I could look out for him, or take him to school and pick him up for you."

"Justine . . ." Richard spoke slowly in order to be delicate. "The offer is nice but no, thank you. Raising Nathan is my responsibility. Besides, I'm not staying in this apartment any longer than I have to. I'm going to break the lease and purchase a home. You can stay until then, but that only gives you a limited amount of time. You need to find yourself some place to live."

"But—"

"I'm sorry Justine, but that's the way it's going to be." Justine was silent and Richard could see by her expression that she was pondering over what to do. Poor thing, he thought, poor bewildered thing.

23

Time waited for no one, and Richard eventually purchased the home of his dreams in Barrington, Illinois. He and Justine attended Rubylee's trial and listened as the jury handed down the painful verdict of guilty. The judge sentenced her to fifty years behind bars. Rubylee was limp and lifeless as the sentence was handed down. All of this was so unfortunate. So many lives had been affected by this woman's greed. Estelle died because Rubylee leaned on her too hard. Red was killed by her gun. Justine was forced to be responsible, which was something she wasn't capable of; a few weeks later she ended up behind bars for driving a stolen car. Keysha lost a mother, a grandmother, an aunt, and a place to call home. She ended up staying with a relative on her father's side somewhere in Tennessee. Nathan had lost a mother and a grandmother. Richard pondered the amazing effects one person's actions could have on so many lives. Nina had attempted to put a little bit of distance between them, which Richard felt was out of some feeling of guilt. Nina explained that she felt he needed time to mourn, reflect, and heal. All of this was true, but Richard didn't like the idea of her pulling away from him.

"Nina," he explained, " I'm not going to lie to you. I miss Estelle a great deal, but our marriage had died long before you and I ever got started. I was no longer committed to the marriage. Estelle allowed Rubylee's interference to destroy us."

"Richard you don't have to—"

"No, I need to say this," he continued. "Regardless of all that has happened, Estelle and I were headed for doom. I didn't want her anymore, I just didn't. Believe me when I say that I was not going to stay there with her."

"Richard you've made me feel so alive and wonderful. If I'm going to be honest, I have to admit that I want you in my life. But I want you to want me as much as I want you. I don't want to become someone that you're just tolerating. I want to be someone that you love coming home to and someone you like talking to. I want to be your friend, your lover, and at some point your wife. I don't want to be a rebound thing any more than you do. Let's just give each other some time, okay?"

Richard pouted but agreed with her. Before long, spring, summer, and fall had come to pass and the end of a tragic year was coming to a close.

It was now Christmas morning. Richard had the radio on and listened as Nat King Cole sang the Christmas song, *Chestnuts roasting on an open fire, Jack Frost nipping at your nose . . .* Nat's smooth voice filled the house.

Richard stood in the kitchen washing the few dishes in the sink and looking out the window at the large snowflakes falling onto his driveway. During the month of October, Richard and Nina had begun seeing each other again but this time, things felt so much better because there was no deception going on. John the fireman had come to town from Atlanta for the holidays to see Rose. Richard insisted on having everyone over to his new house for Christmas dinner. He had planned to have the food catered, but Nina insisted that she cook instead. As Richard scrubbed the burn marks off a pan he'd burned cheese into, he glanced out the window at a car pulling into his driveway. He wiped his hands on the towel that was lying next to him and watched as Nina stepped out carrying a few bags of groceries. Richard opened the kitchen door. A gust of cold wind came along and nearly blew Nina down.

"Hey, I heard that there was a fine-looking man in here who was in need of a good cook," Nina said, stepping in out of the cold and walking into the kitchen.

"Well, actually, I'm looking for a full-time wife," Richard replied as Nathan came running into the kitchen.

"Daddy, can you come in the front room and play with me?" Nathan pleaded for his attention.

"Okay, Nathan. Give me a minute to help Nina." Nathan turned and was about to rush out of the room. But Richard called to him.

"Aren't you going to say hello to our guest?"

"Hi," Nathan said.

"Hello, Nathan," Nina replied. Nathan ran out of the room and back to his toys.

"Well, let's see what a sister can stir up for two fine brothers," Nina said as she began unpacking the bags she'd brought in.

"Let me help you," Richard offered.

"No, you should go in there and play with Nathan. I'm a big girl and I know my way around a kitchen."

Richard came up behind her and slipped his arms around her waist. "Are you sure?" he asked, as he nibbled at her neck.

"Yes," Nina replied, pushing him away from her with her behind. "If you're a good boy, you'll get some dessert later," she said teasingly.

Richard tapped her on her rump. "Well, I've got a big appetite. What's for dessert?"

"Your favorite," Nina responded.

"Oh, and what might my favorite dessert be?" Richard asked, loving the tone of her voice.

"Coochie surprise." They both chuckled for a moment. Then Richard spun her around, embraced her, and looked her in the eyes. "I've got a special dessert for you as well."

"Oh, really?" Nina was intrigued. "What is this special dessert called?"

"Lollypop delight. It has a chocolate shell and a cream filling that will make your mouth water."

Nina began laughing. "I must say, it sounds so delicious that I can hardly wait to get a mouthful of it." Nina allowed the tip of her tongue to slide across her upper lip as if she were licking the remains of her dessert.

"Baby, you certainly have a way with words," Richard laughed. Nina released herself from his embrace, placed her hands on her hips, and made another sassy gesture with her tongue. She then allowed her eyes to fall downward and focus on Richard's manhood.

"I just love pleasing my man."

"Baby, I love it when you talk to me like that." Richard was eager for some action at that very moment.

"I love you." The words slipped out of Nina's mouth before she had a chance to take them back.

Richard exhaled as he embraced her once again. "I love you too, baby. I really do. Have you reconsidered my offer to move in with me?" Richard asked.

"I'm afraid, Richard. I mean, Nathan will probably disapprove. I can already tell that he doesn't like me very much and—"

Richard shhhh'd her with his finger. "Nathan will adjust. I want you, Nina."

"Do you really?"

"Yes, I want you more than a bird loves flight."

"Well, with words like that you're making it hard for a sister to turn you down."

"I'm serious, Nina."

"So am I, Richard."

"So, is that a yes?"

"Yes, it is," Nina responded, feeling herself glowing on the inside.

"Baby, I'm about to make you the happiest woman in the world," Richard replied as he kissed her passionately.

Nina pushed herself away from him with one hand. "Go

play with Nathan while I cook. Rose and John will be here in a little while, and you should take some time to be with him." Richard absolutely adored her reminding him. "Now go on," Nina said as she patted him on his behind. "You've got to play with him to make sure that he sleeps all night long." Nina moved over to the counter top, and pulled out some strawberries and some whipped cream from the grocery bag. "I've got plans for you tonight, mister."

"Well, alright Nina! That's what I'm talking about!" Richard felt a surge of passionate energy rush through him. He winked at her as he went to play with Nathan.

To my readers, I would love to hear your comments about this book. You can E-mail me at: earlsewell@earlsewell.com, or visit my website at: www.earlsewell.com